15
Midlife Demon Hunter
THE FORTY PROOF SERIES
SHANNON MAYER

HiJinks

Midlife Demon Hunter

HiJinks Ink Publishing
www.shannonmayer.com

Mayer, Shannon

ACKNOWLEDGMENTS

Thank you to the ladies in the back row. You know, to the ones who cheer the loudest, who support their fellow women even as they themselves struggle. The ladies who stand up for what's right and for taking on challenges that others shy away from. Thank you to the women who have led by example by showing the kind of life I want to live. Full of laughter. Full of love. Full of life.

Living fearless.

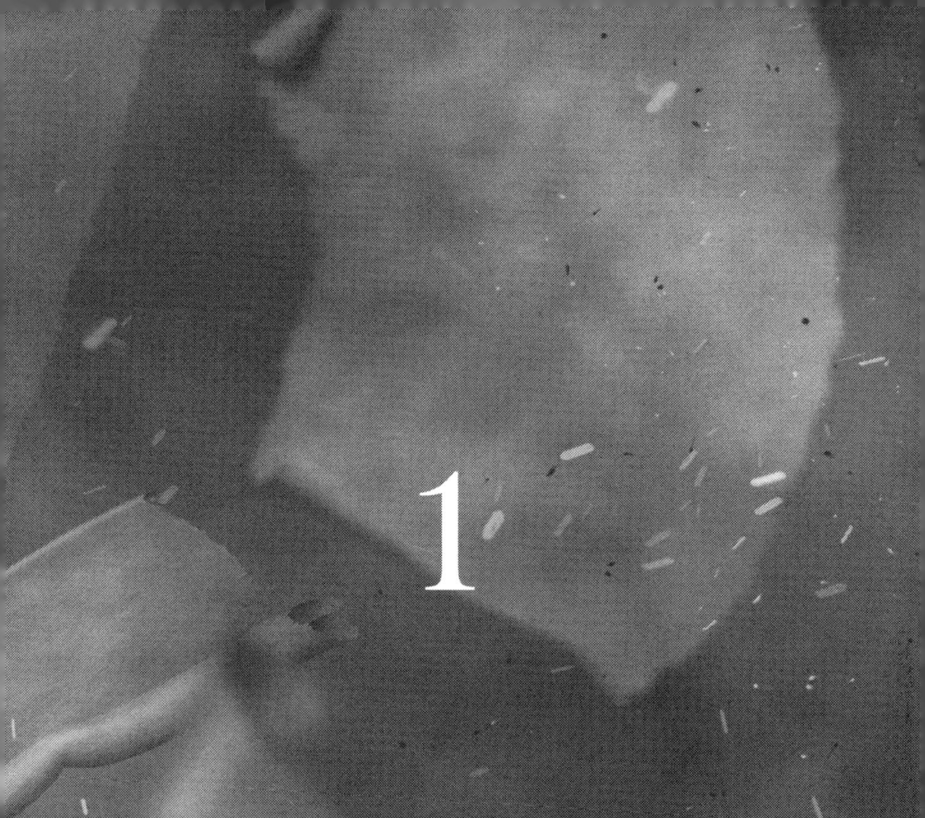

1

What happened when a bigfoot was in love with a fairy who regarded him only as a friend, and a siren was falling hard for the bigfoot who didn't notice her? That might sound like the start to a joke, but it didn't feel so funny from my perspective in the middle of what had become a daily soap opera of sad puppy dog eyes and unrequited love.

I stood by the sink in my gran's house, watching as Eric, said bigfoot shifter, bent in front of the oven. We were into April in Savannah in a house that lacked air conditioning, and the open windows didn't make it any cooler since the oven was constantly on.

But Eric persisted baking in this heat because…

"You know I bake when I'm stressed," he said under his breath. "What do I do, Bree? How do I get her to see me?"

Yes, the irony was not lost on me that the bigfoot who was the current hide-and-seek champion of the world wanted to be seen. By a wee tiny fairy.

"Good grief, you're asking me for love advice? Have you noticed the mess I'm in?" I snorted and dunked my hands back into the soapy water, viciously attacking a series of cupcake molds that had blackened with all the baking he'd been doing.

I'd been ignoring a lot of things the last week, not least of all the envelope holding information on my gran's and parents' deaths. Procrastination, thy name is Breena O'Rylee. I'd almost opened it a dozen times, but every time I picked it up, I found myself putting it down. I'd get around to it, I would. Just… not yet. It would be opening a whole new can of worms. So I was putting it off as long as I could and enjoying this short respite from the craziness that had become my life.

"But you're navigating your love life better than I'm handling mine. At least the men you're interested in realize you have intentions toward them. Kinkly doesn't look at me that way. Ever. I might as well be a talking tree to her." He stood up straight, barely missing the oven hood with the top of his head.

One look at himself ought to have clued him in to the problem—he was over seven feet tall, and Kinkly, tiny fairy that she was, fit in the palm of my hand. A counselor by trade, Eric had the college professor look down to a T, from the bowtie at his neck to the khaki pants and leather loafers, and with that background you'd think he could see the issues he and Kinkly would face. I sighed, thinking about what he'd said and circling back to my own love-life issues.

"First of all, I'm not *interested* in either of them." Yes, I could feel that lie even as I said it. "I just got out of a crappy marriage, and I'd like to play the field a little. Date men who aren't difficult. Men who don't have secrets. Is that too much to ask?" I scrubbed a little harder at the pans, not sure if I believed my own words. "Besides, if you haven't noticed, Crash has stayed away for over a week without contacting any of us, even Feish, and now she's getting fussy about him being 'missing.' And Corb *still* hasn't come by to apologize for coming on so strongly while he was under those mages' spell. Neither one is ringing any of my bells. Really, at this rate, Robert has a better shot than either of them."

A laugh burst out of Eric. He fumbled the pan he'd just retrieved from the oven, and a croissant slid off and bounced on the floor. I dried my hands and scooped up the flaky pastry, hopping it from hand to hand, blowing at it and tearing off pieces while it was still too hot to eat. I didn't care. The minor burns were worth the flavor.

"The skeleton would make a better date?" Eric carefully set the first pan on the counter. "You're kidding me, right?"

I grinned up at him and winked. "He likes to drink whiskey with me, never fails to show up when I'm in need, and doesn't try to boss me around. Right now, aside from the fact that he's dead and nothing more than an animated skeleton, he's the perfect man."

He wasn't bad looking either. Back in the day, I mean. I'd finally seen Robert—pre-death Robert—during my own death-adjacent experience last week. Jet black hair, icy blue eyes that had some serious intensity to them, and a lean build—he made a nice package, all in all. Of course, he wasn't alive, so no point in crying over spilled milk.

Or in this case, crying over a skeleton.

Eric put another pan down and bent at the waist so we were eye to eye. "You mean, maybe I should find a skeleton woman?"

"I could ask Robert if he has a sister," I drawled, then popped the last of the croissant into my mouth. "But seriously, if you like Kinkly, tell her. The worst she's going to say is she's not interested. The best is that she might say, *yeah, let's try this thing on for size.*"

You might wonder why I didn't tell him that the more appropriately sized part-siren was interested in him.

Simply put, she had asked me not to. Suzy wanted him to like her for her, something she'd never had in a relationship before. In the past, she had always spelled the men she was interested in—forcing them to be with her whether they wanted to or not. Without using her siren compulsion, she was as shitty at relationship stuff as Eric.

The upside? Nobody had a broken heart yet. *Yet* being the operative word. I didn't think Kinkly would be hurt—she was oblivious to Eric's affections. He wasn't wrong that she seemed to view him as a piece of the scenery more than anything else, perching on his shoulders or the top of his head for better vantage points.

It was Eric and Suzy who had me worried. Really, you'd think it would be simple, but damn it, I knew from firsthand experience that love and matters of the heart were far from simple.

Let me see if I could put my own drama in a nutshell.

I was a forty-one—chasing forty-two—year-old divorcee. My ex-husband, who I most commonly refer to as *Himself* but was otherwise known as Alan (You know the superstition about evil being summoned when you use its name? Well, I believed it.) took me for everything in the divorce, including my gran's house, which he sold out from under me.

I was pretty sure he used someone in the shadow world to help him doctor documents and get them shoved through the legal system. It was the only thing that made sense. Plus, he'd tried to break into Gran's house to steal her book of spells and the talisman she'd given me.

From there, we go to Corb, Alan's black sheep cousin. Younger than me by more than a handful of years, buff as they come with smoldering dark green eyes and everything you'd want in a bad boy, right down to the cupboards full of so much lube, he could have an orgy and not run out.

Anyhoo, he'd inadvertently offered me a place to stay while I got back on my feet after the divorce, and to his surprise—and maybe even my own—I'd taken him up on the offer. And he'd kissed me, and I'd slept—platonically—in his bed one night all curled up next to him. Cue the sighing.

Enter the third and final player in my little love-life drama. Crash. One hot hunk of a fae blacksmith who had also, at one point, been the fae king. He'd made the knives I carried to keep me and Savannah safe, and I'd seen his bare ass more than once. And did I mention that his kisses set my body on fire like I was melting from the inside out? Panty-melting indeed.

The thing was I knew when I was playing out of my league. Because I'd also seen Crash at a fae party joint where he'd had a beautiful girl under each arm. Girls, not women. So I knew his type, and I was not it by a long shot, by at least twenty years.

And yet, he'd given Gran's house back to me (sort of—his name was still on the title too), and I'd heard him and Gran talk about me while I was asleep. Still, he'd been gone for a week, and every doubt I'd had about him had come crashing back. Wordplay intended. On top of it all, I had no real desire to choose between the two men. There was a part of me that very much enjoyed flirting with both.

What can I say? It had been a long time since I'd felt this much sexual chemistry, and my mature libido was out of control and pushing me to keep my options open.

"Hello, earth to Breena," Eric waved a hand in front of my face. "You in there?"

"Sorry, wandered off in my head, fell off the path, and got sucked down the hole of where the hell did I go wrong in my own love life?" I laughed, turned, and dunked my hands back into the soapy water. "Just tell Kinkly," I said again. "That's the best way to find out. And then you can move on if it isn't a fit."

Which it literally could be in so many ways.

He sighed. "I know you're right. Of course I do. I just never thought it would be so hard to tell someone how you feel."

"What would you suggest to one of your clients?" I asked. From where I stood, I stared out the window at the house next door. Eric answered, but his voice slid into something of a drone, a buzzing that filled my ears as I fixated on the eyes that could only belong to Matilda. The ghost had tried to push her way into Gran's house last week, but we'd managed to keep her out since then by maintaining the garden and the protective spells Gran had laid on the house via the plants. Unfortunately, it didn't keep Matilda from watching us.

Which was what the freaky neighbor ghost was doing now. She stared at me from the window of the Sorrel-Weed house, clear as day...until she disappeared. One of the windows on the upper floor of the infamous house seemed to flicker. I leaned over the sink to see better, and there she was on the second floor, looking at our house again. I found myself turning away from Eric and hurrying out of the kitchen. "I'll be back, hang on a second."

Up the stairs I went with only a slight twinge in my right knee. No matter that I was getting stronger every day, that knee was being a pig about not hurting. I used the banister to help me get to the top of the stairs faster, then hobble-jogged to the windows on that side of the house. I ducked into the first room, which was now Suzy's. She wasn't there—she and Feish were out shopping.

The window didn't line up with any in the house next door. I ducked into the next room, which was Gran's.

"Bingo," I said softly as I strode in. Matilda stared into the room, her eyes on mine, her face sad. She lifted a palm to the glass and pressed her hand against it.

"What does she want?" Gran appeared by my side and glowered at the other ghost. Like two dogs stuck in adjacent apartments, they had taken to barking back and forth on a daily basis. They seemed to genuinely dislike each other. But this was different than the usual. Matilda had never come up to this window before. She'd mostly stayed in the lower levels of her house. She pointed at us, then made a slashing motion across her neck at Gran.

Gran lifted both fists, her long skirts swinging with the motion. "Matilda, stop being a bitch!"

I fake gasped and put a hand to my chest. "Gran! I can't believe you cussed at her."

"Ah, well." She turned from the window with a final wave of her hand, like a queen dismissing the court. "It's not like she can hear me. And she really is being a tyrant lately, trying to draw me out of the house so I'll engage with her."

She strode away, her form going transparent in a splash of sunlight, then solidifying again as she stepped into the shadows. I was lucky, so very lucky, I still had her with me. She'd died seven months prior, and I hadn't been able to even attend her funeral—courtesy of Himself. I'd thought I'd lost my last chance to talk to her, to lean on her advice, to tell her I loved her. But I'd found her here in the house we'd lived in together.

I turned back to the window, fully expecting Matilda to be gone. But she wasn't. Her eyes locked with mine, because like Gran, she knew I could see her.

Worse, she'd been joined by a much darker figure that cast a shadow on her from behind. Long spindly fingers wrapped around her upper body, digging into her spectral flesh and slowly pulling her deeper into the darkness of the house. The malevolence of the deliberately slow movements, the look of fear and horror etched into Matilda's eyes, the lack of fight in her—it all sent chills through me that left my knees a little wobbly. This certainly hadn't happened before.

"Duck me," I whispered as I stepped back, too, away from the window. On second thought…I reached forward and grabbed the sash, pulling the curtains closed, blocking the view of Matilda and her new friend that I didn't want to meet, never mind see. Gran had never mentioned a darker entity next door.

Sure, the supernatural world wasn't new to me, but that didn't mean I wasn't affected by it, or the special shades of ugliness that occasionally popped into my line of view. I didn't realize I'd backed all the way out of my gran's room and into mine across the hall until my hand touched the side table by my door.

My fingers brushed against the yellow manila envelope that lay there. The one I'd meant to open a week ago—and several times since—but like I said earlier, every time I picked it up, I seemed to chicken out at the last second. My eyes were locked on the window across from me, even though I could no longer see Matilda or the critter pulling her into the darkness. I slowly picked up the envelope and pulled it to my chest as if it would somehow block them from seeing me.

The envelope felt heavier than it actually was, a literal weight in my hands.

"You're freaking yourself out," I muttered as I backed up the last few steps and shut the door. The minute the barrier was in place the tension slid out of me. As if I'd cut off prying eyes. I shuddered. "I gotta ask Robert if he can get rid of her," I mumbled to myself.

A tap on the door about stopped my heart. I took a step back, crouched, and peered under the oversized crack at the bottom. Shadows of a pair of feet, nothing more. If it had been any of my friends, they would have announced themselves.

Who the hell had broken into my house this time with Eric downstairs?

"What in the world are you doing?" Gran said behind me, and I squeaked...and maybe peed myself a little.

"Damn it," I whispered. "I'm trying to see who's out there."

"Well, isn't it obvious? You said his name. It's Robert. He's like a damn golden retriever. Irritating as Matilda if you ask me," Gran grumped and promptly walked past me, through the door and out of view. I frowned after her.

"Who put a murder hornet in your panties?" I muttered after her.

I opened the door up to see the swaying form of Robert. His long dark hair hid his face, and the rags he wore—if he could be said to be wearing anything—covered his literal skeletal frame. Enough so that if you didn't look too hard, you wouldn't notice that he was a skeleton. If indeed you could even see him. Like Gran, he didn't seem to be visible to everyone.

"Robert, what are you doing here?" Was Gran right? Was just saying his name enough to pull him in from his hiding spot? I usually left him outside in the garden. He liked it under the new, larger-than-it-should-have-been oak tree, although maybe it was something about the magic of the fae relic buried beneath it that spoke to him.

He reached out a finger and tapped the yellow envelope. No questions, just a tap of a single finger bone, followed by a waggle of said bone.

"Yeah, I know. I know! Okay, I should open it and see what it says, right?" I nodded even though I didn't want to open it. Robert tapped the envelope again. I sighed. "Fine, I'm opening it. Don't get pushy."

"Friend," Robert said.

"Friend," I said as I put my finger to the opening of the envelope that held not only information on my gran's death, but on my parents' deaths thirty years ago.

The minute I opened it, this quiet we'd been enjoying would be gone—I just knew it. Whatever darkness was trying to dig into Savannah would wake up, like peeling back the curtains and staring into the eyes of a demon. I shuddered and shook my head.

"Like a Band-Aid, just rip it open," I whispered.

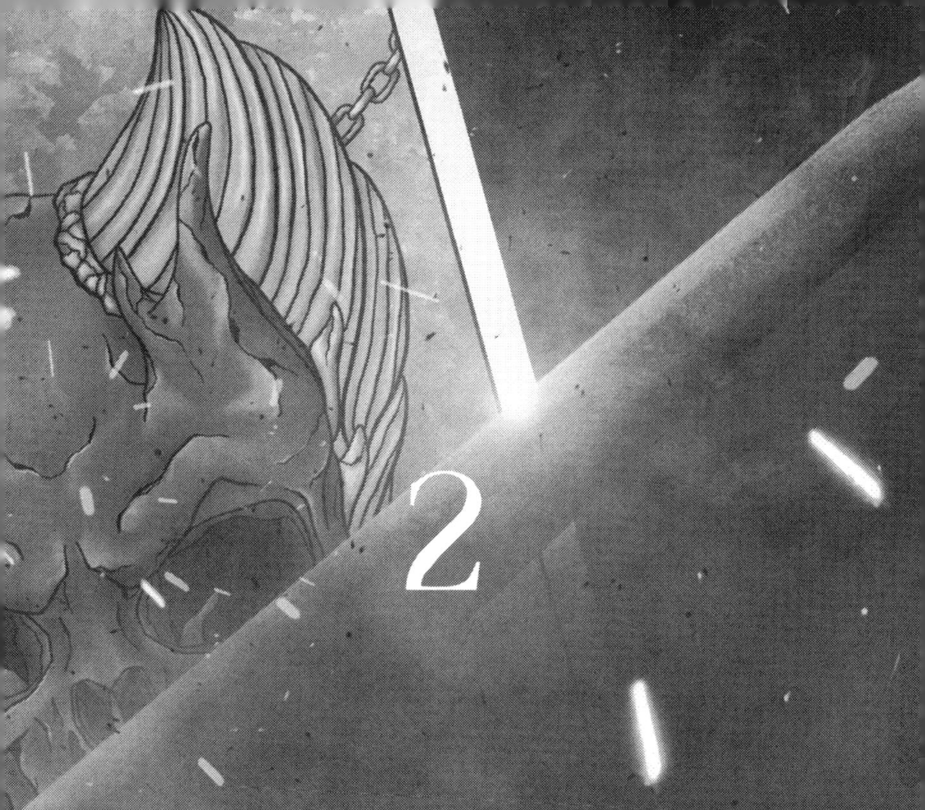

2

I backed farther into my room, slid my finger through the edge of the yellow manila envelope, popped it open and dumped the contents onto my bed in a quick move before I could yet again change my mind. A whoosh of air seemed to fly through the room, dancing across my skin like a whole army of tiny ants crawling across it, biting me here and there. I smacked at my arms and legs, shuddering as the sensation slowly faded, leaving me tingling all over.

That's what I got for freaking myself out.

The paperwork had its back to me, as it were. Maybe that was good. I could put off looking at it for a few more moments.

"I don't know if I'm ready for this." I glanced at Robert. "I mean, I know that Gran's death was probably a murder. And I know that it's likely my parents were offed by someone too. And it's one thing to think about that and want justice. It's another entirely to look at pictures that might show them dead." Or worse, not just dead but altered beyond recognition, something horrific enough to change what memories I had of them. I put my hand against the papers as if I could sense how bad it was just by touching them.

Shaking more than I cared to admit, I forced myself to pick up the stack and start to turn them over.

A boom of *something* against the front door spun me around, breaking my concentration, and I scrunched the papers then stuffed them back into the envelope. The banging on the door continued, quickly becoming a heavy-handed fist by the sounds of it. "Get that, Eric, would you?" I hollered down.

Only there was no Eric answering the door. Where the hell had he gone?

The banging thumped again and I hurried down the stairs. "Hold your horses, would you? You're going to break the damn door!"

I grabbed the knob and swung the door open. The person on the front porch was someone I would have happily kept on avoiding if she weren't trying to hammer the door down. Her hair was pulled into a neat-as-a-pin bun, tight enough to give her a facelift. Her eyes were narrowed and she leaned heavily on a cane I wasn't entirely sure she truly needed.

Missy, Gran's old frenemy. The literal witch who used to strike me with that very cane.

"That's quite the knock you have there." I leaned against the door jam.

Her entire body vibrated with energy. "Aren't you going to invite me in?"

I grimaced. "Seems like a bad idea, inviting bad mojo into my home, don't you think?"

Her eyes went from narrow to furiously bug-eyed in a flash. "I am…this book…" She kept starting and stopping with her words. I'd seen her this angry only once before.

When I'd lit the bottom of her long skirts on fire for telling me I was a stupid, useless git. It had gone better than expected because she hadn't noticed the fire right away, giving me time to put enough distance between us so I could feign innocence. Not to say that she didn't suspect me, I'm sure.

She held up the red leather-bound book I'd exchanged with her for information. "The spells… where is she, I want to speak to her."

I turned my head, fighting a grin. The book I'd given her was, of course, useless. Truly nothing more than a book of spells for beginners wrapped in the crimson cover that had originally bound Gran's book of spells and information about the shadow world. I'd been waiting for this visit, to be honest. I hadn't thought Missy would want to talk to Gran, though. I'd figured she'd be pissed at me for pulling a fast one.

She'd given me help for a bum book. "Gran, Missy is here to speak with you!"

Gran floated down the stairs, stopping just behind me. I stepped back so the two old "friends" could talk. Curiosity kept me close, that and the fact that I didn't trust Missy further than I could throw her.

"Yes, Missy?" My gran clasped her hands in front of her. "What can I do for you?"

Oh, that was pretty formal even for Gran.

Missy held up the book with one hand and jabbed at Gran with her walking stick with the other. Not that it would hurt her, but the indignity of it was meant to wound. "What clouding spell is on this book? I've tried them all!"

I turned my head and coughed to cover up the jaw drop I'd experienced. Missy thought the book was still the real book, but covered with a spell?

"Then perhaps you aren't the witch I thought you were," Gran said.

Missy let out a low hiss that filled the air. "May I remind you that you are dead, and I am not?"

"I'm quite aware," Gran said, her words dry as a popcorn fart. "The fact that you feel the need to remind me makes me wonder if dementia has finally begun to set in. Was your mother not affected by the brain fog? Perhaps you need to speak to a doctor before you try any more spells. I'd hate to see them backfire on you."

I couldn't resist. "You mean like when she set herself on fire?"

Gran nodded solemnly. "True, I often forget about that slip. Terrible."

Missy vibrated where she stood. "Celia, you have no power." She thumped the doorframe with her cane as if she'd like to thump Gran the same way. "Tell me how to read the damn book!"

Oh, she broke out an almost-a-cuss word.

Still shaking, she hit the frame of the house again, and Gran actually took a half step back. "You wouldn't dare."

Missy spun, and leaning heavily on her cane, she strode down the steps and through the garden, switching off the heads of plants as she went like a petulant child.

The gate slammed behind her and I watched as she left a veritable cloud in her wake.

"You're going to have to be careful of her." Gran shook her head. "I can't stop her like I used to."

"I'm not worried. Nothing in that spell book, remember?"

Gran reached out and brushed a hand over my face. "But when she figures out that she's been duped, it will be a dangerous moment for you. She's not evil, Breena, but she's dark. There is a difference."

Her words unsettled me for reasons I couldn't pinpoint, but I found myself stepping out of the house and following the path out to the gate. The air in the garden felt tense, tight, and not unlike the coming of a storm.

I didn't like it.

Our neighbor's little girl, Charlotte, was across the street jumping rope. She paused and waved at me, flashing a big grin with a single missing tooth, her long dark hair in pigtails off to the sides of her neck. I waved back, forcing a smile. "Hey."

"Is Eric baking cookies today?" she asked. "He said I could come get some before I leave for New Orleans."

"I think he just stepped out but come by later. I'm sure he'll have something," I said, wondering where he'd gone. Maybe to talk to Kinkly?

"Oh, that's great. I told my auntie and uncle that he makes the best cookies, and I said I'd bring some with me this time." She leaned on her fence and stared across the street at me, waiting for a car to go by before picking up her thread. "My mom is being deployed again. I don't know for how long. So I want to take enough cookies to last me for a while."

I swallowed the prickling worries I had running through me. "But you'll have fun with your auntie and uncle, right?"

She shrugged. "I guess. They live in an apartment. It's smaller than our house here, but they think our place is haunted. Which is funny, because I'm pretty sure they have a ghost living with them." She sighed and leaned hard on the fence. I looked past her to the house and nodded. I didn't think it was haunted, but I knew there was something supernatural living in the basement. I'd seen a tiny figure darting in and out a few times in the shadows of dawn and dusk.

"You know, they're probably right. Most places in Savannah have a spirit or two. But like my gran, they're there to watch over the people who live here. To protect them."

Charlotte grinned. "I know that. Our ghost is named Bridgette. She talks to me sometimes through the vents."

Of course she did. That earned a real smile from me. "Come over later, Charlotte. You can have as many cookies as you can carry."

She gave me a double thumbs-up and went back to her jump rope. She was a sweet girl, and I felt bad that her mom was being deployed again. That was the life of an army brat, though—you went where your family went, or you got shipped off to another family. At least according to her mom, Ryoko.

I gave her a last wave and headed back into the house. My mind was all wrapped up with Missy's visit. She'd threatened Gran, which I didn't like, but then again, what could she do to a ghost? Not much, methinks.

The kitchen was a mess, so I started in on the dishes. I couldn't help myself. My years with Alan had made me a little bit…crazy about a clean house. He'd never done the cleaning himself—no, he hated cleaning—but he'd always been quick to tell me what I'd done wrong and how I could do it better, all the while acting as though he never made a ducking mess.

"Son of a mother ducking donkey!" I all but threw a pan into the water, sending a splash of suds out onto the floor.

A throat cleared. "I know I haven't been around."

I spun to see Corb standing there, staring at his shoes. "Look, I'm sorry. I know I was a bastard. I wasn't honest with you, and I should have been, right from the start."

A sigh slid out of me. "You aren't the bastard. Alan is."

Corb didn't look up. "I messed up too, Bree. I…"

I waited, but he struggled to find words. So I helped him out.

"Look, did you divorce me after treating me like shit for twenty years? Constantly nitpick my faults? Pin me with every debt we ever accrued together and then some? Lawdy gawd only knows what the final tally is! And I let him, that's the worst part, Corb. I let him because I thought that was what a wife should do. I thought I had to stick it out."

I breathed out the words and my knees failed me. They damn well buckled as a hot flush of horror slid through me. As much as I wanted to just hate Alan and his games, I had played a part in them, and I had to own that.

I'd let it happen, afraid to rock the boat.

"How, Corb? How the…how did he do this? No judge would have approved this B.S. This is not how the legal system works!"

I was on my butt on the hardwood floor, looking up at the underside of the table as if there were answers to be found etched into the wood. Corb lowered himself into a crouch beside me.

"Best I can tell, he had some help from the shadow world. You were right about that, though I wasn't able to get many details. I've been looking since you asked me." He reached out, carefully took my hand and then covered it with his other hand. "It's how he moved up the ranks so quickly in his office. How he made partner without truly putting in the work. I think he's been at this for a while. The signs are all there now that I'm actually looking for them."

I bit my lower lip and looked at him. "That's how he screwed me over." I'd known it. I'd known there was no other way Himself could have gotten away with so much.

"Yeah, it's how he screwed you over. Completely unethical even in the shadow world, but you know how seriously supernatural people take their bargains. There must be a copy of that deal somewhere. We just have to find it. He tried to steal your gran's spell book and her talisman she gave you; that had to be part of the deal." He sat and scooted around me until I was in the cradle of his arms, his legs to either side of me. "Whoever he's working with has some major mojo. I'm sorry I ever discussed this world with Alan. I never would have if I'd thought he'd take me seriously."

His words slowly sunk in and I closed my eyes. "That's why you were at his office building that day I ran into you? You were telling him about the shadow world?"

Because Corb had been there the day I'd found out that Himself had taken my house out from under me and had me evicted (Gran's house wasn't the only one he'd stolen). I'd gone to his office to confront him, only to find Corb in the elevator. He'd walked to Himself's office with me, so both of us had gotten an eyeful of Alan banging the tar out of his new lady lawyer friend. I couldn't have cared less at that point. We were already divorced—if only by days—and even if we hadn't been, I wouldn't have cared anymore. Thinking back, though, the look in her bright hazel eyes irritated me still. Like she relished hurting me. As if it had been personal for her too.

Maybe it had been.

"No," Corb said slowly as if he wasn't sure he wanted to keep going. "I'd already told him about it by then. He asked me to come down and look over this contract he was signing with someone in the shadow world. Must have been the last of all this shit. I didn't end up looking at it because I was busy helping you get out of the building before the police caught up."

Yes, there were police involved, and a high-speed chase through downtown Seattle prior to my arrival at Alan's office. What can I say? When I'm riled up—aka evicted from my own house—you really shouldn't cross me.

It had surprised me when Corb had reached out on Facebook and offered me a place to stay—and like I said, it had surprised him even more when I'd shown up at his doorstep, interrupting a hookup session.

"I'm sorry, Bree. I had no idea he'd—"

I waved a hand. "It's not your fault he's a useless limp dick. Good for nothing but disappointing everyone." I paused a moment, a thought coming to me before I pressed on. "Is that why you offered to help me? Because you felt responsible?"

"To ease my guilt?" Corb nodded and rested his forehead against my shoulder. "Yeah. Initially. There's more, though."

I wasn't sure I could handle more right in the middle of my pity party. "Another time, okay? Was there a reason you came by today? Or was it just to confess that you're a bastard?" If he knew who was helping Alan, I wish he'd just come out and say so.

He didn't lift his head. "I came to apologize. I made moves on you when you were drunk, when you were not in a good head space. You'd just killed a man, and—"

I twisted around. "And? Did we have sex and I don't remember? Because that would be a shame."

"What?" He snapped his head up, eyes wide. "I don't think so, did we?"

I rolled my eyes. "Corb, you were under a *spell.* And I am a grown-ass woman. If we'd knocked boots, it would have been because I wanted to. If anyone would have been coerced, it would have been you, and I'd be apologizing for taking advantage. Besides, I know exactly how to cut your balls off if you made a move I didn't like, okay?"

The relief on his face would have been funny if not for the fact that I'd threatened his balls. Okay, maybe that made it funnier. What I knew was that

Crash had threatened Corb at some point and made it clear that he needed to apologize. While I appreciated the notion, it wasn't really needed. I wasn't so precious that I was offended a younger man had hit on me. Even if it was because of a spell.

Robert slid into view, just behind Corb. "Friend. Coming."

I looked at Corb. "Kind of late, Robert."

"Other."

Corb lifted his hand to my face. "I do care about you, Breena. Not like…not because you were family for years." Something along his jaw ticked and he ducked his head close, pressing his lips to mine, surprising me. Just a quick kiss and he pulled back. "Okay? Can we start again? Maybe I can take you on a proper date where the restaurant doesn't blow up?"

I was confused, mostly because there were too many emotions galloping through me. Worry about what Missy was up to. Anger that Alan, who'd always ridiculed me for believing in magic, had used it against me. Confusion and uncertainty because of Corb's confession. And then a hot flush of desire hit me, so wild I thought it would strangle me. I blinked a couple times and found myself looking past Corb, spotting the source of the sudden heat curling through me.

Crash stood in the back door, his eyes on Corb and me sitting there wrapped up in each other's arms.

At another time in my life I would have stuttered and tried to explain. At another time I would have felt embarrassed to be attracted to two men at once. But that was then, and I was a new kind of cougar.

I grinned up at Crash and winked. "Want to join us?"

3

No, I really wasn't into a threesome, despite my question, but Crash and Corb didn't know that. And their differing reactions as I sat there between Corb's knees on my kitchen floor opened my eyes more than a little.

Crash gave a slow grin. "I doubt you could handle both of us at once."

Corb let go of me and pushed to his feet. "She's bluffing."

I sighed and slowly pulled myself up using the edge of the table. "The young ones never think I'm capable. But the truth is I could show you both a trick or two, right, Robert?" I looked to my skeleton buddy for support.

He lifted a hand and gave a bony thumbs-up.

Corb raised his eyebrows. "I can't see this Robert you've been talking to all this time. You know that, right?"

I looked at Crash. "What about you? Can you see Robert?"

Crash narrowed his eyes, staring at the space next to me where Robert stood swaying. "I can see a shadow if I pay very close attention, but he slips through my vision."

"Weird. Because Sarge and Luke can see him. And Eric," I said.

"He is between two realms, straddling them, if you will. Eric can stand between realms too. That's how he keeps from being found by humans." Crash walked farther into the kitchen and went straight to the stash of pastries Eric had been baking. Seriously, where was my bigfoot roomie anyway? Had he gone to talk to Kinkly? That seemed the most likely reason for his sudden disappearance, but he'd been gone a long time. Silently, I wished him luck. Better luck than I was having. Then again, I had two hot guys hanging out in my kitchen, so maybe my luck wasn't the problem.

Crash scooped up a jam-filled flaky confection and took a bite. "Shifters can often sense the dead. Like any animal."

Corb moved to stand a little closer to me. I took a step to the left. "If you pee on my leg to mark territory, I'll seriously kick you in the shins."

He shook his head—an *oh, Bree* kind of shake—then turned his eyes on me. "So I'll pick you up for dinner tonight?"

Really? He was really going to push this now? I sighed. Of course he was—he was peeing on me without peeing on me. "I'm not going to turn down a free meal. But not tonight. Tomorrow would be better."

"I'll pick you up at five." For a moment, I thought he was going to try for another kiss, but he must have gotten the hint from my narrowed eyes because he backed up and made his way to the front door. I sighed and sat at the table.

"Bad news?" Crash said around a mouthful of pastry. I lifted my eyes to his, fighting the need to throw myself bodily at him. Gawd in heaven, he was hotter than sin and twice as enticing.

"Same old. I hate my ex. Wish I could stuff him in a body bag and drop him into the river," I said.

"I don't much like my ex either," Crash said.

I looked up at him and laughed. "Yeah, she isn't my favorite fairy queen, I'll say that."

He popped the last of the pastry in his mouth and licked his finger, and I had to look away as my face heated. Yup, too many dirty thoughts rolling around in my brain. Way too many.

More than my face heated as I turned my back on him, trying to get my wildly treacherous hormones under control.

"Breena, is there something I can do to help?" Crash asked.

I wanted to say yes, I really did, and tell him he could start by throwing me on the table and having his way with me repeatedly.

But my worry about Alan interrupted my hormone fest. Who the hell knew what Himself was up to, or how deeply the hypocrite had entrenched himself in the shadow world? And while I knew Crash would happily help with that problem, too, I wanted all the joy of kicking Alan in the balls, physically and in the wallet. And I wouldn't pass up a serious metaphysical wallop either. I'd take any of the three. Besides, Himself and his threats weren't dangerous to my health, just my…anything I owned.

And that's when the penny dropped.

I groaned. The house. I turned to face Crash. "You need to take my name off the deed. If the loan sharks or whoever is recalling the debt find out about that, they'll take the house."

Crash's eyebrows shot up. "Who told you?"

"You did."

He leaned back on the counter, folding his arms over his chest, which flexed his biceps under his plain black T-shirt. Damn it, all the hotness in one package. It wasn't fair. "You were awake when I was talking with your gran?"

"Yup. I've been telling you all I'm a good faker. Just ask my ex." I winked and he laughed.

"I'd know."

And just like that, the heat at my core turned to lava. I couldn't look away as he stared at me.

"I'd know," he repeated. "Even if we shouldn't."

"Heard you the first time." I struggled to breathe. He was...too much. I knew it. *He* knew it. This was a bad, terrible, idea.

But, oh man, did I ever want to jump his bones. I mean, my libido had been riding high ever since I hit forty, like through the roof, but Crash just flat out hit every sexy button inside me. Mature, built like a brick house, fantastic eyes, an amazing kisser...I could keep adding to that list all damn day. But the fact remained that he was a fae king. Or had been, I wasn't really sure if he was still a king given that he'd divorced the fae queen. He worked in shady deals that I couldn't ignore. And then there were the girls he'd been with...I couldn't compete with that.

I backed up as he approached me until I bumped into the wall. "This is a bad idea, Crash."

"I know it is. I'm aware that this is probably the worst idea, but do remind me why again," he said, and I realized he was stalking me and I was acting like prey. That thought was like cold water.

I stood a little straighter, put a hand out and jabbed two fingers into his too-hard abs, stopping him in place. "Because. You said it yourself, the fae would use me. I recognize that you are way out of my league. I'm not stupid."

He stopped his approach and opened his mouth, but I cut him off, diving into the deep end in a way that my younger self would never have dared.

"The thing is, you know I've got the hots for you. And for some reason, you promised my gran to look out for me. And that means you have a leg up on me.

So you don't have to pretend, okay? You're looking out for me, but I get that you don't actually like me like that. I mean, I know you like me as a friend—"

"Stop." He held up both hands, palms facing me, and my mouth clicked shut, cutting short the rambling I'd fallen into. "Bree, just stop." Crash blew out a breath and the intensity in the room slid down a notch. "I'll get your name off the deed before the day's end." He paused and the weight in his blue and gold-flecked eyes pinned me in place. His eyes dilated, and for just a moment, I thought he'd say something like *screw it, let's do it on the table*. But before I could say *yes, please*, he closed his eyes, cutting me off from whatever he was feeling. "Have a good night with Corb tomorrow."

He turned and walked out of the back door, the screen flapping and banging behind him.

I was leaning against the kitchen wall, breathing hard, my body cursing me for not dragging that delectable man upstairs for some serious afternoon delights. I opened my mouth to call him back, but I had enough sense to shut it before I could. Hooking up with him really was a bad idea—I knew it in every ache of my body.

"That man is going to be trouble, Gran."

She snorted from somewhere in the other room, but otherwise, kept her thoughts to herself.

The front door opened, the sound of footsteps met my ears, and then Eric brushed past me, his chin to his chest. He didn't seem to notice me as he went straight to the fridge and pulled out a can of pressurized whipped cream. With a flick of his thumb, he popped the lid off, held it over his mouth and depressed a whole pile of the chemical-laced concoction.

"You talked to Kinkly?" I asked.

He nodded, swallowed the cream, and looked at me. "It didn't go well."

I walked over to him and motioned for him to give me the can. I sprayed a bunch of the fluffy sweet stuff into my mouth, choking on the amount as I swallowed it down. "I just turned Crash down."

Eric groaned. "This is terrible. She laughed at me, and not in a mean way—she genuinely thought I was teasing her." He sprayed more whipped cream into his mouth and then handed it back to me. I took my shot.

"He said I was right, it was a terrible idea." I started to giggle. "Oh my gawd, I turned down the hottest guy I've ever known. Because I was afraid he'd use me for some nefarious purpose. Like having red-hot sex until I can't think straight." What was wrong with me? I totally should have gone for it. I could keep my heart and libido separate, couldn't I?

Eric looked at me. "I got on one knee and proposed to her, and she laughed louder." He took another squirt of whipped cream, but his lips twitched. "We are both losers."

I burst out laughing so hard, tears crept into the corners of my eyes. I took the can of whipped cream from him and saluted him. "We *are* both losers."

Eric started to laugh, a braying noise that only made us both laugh harder as bits of whipped cream flew out of our mouths. Which was how Suzy and Feish found us, on our butts, laughing so hard that tears ran down our cheeks, whipped cream smeared on our faces.

"What in the world happened to you?" Suzy crouched beside Eric and swiped whipped cream off his mouth and tucked it into her own mouth.

My eyebrows shot up, but he was as oblivious to her as Kinkly was to him. "Oh, you know, easing a broken heart," he mumbled.

Suzy grinned and flipped her long blond hair forward. "I have a much better remedy than whipped cream. Although that's not a bad addition."

Eric sighed. "I'm all out of self-pity for the day. But thanks."

Feish snorted and put her hands on her hips. "She wants to get you in the sack, Bigfoot."

I choked on my mouthful of whipped cream as Eric's head swung around to stare at Suzy. "What?"

And for all that was holy, the half-siren blushed. "I like you, Eric. You're sweet and kind, and handsome. And…you make me smile."

I scrambled to my feet, grabbed Feish by the hand, and hauled her to the back door. "Time to go."

"Wait, what are we doing? I want to see what he says!" Feish tried pulling me back the other way, but I didn't release her.

Of all the times we needed to be out of the house, Suzy and Eric potentially getting together was high on the priority list.

"We'll find something to do," I said.

Heaven help me, I found a little more than I'd bargained for.

Again.

4

Where are we going?” Feish let me drag her down the street, away from my gran’s house where Suzy and Eric may or may not have been hooking up. I certainly didn’t want to be there to find out. I silently apologized to Gran for leaving her behind. I mean, it wasn’t like I could take her with me, but still…she’d be mad when I got back.

“I don’t know, anywhere but the house,” I said.

“I think Boss is back.” Feish got this sly look in her bulbous eyes.

I shook my head. “I turned him down. Or he turned me down. Both maybe.”

Her fish mouth bobbed open like she was gasping for air. It was a disconcerting look for sure. “Whaaaat?”

"Look, I know he's out of my league!" I almost shouted. I could feel my control slipping as we drew closer to Centennial Park. Really, it wasn't a park but a graveyard that extended well beyond the walls that were supposed to contain it. The closer I got, the more my agitation increased, until I was all but vibrating with it.

Because what had happened in the kitchen still bothered me.

"You too good for him anyway," Feish said softly. "He's used goods."

Her assessment of Crash put me over the edge of crazy laughter. I stopped at the brick wall surrounding Centennial Park and leaned against it as I laughed till I had to cross my legs. Tears streamed down my face as I clung to the wall. Used goods. Crash was used goods?

Like…was that something he (or any man) would ever worry about? Doubtful.

"Why so funny?" Feish asked. "He was a ladies' man for long time. Not now. But long time."

That made me remember those girls who'd been under his arms at the fae in-between we'd stumbled into. They'd been stunners, ten plus on the scale, and younger than me by half my years.

The thing was, whenever I was around Crash, I forgot all that. He drove it out of me, or rather my desire for him did. Whenever I was near him, I was filled with the heated wish to explore every muscle on his body with my mouth. I pressed my forehead against the coolness of the bricks, calm slowly suffusing me.

"I'm hungry," Feish announced suddenly. "Let's go to the Pirates' House. I want pecan pie." She looped an arm through mine and dragged me in the general direction of the restaurant. The last thing I wanted was food. The chemical whipped cream felt like it was curdling in my belly, which, let me tell you, was a crappy feeling. I let her lead us for a few minutes before I realized we weren't heading toward the restaurant at all. What was she up to now?

"I'm not hungry."

"I am," Feish insisted, pulling me to the left. I pulled back. We were down by Factors Row, and a set of eight long, hairy legs dangled down from the walkway above. I looked at Feish, who shrugged.

The legs belonged to Jinx, a shifter of sorts who frequented Factors Row. Really, she was more of a trickster who could change shapes as an added bonus.

"Jinx, what are you editing now?" I called up to her, and she scrambled away. A red pen fell from the rafters, along with a series of papers that floated down like oversized snowflakes.

"Nothing!" she yelled as she dropped to the ground and scooped up the papers. They stuck to the toxic hairs that covered her legs. "I'm not editing."

"No?" I picked up a sheet of neatly printed paper that had landed near my feet. The series of red marks across the page would no doubt be the bane of any writer's existence. "Looks like you're editing to me."

"Proofreading," she snapped, one hairy leg yanking the paper away from me. I made sure to not touch her.

The spines in her hairy legs were a bad match for me, and the last time I'd encountered them, I'd needed a lot of help—namely from Crash—in order to come out of the stupor she'd put me in.

"What are you doing here?" Jinx scuttled sideways, hugging the papers to her chest, not unlike the way I had held the manila envelope filled with papers about my family's deaths.

"Looking for trouble," Feish said. "You hear of any jobs? I think you might know of one."

I shot a look at Feish. What the hell was she going on about? Our new odd jobs group, which we had yet to call anything but Gran's Girls, had heard about a couple of potential jobs this week, but none were really promising and hadn't panned out. Still, I wasn't positive I wanted to ask Jinx for help. She was definitely trouble with a capital T.

Jinx looked hard at Feish and then gave a slow nod. "Goblin looking for help yesterday." She tapped one long spindly leg against her mouth, which drew my attention to her long, curved fangs.

"We want that job," Feish said.

"We do?" I looked at Feish, who was trying hard not to look at me at all. She kept her eyes fixed on the giant spider.

Jinx rubbed one fang with the tip of her foot. "If I tell you about him, will you bring me a book on editing?"

The weirdness that was my life and Savannah had no bounds.

Feish clapped her webbed hands together. "Right now."

Apparently, this was happening.

I sighed. "Sure thing. One book on edits, coming up."

Which was how I found myself back in the used bookstore on River Street. The owner narrowed his eyes at me, looking me up and down. "Do I know you?"

"Nope." I strode into the place like I hadn't loudly (and a tad aggressively) demanded a copy of *Charlotte's Web* on my last visit—also for Jinx. I made my way through the store to the non-fiction section to find a bunch of books on how to write. Fewer on editing, but there were a couple.

I pulled out one that was super thick, the edges turned down, and had lots of highlights and marks on its pages. That would do the trick. I tucked it under my arm, ready to go.

Feish tapped me on the shoulder. "I'm looking for a good book on romance. I want to understand how it should happen between two people. Where should I start?"

I schooled my face because I didn't want to hurt her feelings if she hoped to find herself a man. "Well, try the romance section. See if they have any of Denise Grover Swank's books. They're super fun. Perfect amount of heat and giggles. You can't go wrong with her."

Feish gave me a wide grin and hurried off down another thin alleyway of books. Apparently, we weren't in any hurry to get back to Jinx, so I let my feet take me where they would. The place was a maze, and I was happy to get lost in it for a while. I certainly didn't want to head back home anytime soon.

Given the way that Suzy had been eyeing Eric like the first meal she'd been handed in weeks, they'd be at it for a while. Lawdy jaysus, at least someone was getting laid.

I grimaced again at the thought of Gran being stuck in there with them, but then I found myself grinning. I was so going to get an earful when I got back and that just made me...happy. Because it could be far worse. I could be without Gran entirely. I'd take her being mad at me from time to time if it meant I got to keep her in my life.

My fingers brushing across the spines of the shelved books, I stopped dead in my tracks when one book heated and all but glued itself to my fingertips. Slowly I turned and looked at the item in question. There were no words on the outer edge, and when I pulled it out, the cover didn't have anything on it either. It reminded me of the way I used to cover my textbooks with brown kraft paper.

I flipped it open, and then shoved it back as soon as I saw the interior title page.

Black Spells of Savannah and the Undead.

I turned, flushed with a weird sense of foreboding, and immediately stumbled over someone.

"Oh, I'm sorry." I hit the side of the aisle and looked down at the person I'd stepped on.

Oster Boon, the leprechaun with fangs I'd bought Gran's red leather-bound book from, stared up at me. He smiled. "Breena, I see you are still alive. That is rather shocking."

"Pardon...what?" I stumbled over the words. "What do you mean by that?"

"Well, seems like you've stirred the ants' nest quite sufficiently." He smiled and there wasn't anything about it that screamed mean, but I still took a step back. "Just wanted to make sure you remember you owe me a favor. Try not to die before I call it in."

I wanted to wrinkle my nose and tell him off, but he wasn't wrong. It was part of the deal that had allowed me to reclaim the book. I *did* owe him a favor. "Are you cashing it in now?"

"No, no," he waved his hands in the air, "I just wanted to remind you. That's all. Oh, and you should take that book."

He tipped himself forward in something that resembled a bow at the waist before he turned and strode away. Just a reminder, my ass. How had he known where to find me?

But he'd just told me to take the book of *Black Spells of Savannah and the Undead,* and I'd barely opened it. Had he put it there? I hurried to catch up to him, but he was already gone, the slippery little leprechaun.

I turned and stared at the aisle I'd hurried through. Putting my hand back on the shelves of books, I let my fingers trail along the spines again. Because maybe he was wrong and maybe...the same sticky hot feeling rushed through my fingers and I jerked my hand back.

Damn book was apparently coming home with me. I grimaced and pulled it out, stacking it on top of the book on editing so I didn't have to touch it.

Muttering under my breath about how stupid this was and how I didn't want a stupid spell book that felt like death incarnate, I made my way to the front counter and put the two books on the table. Feish hurried up beside me. "They had two of Swank's books. I can't wait!" She set them on top of my two and the shopkeeper rung them up, giving me the stink eye the whole time.

I paid the bill with a twenty, took my change, and said nothing else. Feish quickly noticed I was quieter than usual.

"What's wrong?"

"Oster Boon was in there. He reminded me that I owed him a favor." I held up the mid-sized, deceptively simple-looking book. "This was in there, too, and he thought I should take it since it stuck to my damn finger."

Feish took it and flipped it over in her hand. "A blank notebook?"

"Open it. Read the title page," I said.

She did as I asked and all but threw the book at me, her face paling around the gills to an even paler yellow-green. "That is…that is bad. Maybe the worst kind. Could be how to raise a demon in there."

"Yeah. I figured it was something bad like that." I made myself open it again. Scratched under the title was a very faint signature. So shadowy, I couldn't make it out. I closed it and put it into my hip bag.

"Agreed, agreed. But bad. So bad." Feish shuddered and made a burbling sound as if she were underwater. "Keep it safe, maybe."

"Yeah, that's the plan," I said.

We made our way back to where Jinx waited. I held up the book on editing which she plucked from my fingers. "It looks well used, which made me think it would have a lot of good suggestions..." I trailed off as she began yanking pages out and eating them. "Well, whatever. Tell us about this goblin who needs help."

Please *gawd* don't let him be in the wildlife preserve. We'd already had two major cases out that way, and I'd had enough of trees and marshy water for a good long while.

"West of the city is the goblins' territory unless you go through Faerie land to get there," Jinx said around a mouthful of paper, "but this goblin is hiding in the Marshall House downtown. Away from his people. Says someone is trying to steal a family heirloom. Wants to talk to you."

I wanted to smack my hand against my forehead. That hotel was seriously haunted. I'd walked by it a few days ago, the first time since my return to Savannah, and I'd felt the malevolence from a simple walk on the other side of the street.

Likely because of the same reason I felt the house next to Gran's had amped up its "freak out Breena" vibe. Something had changed in me, making me more susceptible to the undead.

"Are you sure?" Please, please be wrong. And then the rest of what she'd said clicked. "Wait, he wants to talk to *me*?"

"He said that's where he's hiding. He asked me to find out if you would help him, but not Crash. He doesn't want Crash to know."

Feish bobbed her head along with Jinx. What the hell? Had these two had a prior discussion about this? I was betting every dollar I'd stashed away that they had. They were up to something.

That thought had me frowning. "Why would he not want Crash to help him in the first place?"

Feish tapped my shoulder. "Goblins are Unseelie. Darker fae, but not darkest fae. Boss is Unseelie too. But there is a rift between him and the one who says he is king of goblins. So goblins don't always trust the Boss because the king kills those who go to Crash."

I muttered a line of lyric from the real Boss, the words flowing off my tongue without thought. "The highway's jammed with broken heroes on a last-chance power drive. Everybody's out on the run tonight, but there's no place left to hide."

Jinx and Feish looked at me.

"Is she okay?" Jinx asked. "Did she get hit in the head?"

Feish shrugged and wobbled her fish lips. "No idea, she is just kind of strange, I think."

The irony was not lost on me that a river maid with gills and fish lips along with a talking spider who thought she was an editor thought yours truly was strange.

I waved a hand at the two of them. "Never mind. Jinx, why didn't you tell Crash?"

She paused from shoving chapter thirteen into her mouth at a rate that would have choked a horse to speak around the pages.

"No. He didn't come by. You showed up first. First dibs," Jinx mumbled and then sighed. "So good. This book is just magnificent."

So weird.

Well, a job was a job, and if I couldn't find a way to reverse all the debt Himself had managed to foist onto me, I needed every job I could find.

I looked at Feish. "I guess it's time to pay the Marshall House a visit."

5

The plan was for me to drop our stuff off at Gran's house and for Feish to get us food—she was still hungry—before we met outside the Marshall House to speak with a goblin. A goblin who wanted me to help him, and to keep it a secret from Crash.

Curiouser and curiouser. The intrigue of it had me more than a little excited.

Our plan was solid, but I got derailed in an unexpected way.

I snuck through the back door at Gran's, quiet as I could, and stuffed the black-spell book and Feish's new romances into the cupboard next to the fridge. When I came back later, I'd show the book of spells to Gran and ask where she thought I should hide it.

My fingers lingered on the cover. I swallowed hard, and at the last second, scooped it up and shoved it back into my bag.

"You are going to be trouble," I whispered.

A creak from upstairs made me wince. I did not want to hear Suzy and Eric knocking boots, thank you very much.

"Sorry, Gran, you're on your own," I whispered.

I hurried out the door into the backyard. I turned and came face to face with a ghost I did not like one bit. I had to clamp a hand over my mouth to keep from screaming.

Matilda, the ghost from next door, had returned. She crept onto our property slowly as though it pained her, and kept pointing to her neck as her head flopped off to the side. "Gah, get out of here," I whispered and made a shooing motion with my hands.

A dark chuckle rolled out of the Sorrel-Weed house.

Yes, send her back to me. Send me the old woman too. I would like them both to serve me.

Chills rippled over and through me, and I *grabbed* Matilda and yanked her behind me. Don't ask me how, because I couldn't understand it in that moment. "He's hurting you, Matilda?"

I own her. You can't have her, dark one.

Smoky black tendrils shot out of the house next door, wrapped around Matilda as if they were ropes, and just like that she was sucked away with a violent jerk, a silent scream on her lips as she was drawn into the house.

The breath in my chest froze, and my limbs shook like leaves in a windstorm. I stepped backward, keeping my eyes locked on the house across from me—back and back, I went until I was going down the steps that led into the basement below the house. I fumbled with the doorknob behind me, swung the door open, and shut it, finally blocking the sight of the house and the darkness within.

How the hell was I going to deal with that place being right next door? Since my nearly-all-the-way-dead experience the week before, the Sorrel-Weed house's darkness seemed to get worse every day.

I leaned my head against the door, the knowledge that I would have to go back out, that I would have to cross the lawn and pass by the stupid house freaking me out. How was no one else feeling the monstrosity lurking in there? I'd been looking through Gran's book of spells, but there was nothing in there about banishing a house spirit. Maybe that *Black Spells of Savannah and the Undead* book had something. I shuddered at the thought of using that book. Not that I had any gift for spells, anyway.

"Crash, you in here?" I called out, the heat of the day not fully permeating the basement. But the forge was going, and the sound of the flames was weirdly soothing, as if they would burn out the voices of the ghosts next door.

"Yes." His voice was rough and solid, and it provided me with the steadiness I needed in that moment. I smoothed my hands over my face, unable to turn to look at him. He'd rejected me, and I him, only hours before, and we'd both agreed it was for the best.

I couldn't stop the shaking in my legs though, couldn't ignore the need to let the fire between us drive out the darkness that was trying to lay claim to me by digging into my soul. Because whatever was in the Sorrel-Weed house was darker than anything else I'd run into in the shadow world, and that was saying a lot.

"Breena, are you okay?" The concern in his voice undid me.

"Nope. That's a nope," I whispered.

Then his hands were on my shoulders, turning me, and I buried my face against his chest.

"You're freezing." He swept me up into his arms and carried me closer to his forge. He sat on a chair, pulling me down with him. "How is that possible in this heat? What happened?"

My eyes remained wide open, because I was suddenly afraid of closing them. "Just give me a minute."

He didn't push, and he didn't let me go either. The minutes ticked by, and the pounding of my heart finally slowed, though the fear was still at the edge of my mind. Like if I let it, it would crawl over me again, freezing me in place and stealing the new life I'd made for myself. "That house next door. It's harboring something darker than just a nasty ghost." I shuddered. Even saying it out loud felt like a risk—as though I was calling it to attention.

"It's always been dark," Crash said softly. "The history there is ugly."

"It's worse now. Something has changed. There's an…entity in there that's hurting Matilda. Before, she was in there alone," I said with absolute certainty. I rubbed my face.

His arms cinched tighter around me. "I believe you, but I can't see it. You seem to have an easier time picking up on the dead."

I looked up at him, changing directions because I did *not* want to think about the critter haunting the Sorrel-Weed house. "Crash, what the hell were you doing with those two girls young enough to be your daughters?"

He stared down at me. "I thought this was a terrible idea. All of it."

"Oh, it is, that hasn't changed." I shrugged. "Doesn't mean I don't want to know—"

"That we don't feel something when we are in contact with each other?" He arched a brow. "Is this helping you push back the fear?"

"Distractions are a beautiful thing," I said, knowing that I needed to go. Feish was waiting for me, and whatever was in the Sorrel-Weed house would still be there when I came out, no matter how long I waited in the basement with Crash. He couldn't really protect me, but when I was with him, I felt safe—even though it was probably an illusion. It was why I'd sought him out just now if I was being honest with myself.

He bent his head, hair falling over his forehead, and his eyes locked on mine then slid down to my lips. "It would be a beautiful thing even if it's a bad idea."

Oh dear. I clung to my one touchstone in the raging sea of hormones and desire. The thing I used to remind myself that he didn't really want me. "The girls? You just like them young?"

His jaw ticked and he pulled back, a flash of irritation on his handsome face. "You are not the only one with a job to do. One of mine is protecting the younger fae, and in a place like that, what you saw needed to look the way it looked."

I couldn't help the dry sarcasm. "Right, it needed to look like the three of you…" I left it open for him to finish the sentence, thinking I'd push him into the depths of anger. That's the way Himself would have responded, defensive and childish. Mostly because he was usually guilty as could be when I finally confronted him about something that had to do with other women. He'd told me more than once his relationships with others were none of my business.

I wasn't falling for that stupidity again.

But not Crash, there was no defensiveness. Nope, Crash *chuckled* at me. "There are fae men who would hurt the younger women badly if they didn't think there would be repercussions. I have a fairly good reputation for handing out repercussions to those who cross me or hurt those who are under my protection. It is my job as an elder fae."

Well, damn it. That was some serious white knight business that was all kinds of sweet and chivalrous. "Damn it, I didn't want to like you more," I muttered.

I waved a hand between us as if that would cut the sexual tension. Only it didn't work. He caught my one hand and raised it to his mouth where he pressed a kiss to my wrist that involved lips, tongue, and a nip of teeth.

Fire, electricity, and a steady thrumming low in my body sprung to life, awakened by that simple touch, by the kiss that hadn't even landed on my lips. Far too easy to imagine his mouth other places.

All the places.

I swallowed hard. "You shouldn't do that."

"Why not?"

I went with complete honesty. "My clothes will fall off."

He burst out laughing. "Gods, Breena, you always manage to catch me off guard."

I used his distraction to slide off his lap and what was getting seriously hard down there. "I should go. Thanks for…helping me. Again."

He didn't step toward me. "At some point, we will have to discuss this."

I didn't fool myself into thinking he meant something like a blacksmithing training session or another discussion about the house next door and the darkness within it. He'd be there for those things, too, I had no doubt, but he was talking about when I was ready to ride him like a pony into the wee hours of the morning. Maybe several mornings. I swallowed hard. "I'll keep that in mind…should Corb not be available."

Oh, yeah, I went there. I was trying to push him away, but he was on to me.

He laughed softly. "I doubt he'd be able to keep up with you. There is some supernatural blood in him, but not enough to handle all that you are, Bree."

"Corb is supernatural? What is he?" Those two questions flew out of my lips, and on the heels of it came a thought I did not like one bit. Was Himself supernatural too? Was that how he'd screwed me over, not because of some connection Corb had accidently given him? No, that couldn't be it. Corb said he'd introduced Alan to the shadow world.

"That will be his story to tell you," Crash said. "Not mine." He stood and turned to the forge, his back muscles pulling on the T-shirt he wore, and the urge to run my hands over him had me clenching my fists.

I forced my feet to move toward the door, barely shuffling because of the waves of desire ripping through my body just from thinking about Crash and everything he'd just offered me. About all that he could be to me if I let myself trust him fully. But I'd been burned badly by Alan, and I wasn't about to let my hormones be the deciding factor here.

Out of the basement door, I climbed the steps to the backyard and felt the presence of the darkness in the Sorrel-Weed house as keenly as before, cold and dark and ducking ugly. But now I was all jacked up on libido with nowhere to spend that coin. Perfect. The wild sexual frustration protected me from any fear I might have felt.

"I'll deal with you later, jackass!" I snapped and pointed at the house as I strode by. "You come on my property, though, and I'll pull all your bits apart and stuff them into the beyond! See how you like them apples, dink face!"

I had no idea how to do any of that, but the darkness seemed to pause, uncertain for a moment, caught in the onslaught of my frustration which spilled out as anger.

That moment of hesitation from whatever was in the house next door was all I needed to get by the critter, out of the backyard, and onto the street. There was still a sensation of eyes on me, but it was far weaker out here, away from the two houses.

"Duck me," I whispered as I found myself wobbling down the street, a strange mix of hormones, fear, and frustration propelling me forward.

By the time I reached the Marshall House, I'd mostly composed myself. At least I was walking normally, and the libido had faded to a dull thrum. Feish waited for me across the street from the hotel, her hands tucked behind her back.

"Did you pick up something to eat?" I asked.

"Yes, it was good. You want some?" She pulled her hands out from behind her and held out a grease-soaked paper bag.

I took the bag and peeked in. A trio of oily hush puppies waited for me, and I ate them quickly, not caring they were cold. I was hungrier than I'd realized.

"You got to eat better," Feish said. "Vegetables and fruits, or you be getting red spots all over your face."

"Then you should have brought me vegetables and fruit," I mumbled around a mouthful.

"I wanted greasy food," she mumbled back. "I didn't think you'd eat the last of them."

As always with Feish, her reasoning was just a little off kilter. I wiped my fingers on the paper bag and tossed it into the trash.

"Let's go talk to this goblin. See if we can snag us a job. Should be easy since he's looking for us." I jogged across the street, easily dodging the traffic slowly making its way through Savannah's shopping district, Feish on my heels. The four-story hotel was painted green, and the the window-covered front of the building was inexplicably dark for this time of day. Or maybe it was just me and my overly active imagination. Yes, it could be just me.

As we stepped into the lobby, a noticeable chill slid over my skin.

Then again, maybe it wasn't just me.

I grabbed Feish and stopped her beside me as the cold wrapped around my wrist and tugged me toward the stairs.

"Feish. A ghost is pulling on me, I think." Or a ghostly energy anyway. Normally I could see ghosts, but I didn't see anything of the sort.

I reached into my pocket and pulled out Robert's finger bone and set it on the ground. A moment later, he materialized at my side, swaying ever so slightly. Feish blinked her bulbous eyes at me, the extra layer of thin transparent skin flicking over her eyeballs.

"You think we need Robert?"

"He's got an eye for these things, and has saved my bacon more than once," I said softly as I took a few steps forward. The pull of the strange energy still tugged at me, but something else had caught my attention, holding my feet where they were.

Ahead of me stood a cluster of three men in suits and ties having what looked like an intense discussion. Two were average height, the third barely four feet tall, though he held himself up straight and acted as though he ruled the room. That alone wouldn't have interested me, but a fourth man strode up to them, shook their hands, and motioned for them to follow him deeper into the hotel.

Seeing that last man set off my Spidey sense. The fourth man was Davin, the only council member I knew. Mid-thirties, he was smarmy, a liar, and I didn't like him. He'd helped Sarge and Corb go undercover to dig out the poisonous roots of Hattie and her crew's organization, but from what I could tell, he hadn't been entirely honest even with them.

"Feish, are those other three guys council members?" I made myself step to the side, tucking us behind a tall plant. Not exactly hiding, but at least we were out of their direct line of sight. Given that the council had summoned me to speak about my involvement in the shadow world—and I'd ignored said summons—I didn't want to land on their radar again.

Far as I was concerned, the council was full of misogynistic pricks who kept women and others they deemed as "lesser," like half-breeds or weaker supernaturals, from any position in which they might get a say. Not my kind of people, and I could only imagine the way our conversation would go. Them trying to boss me. Me telling them to duck off. Hardly productive.

Feish peeked around the edge of the plant. "Yes, two of them. Roderick is one. The other is Bruce. Third is a goblin named Derek. They are all going toward the main ballroom."

From between the plant's sparse leaves, I watched as they went, taking note of the men, making sure they were completely around the corner before I stepped out from behind our hiding place.

"You think Derek is our guy?" I asked quietly.

"No," Feish burbled. "Derek would not ask Jinx to pass on message. Not his style."

It didn't surprise me that she knew so much about a goblin. Feish was a font of knowledge when she wanted to be.

"Come on." I motioned for her and Robert to follow me as I hurried across the main floor to the stairs. Maybe it wasn't the smartest idea to head upstairs when some sort of phantom energy wanted me to do exactly that, but we needed to get away. Plus, we had no idea where the goblin was hiding, beyond that it was in this hotel, and it seemed likely he'd choose the most haunted floor, somewhere there'd be fewer humans. I sent Feish up first, then me, then Robert trailing behind.

Only Robert didn't follow up the second flight. I stopped and peeked down around the corner, hearing voices.

A man's low Southern drawl rumbled into my ears. "Robert, what are you doing here, old friend?"

"Friend," Robert growled in a way that did not for one second make me think he meant it. Who the hell could see him?

"Well, I was your friend for a very long time. I'm surprised to see you up and about. As it were."

I glanced at Feish and motioned for her to be quiet and stay where she was ahead of me.

"Going." Robert's voice was still growly. He didn't like this person who had cornered him, which meant I didn't like him either. And the fact that the guy could see Robert meant he wasn't human. Reason enough for me to pull a knife.

Freeing one blade, I headed back down the stairs, cursing the fact that I'd to have to walk up this section twice.

"I realize you're going," the man said, "but who are you with, Robert? Who called you from the grave?" That Southern drawl didn't sound threatening on the surface, but it was what he wasn't saying that worried me. Who was strong enough to bring Robert forward? Who was Robert working for? Was it possible the skeleton was here to watch me for less chivalrous reasons than biting off werewolf ears and keeping me safe?

I took the last step around the winding corner and pointed a knife at the man holding Robert. "Hey, that's my friend you're interrogating."

Robert's swaying slowed, and his voice eased off on the growling. "Friend." This time the word was far softer.

The man with him was—*of course*—one of the councilmen who'd been with Davin. His eyes lifted to mine, deep green with a flash of silver around the edges. I hadn't taken much note of the other suited men in the lobby, my eyes had been mostly on Davin.

This one had sandy blond hair that was long enough to brush the tops of his shoulders, but it was slicked back. He was of a medium build, fit but not overly muscular, and a little taller than me. Not by much, though. His suit was expensive and made to fit his body, which spoke of money or power, or both. On one hand, he wore a large ruby ring that sparkled when the light caught the edges. His eyes landed on me and didn't leave. He didn't answer my question.

I didn't lower the point of my knife. "You bothering *my* friend?"

He shook himself, his eyes sliding off me and dropping back to Robert. His perusal didn't feel sexual in any way, just very interested. Like he was wondering just who the hell I was. I was wondering the same thing about him. Council member for sure. But which one, Bruce or Roderick?

He gave a slight bow at the waist, one hand pressed to his chest in a rather old-fashioned move, especially for standing on the stairs of a haunted hotel. "I'm sorry, you caught me off guard. I've known Robert for years. Or I did, when he was alive," the councilman said. Robert was suddenly moving, positioning himself between me and the councilman in a protective stance.

"He doesn't much seem to like you," I pointed out, not liking how this was going. Robert's intuition had always been spot on in the past. If he thought this guy was dangerous, so did I.

The councilman sighed. "Robert is particular about who he likes. I wronged him once, and even though it was long before his death, it ruined our friendship. He still won't let me forget it." He paused and gave me a small smile. "I assume you are Celia's granddaughter, the one who refused our summons?"

Well, crap, so much for dealing with this situation incognito.

6

Standing on the stairs of the Marshall House, facing an unknown person on the council, I went for bravado, as Suzy would have done. Keeping my knife up, I flicked the tip at him. “What’s it to you?”

The councilman’s eyebrows rose to his hairline, which was something to behold. “You are definitely her granddaughter. I’ve seen that look on her face before. Fierce.”

I narrowed my eyes. “Who are you?”

“Roderick.” He bowed again at the waist. “And you would be Breena O’Rylee?”

“I’m not bowing,” I said. “And I’m not coming to talk to you and your council member friends. The one I’ve dealt with is something of a dick.”

He sighed. "They are rather pretentious."

"This from the guy with a cravat," I pointed out.

He touched the material around his neck and then laughed. "I am old, Breena, and I find I can't quite move beyond the styles of my youth. But I suppose it would look pretentious to someone as young as you."

I wanted to back up and put more steps between us. Not because he felt dangerous, though—if anything, there was like zero energy flowing off him. Not even a whisper of magic. Which was ridiculous, of course. He had to be a mage of some sort to have earned a seat on the council, and not just anyone could see Robert.

"Well, Roddy boy, lovely to meet you, but I have an appointment to keep." I did back up then, just a single step, keeping my eyes on the council member.

He held out a hand, flipped his wrist, and offered me a card.

"Nope, not interested," I said. "I've had more business cards offered to me from supernaturals since I got here than I care to count. You can keep it. If you need something from me, you can come to me. You know where I am. And, to be clear, I'm going to count this as meeting with your council." I tucked the knife back into its sheath on my thigh. "And you can tell Davin that suit looks ridiculous on him. He needs one that fits his scrawny frame."

Roderick's laughter followed us up the stairs. "I will pass on your message, but do not be surprised if they don't acquiesce. You'll see one of us soon, I'm sure."

I hurried, all but pushing Feish ahead of me as Robert hustled forward from behind, swaying quickly. He was managing the stairs well. Not until we reached the top floor did I pause and listen for someone following us.

No sound of footsteps coming up the cement stairwell, no echoing of evil laughter or ghostly wails. "I don't know how I feel about that guy," I said.

"Roderick is known for being fair for the most part," Feish said softly. "He is a careful neutral on most things that go before the council. Not a bad one to have on your side."

"Friend," Robert growled and shook his head hard, side to side.

"Okay, well, let it go for now. We're here for someone else." I led the way out of the stairwell. Our feet sunk into the thick carpet, plush enough to keep even the loudest walkers quiet.

Light flickered at the end of the hall, and the one bulb went out, casting a small pocket of shadow. Silvery reflections whispered through those shadows, and for just a moment, it looked like a hand was beckoning me. I blinked, and the light was on as if it were never off and there were no silvery reflections.

"Okay." I blinked again but the light remained on. "Feish, did you see the light go out?"

She turned and tapped me on the head. "Your eyes getting old? The light never went out."

I pursed my lips. "Robert? Did you see that?"

"Ghost," he muttered at my side. Well, good, at least I wasn't losing it.

I found my feet wanting to go toward the spot that had called to me.

No. I had to find that goblin and get us another job.

But how?

I knew from Gran's book that his kind had exceptional hearing. Beyond that, I didn't have much of a plan.

"Goblin!" I yelled into the hallway, making Feish and even Robert jump. "We hear you need help?"

A door at the far end of the hallway creaked open, right under where the light had gone out in no small coincidence, and a creature with a tiny face and oversized bat ears peered out of a room. "Who you be?"

"Breena O'Rylee," I said. "Celia's granddaughter. Do you need our help?"

He made a flapping motion with his hands, hurrying us forward. Rather than run—no thanks after those stairs—I picked up a quick pace that had me at the end of the hall in no time. Feish kept up easily, and Robert, as usual, trailed behind.

Up close, the goblin's skin was a deep brown speckled with lighter brown spots, like a natural camouflage. Out in the bush, he'd be hard to spot. Which begged the question, why the hell was he hiding in the city? He stood out like a sore thumb. I narrowed my eyes and tried to see him as a human would. A petite man, barely five feet tall with flawless dark brown skin and big dark eyes stared back at me, the softness to his features making him downright pretty.

That was the fae for you—vanity was the name of the game.

Even his disguise would stand out in a crowd.

"You really her?" he whispered.

"Jinx said you were looking for help. That's what we do. We help people," I said.

"For money."

I spread my hands wide. "I'm not a charity. And to be clear, you asked for my help, didn't you?"

He blinked. "Don't you want to help people just for the sake of it? Like your gran would?"

I smiled and leaned in close. "No."

Now that wasn't entirely true, but I wasn't about to offer up our services for free. That was how you got taken advantage of. And I had no doubt this little goblin had money for payment. They were known hoarders of coin.

"Should I leave?" I asked.

"I could wait for the Hollows to help me. They would help for…" The goblin kept his voice low, so as not to attract attention, but he still hadn't invited us into his room. "Well, not free, but not a lot. They be cheap."

I wasn't sure about cheap, but I wondered if they'd be willing or even able to help him.

"You could." Feish tapped her chin. "But we would tell them you turned down help from Breena, and then they would say you're a waste of time. You have a little problem." She pinched two webbed fingers together, and my juvenile mind thought for a minute she was referencing something other than his current problem. "Nothing important enough for the Hollows to deal with, in my opinion."

The goblin grumbled a series of curse words under his breath and opened the door to invite us in. As soon as I stepped over the threshold, I was assaulted by a smell that was nothing short of the worst locker room smell I'd ever encountered. As if the stink had been roasting in the heat for a few weeks.

"Bums and feet," I muttered, not sure if I should plug my nose and risk tasting the smell on the back of my tongue. The thought made me gag, and it took all my fortitude to shake off the urge.

"This is awful," Feish mumbled, her hand over her fish lips. I didn't blame her, not one bit.

The goblin didn't even notice us gagging on his stench. "Look, I have a family heirloom and someone is trying to steal it." He dug around in a pile of dirty clothes to pull out a packet of pages. Written on something far thicker than modern paper, more like what I would think papyrus would feel like. I ran my fingers over it, the pages almost greasy under my touch. "It's a family tree of sorts that establishes my lineage and the timeline of when my family settled in these parts. All in Goblinese so don't bother trying to read it. I don't want to lose my land, and these give me rights."

He held up the pages, bound with a couple of thick elastics, to his chest for a moment, then tucked them into a yellow manila envelope, then finally laid them on top of what might have been a table. It was hard to tell for sure, what with all the wrappers and containers from fast food joints that covered it. I saw some green moldy bits in more than one container, which partially explained the stench. Was he trying to stink out any possible intruders? I couldn't keep my nose from wrinkling.

"So you want us to find the person who wants to steal these pages of yours?" I asked, working to speak around the heavy smells in the room. Gawd in heaven, this was bad. I was suddenly wishing I hadn't eaten those greasy hush puppies. My stomach rolled, threatening to revolt at the mere thought of grease.

I had to work to keep it all in and focus on him at the same time.

He shook his head, bat ears flapping. "No. I want you to hide them for me. Then guard them. I don't know why they want them—I just know they can't have them. Okay?" He clasped his hands together over and over, flexing overly long fingers that reminded me of Jinx's hairy legs, minus the hair. I could easily imagine his joints bending backward. I shook off the thought as it was so not helping me in the stomach-clenching department.

"Okay, so we hide the family lineage. Keep an eye on them, and then what?"

"That's it. Keep them safe," he whispered. "Three more days of keeping them safe, then that's it."

"Three days? That's it? What happens in three days?" I asked, but as I finished speaking, I got a very sudden weird vibe. I did a slow turn and lowered my voice. "Someone is at the door."

I could almost feel an energy outside there, one that was way too dark even for a ghost, and I had the sudden thought that the entity from the Sorrel-Weed house had somehow followed us here. Of course, that wasn't the case, but it was my knee-jerk reaction.

The goblin shoved the yellow envelope into my hands and pushed me toward the back of the room. "Go out the window. Down the fire escape," he whispered. "Hurry! Three days, keep them safe for three days."

A thump against the door rattled the entire frame. "Grimm!" The booming voice shocked the shit out of me. I stuffed the envelope under my shirt and wrenched the window open. I shoved Feish and Robert out first, then turned and faced Grimm.

"Sign something that I'll get paid. Now. Or I'll leave the whole package here for you and your friends." I reached for the table and grabbed a napkin that was only slightly smeared with food. I dug in my bag for a pen as someone hammered on the door.

"Go!" Grimm hissed at me.

But I'd learned my lesson from Crash's ex, Karissa, screwing me over. No matter who was on the other side of the door, not getting a fae—even a minor one—to sign that they would pay you for services rendered was dumb. I'd done it once. I wouldn't do it again.

I shoved the pen and napkin at him. "Sign it now saying that you owe me."

Baring his teeth, he snatched napkin and pen and signed a quick I.O.U with his name at the bottom. I took them both and hurried toward the window.

I quickly followed the others out. Robert waited for me on the fire escape, and he stepped in behind me, guarding the rear once more.

Another boom behind us and then the sound of splintering wood. I hurried down one flight of stairs, peeked in the window of the room beneath Grimm's—empty—and tried to pull it open. To my surprise, it worked. "Get in!" I hissed at Feish, who had already started down the next flight of the fire escape. She scrambled back up and in, and I slid through behind her and crouched in the dark room. I grabbed Robert and pulled him in after us with a clank of his bones.

I dragged the window almost all the way shut, leaving just the slightest crack so we could hear what was going on. The banging and yelling continued above us for a few minutes, and then footsteps that obviously had no intention of being quiet thundered down the stairwell.

I pressed myself against the wall under the window and Feish did the same. Robert crouched in the shadows of the room, hidden from whoever might look in.

"Davin," a tenor male voice said, "did you see anyone leave? Could they have gotten it?"

Gotten it? Wouldn't he have said "them" if he'd been referring to the pages? I clutched the envelope a little tighter, wondering if Grimm had been hiding something beyond his family history. For the next thirty minutes, feet thundered up and down the stairwell and all through Grimm's room, along with the moving of furniture. Then all the sound abruptly stopped. There had been no sound of Grimm's voice, no squealing of a goblin being tortured. Had he slipped past them somehow?

"I saw Celia's granddaughter earlier." Roderick's voice was faint as if coming from the open window of the room above us. "Could she have been here for it? Is it possible she understands what it is?"

"No." Davin's sneer was obvious, even though I couldn't see his stupid face. "She's as useless as the rest of the Hollows Group. And to think she's got enough balls to go out on her own. She wouldn't know a powerful item like that if it jumped up and bit her in the ass."

I frowned and next to me Feish let out a little burbling growl. I put a hand on her, and she quieted. This was not the time to go defending my honor. Besides, I'd rather be underestimated. That gave me a lot of room to maneuver.

"I will pay a visit to her," Roderick said. "I don't like the coincidence of her being here."

I didn't disagree with him. I also didn't like the timing—what were the odds that we'd arrived just before the councilmen busted down Grimm's door? Was it just my luck, or was something pushing us all together? Synchronicity was a true thing, especially in the shadow world.

"Don't bother," Davin said, a sneer in his voice. "I need to speak to Corb. He was supposed to gain her confidence, and given how successful he is with the ladies, it should have been no problem. She'll spill her guts to him if he presses her."

Son of a bitch. I mouthed the words but kept the sound to myself. Corb's need to confess suddenly made much more sense. He'd been told to get close to me? To *use* me? And I'd fallen for it, at least to a degree.

Mother ducking…I had to bite my tongue to keep the words inside. The worst part was that he'd apparently told Davin I was useless. And sure, maybe he'd done that to keep the council away from me, but what if he actually thought it was true? Well, whatever his reasons, it was a bunch of hogwash. I was not useless.

Damn it, my own insecurities tried to swallow me whole there in that dark room, and I had to mentally fight them off before I could take another step.

Crash had secrets he didn't or maybe couldn't share, and it had been obvious from the beginning that I could be nothing more than a passing fancy for him. While Corb was out of my league, too, I'd thought he was at least honest. Damn it. I was an idiot. I'd let myself believe that maybe one of them—

Nope, I was not going there.

Well, forget Corb. Hell, forget Crash. At this rate, I'd just stick with Robert, thank you very much.

I slowed my breathing and worked to focus on the current predicament I was in. Even if all I had was a sticky napkin as a signed agreement, it would hold up, and I would take it to the bank when I got through the next three days.

I looked at the pages in my lap. Then I pointed to them, drawing Feish's eyes to the stack. Squishing the edges of the pages with my hands, I could feel something hard buried within the stack. My eyebrows shot up as I peeled the layers back at the edges. There, in the middle of the bunch, was a single piece of silver, a fancy coin with images etched onto it and writing in the middle. More of that same Goblinese I couldn't read.

I frowned and rolled it in my hand, the silver catching the little bit of light coming in the window. Was this what they were looking for? I was willing to bet at least a dollar on it. Why did I get a feeling that Crash would not only know what it was, but that he might even have been the one to make it?

Which was reason enough to keep it from him. One of the last things he'd made was a knife that would have been used to off Eric.

I stuffed the silver item into my bag, considered the pages, and then put them in too. My bottomless bag was probably one of my favorite magical items—it ate up anything I put into it and didn't saddle me with the true weight of the item. I pulled my hand out and *Black Spells of Savannah and the Undead* came out with it, stuck to the side of my fingers.

"Crap," I whispered. My legs were going numb and tingly, and I slid the rest of the way to the floor.

The book, though…it flipped itself open. Yeah, you heard that right.

Flipped itself the duck open.

The pages rippled first one way and then the other, settling on a page with a single line on it.

Of demon skin and angel wing.

That one line had my skin crawling as if it were trying to get off my body on its own.

I closed the book, and shoved it back into my bag, but the thing…hell, it fought me. I was wrestling with a damn book. It snapped shut a few times on my finger, and then it grabbed onto the edge of Grimm's pages and *tore* them with a terrible ripping sound, like a sticky zipper.

I punched the book in the cover and shoved it to the bottom of my bag. Grimm's pages were only a little torn, but Jaysus. What the hell had I gotten myself into?

Of demon skin and angel wing. That line, though, it was almost as if I'd heard it before…

"How are we going to get out?" Feish whispered into my ear, giving me more than a little spit. "They will be looking for us, and when they find us, they will search us. They will find everything."

I nodded. "Thinking. Give me a minute." We needed a way to hide my bag. That way we'd escape with the object and the pages, even if we were frisked. I didn't dare leave it behind because Roderick and Davin would no doubt search the building.

I looked at Robert quietly swaying next to Feish, a thought blooming.

"Robert," I said quietly. "Most people can't see you. I want you to take my bag." I handed it over to him. "You think you can take it with you when you turn into a single finger bone?"

Robert slowed his swaying. "Friend."

"Yes, can you hide this?" I pointed at the bag on his shoulder, blinked, and he was gone. My bag had disappeared with him, and the finger bone I carried around lay on the floor.

I scooped it up and tucked it into my bra. If they frisked me that well, they deserved to find a bone in my bra.

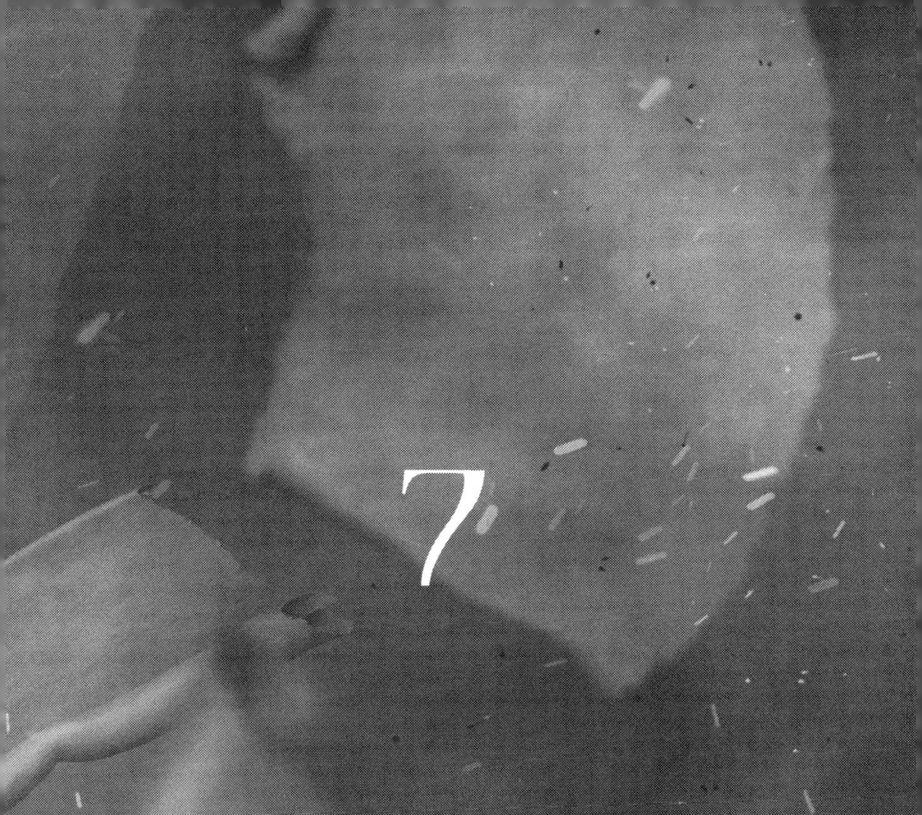

7

We waited another thirty minutes until the voices from Grimm's room slid away and the sound of feet faded, leaving us sitting in silence in the dark in a haunted hotel. Robert's finger bone was tucked between my boobs, and Feish and I moved to the door. The old bedroom in the Marshall House that we hid in smelled musty with disuse, something that had only slowly become apparent to me.

"You pick up on any ghosts?" Feish asked as we waited by the door.

"Just that initial pull and then nothing," I said softly. I wondered at that. I mean, I obviously had an affinity for the dead, more so after my little dying escapade in the graveyard not long ago. And the ghosts here in the Marshall House were notorious for being aggressive, and in some cases, downright violent if they decided they didn't like you. And yet I'd felt nothing more than that slight pull toward the stairs, and then another pulse toward Grimm's hallway and his room.

Almost like whatever entity was here had wanted me to find Grimm and his pages. Or had Grimm himself drawn me to him?

Interesting. I tucked those thoughts away and focused on the present moment.

I twisted the door handle and peeked out. The hallway was empty, which was what we'd hoped for, although we were ready to rumble if we were stopped. Who was I kidding, there would be no rumbling. More like talking smack and making a run for it while they were distracted by my insults.

If we got caught, Feish would let me do the talking. The story we'd concocted was that we were here doing some ghost hunting for a client, nothing more, and if they questioned it, then I would tell them about the silvery shadows that had led me down the hall.

We walked toward the elevator, hit the button, and stepped in. There was no one with us, and partway down, the lights in the elevator flickered. The car slowed and I let out a groan, hitting the button for the first floor.

"No, no getting stuck in an elevator!" I snapped as I jammed the button harder as if that would get my point across.

The elevator stopped completely and the lights went out. "Are you kidding me?" I yelled into the darkness. "Seriously?"

Feish grabbed my arm around the bicep and squeezed hard enough for her nails to dig in. "Feish, ouch, ease off!"

"I not touching you," she said softly.

I went very still and looked over my shoulder, not really sure I'd be able to see anything in the pitch black. The pale, shimmering face of a woman peered back at me, eyes focused and unblinking. I couldn't tell if she was old or young. Only that her clothing was from long since past, likely the eighteen hundreds. Her hair was pulled into a bun at the back of her head with tendrils flowing out from around it.

The hand on my arm tightened and the mouth of the ghost opened.

I heard a word not spoken aloud.

Vampire.

"Oh, for duck's sake, are you serious?" I whispered, and I most certainly did not use the autocorrect of duck.

The ghost gave a slow nod and then disappeared. The elevator lights flicked on and the elevator began to slide downward to the lobby. I hit the second-floor button, running on instinct.

"What are you doing?" Feish whispered. I looked at her to see her shaking and rubbing her arms. I put a hand out to her and she took it. "It got very cold. Was it a ghost? I couldn't see what you were talking to."

"Yeah," I responded, although I hadn't noticed the cold as much as Feish obviously did. "We're getting out on the second floor. We'll find a way out from there."

The elevator stopped a second later on said floor. The doors opened and I peeked out, checking both directions. If the ghost woman was right and there was a vampire somewhere around here, I would do my best to avoid the fanged entity. That was not a critter I wanted to interact with, thank you very much.

I kept a hand on Feish and her webbed fingers tightened over mine, trembling slightly. "I think I'd like to not be with you the next time you ghost hunt," she said.

I slowed as we approached the stairwell that would lead down to the lobby. The light above flickered and went out, and the ghost woman from the elevator made a reappearance and shook her head. She pointed to the door to her left and I went straight for it.

"You see her that time?" I whispered.

"Yes. You think it's a good idea to trust a ghost?" Feish asked. "Especially when the ghost is here in this place?"

"I'm less afraid of a ghost than I am of what she says is in the hotel." I tugged Feish along with me. Not that she was slowing me down, but a growing sense of urgency pushed me onward. Like we had to get out of the hallway before something bad showed up.

I put a hand on the door to the room, fully expecting it to be locked. The knob was ice cold, but otherwise, it twisted easily in my hand. I stepped into the dark room beyond it, Feish behind me.

The door clicked shut, and I found myself staring into a room full of ghosts.

And when I say full, I mean *ducking* full.

Men, women, a few children, all in a variety of clothing representing many periods of time. Some looked fresh, *new* is the only word I had for them, and others were faded like the silvery woman who'd directed me here. Many were dressed in army fatigues from eras gone by, their bodies still showing horrific injuries.

I took a deep breath, my exhale showing the heat of my body clearly in a puff of mist. Feish was shaking hard, and I didn't think it was from fear. "The cold bothers you?"

"I'm a river maid. My body temperature picks up on the environment around me," she said.

"Okay, let's make this quick." I dipped my voice low. "You all know I can see you?" One by one, the various ghosts nodded in my direction. "And you know that something bad is happening here?"

Again, they all nodded.

"Here's the deal," I whispered. "We have to get out of here. If there really is—" I didn't want to say *vampire* out loud as if that would make it more real. Which was kind of ridiculous given that I was having a discussion with a roomful of ghosts. "—that fanged creature here, then we need to go. We need to tell someone."

The ghosts looked at one another, then slowly parted and pointed to the window. Three strides took us across the room, and I shoved Feish toward the old glass. "You go." And on a sudden gut feeling, I pulled Robert's finger bone out of my bra.

"I need the book out of my bag, Robert."

He stood up, between one blink and the next, swaying there next to me, my bag hanging over his shoulder. I reached for it, dug around in it and pulled out the spell book from the used book store. "I'll keep this with me."

Robert collapsed once more without me telling him, and I scooped him back up, handing him to Feish. They both needed to get the duck out of there.

Feish looked up at me. "Why are you staying?"

"Because I have to." I had no good reason, but there were plenty of ill-advised ones. These ghosts clearly knew things. Something about Grimm, I suspected, and also about a vampire who may or may not be hanging out in the hotel. And they were hiding. Some of the most fearsome ghosts known to Savannah were *hiding*.

Feish didn't require much more prompting, and I watched as she made it to the street and hurried off. When she rounded the corner, leaving my field of vision, I pulled my head back into the room.

"Okay, you all need to talk to me. Why are you in here? Are you hiding?" I faced the room of ghosts, waiting for one of them to volunteer information.

The Silver Lady stepped up, her form sliding in and out of transparency. Her hand lifted, palm out to me in a gesture that made me want to press my own hand to hers. I lifted my hand.

Ghostly skin pressed to mine, and the world around me evaporated. Suddenly people were rushing all around me.

"You have to get them out of here." The Silver Lady spoke clearly, only this time she was very much alive and no longer the ghostly woman. Her skirts shushed around us as she hurried between cots of groaning wounded men. "Those that carry the plague are coming."

A doctor who looked suspiciously like Tom closed his eyes. "Mercy will not find any of us if they catch us here with the wounded."

Time passed, everything happening too fast, like a film put on high speed, people rushing around in front of me as if I weren't there, and then the world slowed again.

The Silver Lady stood at the doorway, her eyes locked on it. "They are here. Go. I will stop them."

She held an impossibly thin piece of silver, at least two feet long, in one hand, and in the other she held a hammer. A silver stake. A hammer. Holy duck, she was a vampire hunter.

She pressed the tip of the blade to the door, took a breath and hammered it through. An unearthly wail lit the air and—

I hit the ground hard, bouncing backward through the sea of ghosts. Hands hovered around me as if they'd help me to my feet.

"Okay, okay, so you're a good ghost," I said. "I get it."

She nodded, then reached out and touched my side where I had the spell book. "This?"

Another nod.

I pulled it out and her hand floated over the book, the pages flipping back and forth like they'd done earlier. Maybe it hadn't been the book. Maybe a ghost had controlled it.

The pages slowed and stopped.

Silver moon is the time for the demon skin to be found, and bound, and used to be bidden.

I grimaced. "Demon skin, really?"

She nodded and mouthed three words. *Find the skin.* What in the world demon skin had to do with her showing me how badass she was, I didn't know. But my instincts said she was trying her best to help.

The sound of feet outside the door caught my ears, stopping me from asking any other questions.

The ghosts dispersed so fast that the room's temperature shot up forty degrees in an instant, the sudden change causing sweat to break out along my spine. "Holy crap," I whispered.

The door opened and the outlined figure was distinctly male. "Who's in here?"

I knew that voice. And in a split second, I fell into my role playing and the story I'd prepped.

"Davin, what the hell? Here I am in the middle of a ghost hunt, and I think I had a ghost ready to talk to me, and you just bang down the door like some thug?" I stormed toward him, shoving him out of the way. Bravado was my best bet here. And since he knew I didn't much like him, I cringed and wrinkled my nose as I passed him. "You smell." Actually that was true, he really did stink.

"What?" He stumbled away from me as if I'd kicked him in the shins. Also, not a bad idea.

I wrinkled my nose again. "You smell like"—I sniffed the air as if I were indeed scenting him, but a different smell caught my attention—"fresh grave dirt? Is that a thing? Because you smell like it."

Davin's eyes narrowed. "What are you accusing me of?"

I lifted both hands, turned, and walked into a cravat I'd seen earlier. Roderick looked down at me, his face a careful neutral, and the smell of whatever cologne he wore dispelled the odor of fresh grave dirt. I put a finger to his chest. "This guy smells good. You should ask him for his cologne. Or Corb. Corb's cologne is also lovely."

"It's because of what Corb is that he smells that way. No one can duplicate it," Davin snapped. As if maybe he'd tried and failed? Yeah, I could see Davin trying to pull off Corb's allure.

I was about to ask just what he meant by that, but Roderick stopped me with a lifting of his hand. The third guy from earlier, the one who wasn't a goblin, burst through the doorway leading to the stairwell.

His eyes were wild with anger, and the intensity that rolled off him was enough to steal my breath. That had to be Bruce, the last council member Feish had named.

I couldn't take my eyes off him, and not in a *you're so damn hot, my panties are on fire* way. No. More in a *holy crap what demon have you made a deal with to give you all that dark energy* kind of way.

I kept looking at him, but his face didn't stick in my mind. Like from one second to the next, I couldn't have told you what he looked like, only that he was there. "Who the hell is that?" I pointed at him, but Roderick and Davin ignored me.

Roderick focused hard on me. "Where is your friend?"

The words were spoken in a neutral tone, but they vibrated through my bones with a power that spoke of deep magic that even I, a relative newbie in some ways, could recognize. I gritted my teeth and looked up at him.

"Mage?"

He gave me a subtle nod. "One of the best." No arrogance there at all. I tried to look at the third council guy, but again, his face seemed to slide away. Every instinct in me said to keep my eyes on that one, to try to pin him down.

I gritted my teeth again as my eyes were drawn back to Roderick. "She didn't like the feeling of the ghosts, so she left. Too cold. River maid."

"And yet you stayed?" Roderick's words continued to knock through me like a tuning fork shaking the inside of my bones and turning them into jelly.

I do not like this, Sam I am. I do not like Rod's bing-bang-bam.

Maybe I had a little bit of Dr. Seuss in me after all.

"Working. Ghosts." Whatever magic Roderick possessed, his power pulsed through me in a way that made the hair on my neck want to crawl off. That alone was reason enough for me to try to defy this macho crap and give him sideways answers.

"On a ghost hunt?" he asked, and the power in his voice just about set me back on my ass. He frowned and shook his head. "Why are you fighting me?"

"On principle," I whispered. It was taking everything I had to keep my thoughts to myself. Except... was that even the right thing to do? Shouldn't I tell the council about the vampire and the ghosts being afraid? Should I tell them what the Silver Lady had shown me?

No. Somehow I knew I had to keep it to myself for now. They couldn't know, or something bad would happen. Just like I couldn't tell Crash.

Secrets abounded, and I was keeping most of them.

"She is difficult. I told you we should bring her in and let the council have a round at her," Davin said. "She thinks she's something special. But she's nothing but a washed-up divorcee. She's only here because she had nowhere else to go and nowhere to hide. I heard the bank has her address now. It won't be long before they take everything, including that house of her gran's. Terrible pity that, but once they have everything she owns, she'll be forced to move on."

My eyes shot to him, his words slamming the final pieces of the puzzle into place. I was the queen of guessing, and I had a real doozy to drop. "You helped Alan, didn't you?"

His smile said it all and the rage that shot through me repulsed Roderick's magic as if I'd taken a stick and walloped him a good knock to the noggin. He stumbled back from me. "Dav, I don't think you should piss her off."

The third council member crept closer to Roderick. "What is she?"

"I don't know," Roderick said.

"She's only got the knives that Crash gave her. And those won't hurt me," Davin sneered. "Fae magic is nowhere near as strong as that of a *true* mage. Shall I show you how it's done, Roderick?"

Roderick cleared his voice. "I don't think you should push her. If you do, you'll be dealing with something other than fae magic in the form of knives."

I didn't even look at the other council members. All I could see was Davin offering Alan a deal that would free him from any debt, from his wife, from any responsibility whatsoever. A deal meant to destroy me.

I clamped my hand around Davin's wrist. He looked down at where I was hanging onto him.

"Take your hand off me, hag."

"Hag?" I whispered the word as something within me clicked open wide like a treasure chest letting me see a hint of what I was capable of, a glimpse of the possible. I called the magic to me, feeling for the first time since I'd landed in Savannah that there was more to me than the "washed-up divorcee" some people like him saw. Gran had told me as much, but this was the moment I knew down to my bones it was true.

The Silver Lady appeared behind Davin, solidifying until she looked as alive and real as I did. My rage appeared to be feeding her strength—lines of magic or maybe energy spooled between us, connecting us, as silvery as the name I'd given her.

Roderick let out a low muttered curse and pinned himself against the far wall—apparently, he could see what I was doing. The third faceless one that still gave me the willies, even in this rage high, watched with great interest. I didn't like the feelings that swirled around him, but he wasn't my focus. Not today.

The Silver Lady held her chin high, watching me and waiting for me to speak. "I think you should stay with him," I said. "Keep him company. Don't let him sleep. Let him know what a hag can truly do."

Her smile was slow and wicked, and I found myself answering it.

Davin's face paled as he yanked out of my hold. The Silver Lady put a hand on his shoulder and *sunk into him.* He shivered, and sweat broke out on his forehead that I was sure was cold as ice.

"You will come before the council before the week is up," said Roderick's voice.

I found myself giving him a mock curtsy. "I have no idea where you losers meet, so you'll have to give me the address."

Davin shivered and jumped when he looked into the shadows of the hall. The lights flickered and the hallway went dark. He squealed, high-pitched like a little child. "Roderick, Bruce, get some light in here."

"You're a mage, why don't you turn your own damn light on?" I said, feeling the ghosts in the walls, knowing they were the ones messing with the lights.

"Because that is not where his abilities lie," Roderick said from within the dark hall. I assumed that Bruce was the one whose face was sliding all over the damn place.

Roderick's hand glowed a light purple, and flames prettier than they had any right to be lit his outstretched palm. His eyes turned to me. "I will come gather you for the meeting when they decide to speak with you. It was lovely to meet you, Breena O'Rylee, granddaughter of Celia." Formal, he was being super formal, and I didn't like it. Bruce said nothing, which I liked even less.

Call me suspicious, but he was going to be trouble, Mr. You-can't-see-my-face-no-matter-what-angle-you-look-at-me-with.

"I would say it's been a slice, but I'd rather not lie." I stood there waiting while the three council members reached the stairwell and headed down,

Roderick all but holding Davin together. Bruce stopped in the doorway to look at me.

I put my hands on my hips. "What are you looking at, No Face?"

He might have growled at me, but I wasn't sure because I couldn't see what the hell his face was doing. And then he was gone too.

I didn't ask why they didn't take the elevator. Maybe they (correctly) assumed the ghosts had control of it. The second they stepped into the stairwell the hallway flooded with the ghosts that had been hiding in that one room.

"I'll be back," I said to them. Because whatever the heck was going on was surely tied up with the ghosts in the Marshall House. I just had to find a way to discuss it with them. And I knew the person to ask how best to go about it.

Louis from the Hollows Group was about to get a visit from me.

8

I hadn't been to the cemetery where the Hollows Group trained since everything had gone down with the O'Seans. After I'd faced down O'Sean Senior (His first name had been Patrick. I'd learned that after I'd killed him). Since I'd sort of died and had come back after a chitchat with Robert as he would have been in life. Which meant I'd only been back once after the whole Sarge-firing-me-while-under-a-spell debacle.

All in all, those were great reasons not to go back. But the thing was, Louis, the resident necromancer, was one of the mentors. If anyone could help me understand the whole ghost episode in the Marshall House, it was him. Maybe he'd even have some insight into the book of black spells. What was it with that line *Silver moon is the time for the demon skin to be found, and bound, and used to be bidden*?

It circled around my brain in a way I didn't like.

At least, I was hoping Louis knew something. Because if he didn't, I didn't know where to turn to next.

I patted my bag on my hip. I'd stopped back at Gran's house to find Feish freaking out that she'd left me behind in a room full of ghosts.

I'd calmed her quickly and suggested that perhaps she and Kinkly—who lived in the big oak tree out front—should stay in the garden and do some weeding even though it was after dark. Because I heard things going on upstairs.

Jaysus lordy, Suzy and Eric were still going at it? I didn't want to know. I really, really didn't want to know.

A small smile tripped over my lips as I imagined Gran walking in on them. Just floating through the wall like she was prone to do. Yeah, I was going to do some serious apologizing to my gran after this.

I blinked and shook myself as I drew close to the cemetery gate that led into the Hollows. In the distance, I heard yelling, and my hand dropped to the knife strapped to my thigh. But the shouting was from Eammon, and it took me a moment to register that he was barking at the remaining recruits to move their sorry asses faster.

That made me grin. I was oh-so-glad I didn't have to do the run around the graveyard anymore. I mean,

Suzy and I still worked out, but it was different and more suited to a woman's body. We did cardio, sure, but we also did things like yoga for flexibility, climbing fences for obvious reasons, and exercises to increase our upper body strength. Not just running around a graveyard for miles and miles.

I let myself in through the gate, and Robert popped up to my left, appearing as he so often did. "Hey, I thought you were going to stay at the house?" He'd already returned my bag when I'd checked in, so I figured he would stick behind with Kinkly and Feish. I still had Grimm's pages and his family's silver coin, so they were safe with me, for the moment.

"Friend. Trouble," he said as he swayed in time with my steps forward, his shoulder bumping mine here and there.

"Great," I mumbled, feeling the dull fatigue that had begun to eat at me. Really, you'd think that finding out that I was a quarter fae, plus half something else, courtesy of my father, would have given me some respite from things like body aches, fatigue, running on empty. Nope, not me.

I felt as human as ever despite the whole seeing ghosts and such.

I walked down the pathway to the center of the training ground. A massive tomb with a standing angel on top, one wing broken—not broken as in broken off, but actually carved broken and hanging limp from its back—marked the center of the Hollows's training grounds.

As I drew closer, Eammon was easier to spot. Being a leprechaun had its disadvantages and being invisible in a crowd of taller men was one of them.

But he'd dragged up his waist-high stool from the interior of the tomb and stood on it in the grass, waving his fists about, making him taller than everyone else there. Something had put him in quite the rage.

The other mentors were with him, standing back, letting him do his thing. Tom, the resident mage, saw me first. "Breena, what are you doing here?" He strode toward me and pulled me into a big hug. I hugged him back.

"Couldn't stay away. All these old guys are such a draw, am I right?" I grinned up at him, and he put his hands on my arms.

"You look good, no more bullet holes?" His dark brown eyes were inquisitive as if the question wasn't quite rhetorical. The hole in my leg from Sarge shooting up Eric's cabin had healed to a tiny scar.

"None today." I shrugged. "But the day isn't over."

Eammon flagged me over. "Come on, Bree. Don't be shy. We're all still friends even if we're in direct competition, right, lass?"

Oh. I hadn't really thought of that. I shrugged. "I promise only to take the jobs you turn down, how about that?"

Eammon gave me a sharp look and I smiled. Because the Hollows Group had scoffed at the job that had earned me the most money, and they'd flat out turned down the one that had secured my reputation in the shadow world.

"Smart ass," he muttered.

"Short stack," I threw back.

Louis sniffed. "What are you doing here?"

Corb smiled but I didn't look at him. I would deal with him and his games later. "I actually came to talk to you, Louis. You game for a chat?"

Louis startled and pressed a hand to his chest, fingers splayed wide. "Me? Why me?"

"Are you not the resident necromancer? I need some help deciphering something to do with ghosts." I wasn't sure how much to tell him. Because he and Eammon were right. We might still be friends, but they were not obligated to help me, not one bit. "I can pay you for your time." I did grin at that.

Louis did not grin. "I am not some cheap whore peddling my wares."

"Expensive call girl?" I offered. "I've got twenty bucks with your name on it. Another twenty if you're really good." I couldn't resist even though it was likely he'd spit on me now. The truth was I could already see that he'd say no, no matter what I offered.

A string of curses in French were thrown my way and he bit his thumb at me. I rolled my eyes. "That's an Italian move, isn't it?"

Louis stormed off and his trainee—Chad, if I remembered correctly—was right behind him, trailing his mentor closely. The thing was, when I was around Louis, there was no sense of the dead like there had been at the Marshall House. No sense of ghosts or anything...and then there was the fact that he couldn't see Robert. I'd always thought that was strange. Shouldn't a necromancer be able to see an undead skeleton? Hell, even Roderick could see Robert.

I turned to look at Eammon. "Is he even a necromancer?"

Eammon seemed as shocked by my question as by the possibility I raised. "Well, of course he is. He is one of the best—"

I held up a hand. I'd learned recently that the Hollows wasn't the well-regarded group I'd initially believed them to be. They were considered the duck-ups of Savannah. They only took on trainees not desirable to the more prestigious Savannah Council Enforcers or SCE. "Okay, fine. Maybe I'll ask Annie."

Tom shook his head. "No, I wouldn't do that."

"Why not?" I frowned. "Annie's one of the good ones."

Tom shook his head a second time. "She's been off lately and been downright mean with a few patrons. Not like her, but something has her on edge, so just steer clear would be my suggestion."

Beside Tom, Corb gave the slightest nod. "I agree with him, steering clear of Annie if you can would be best, at least until someone talks some sense into her."

Well, so much for that idea. I was disappointed. Annie was one of the few people I would've liked to have known better.

"All righty then. I'll find someone else to talk to. Nice to see you all. Come by for tea sometime."

I turned my back on them and started back the way I'd come, stopping after a few feet because a rather large handsome man hurried to get in front of me.

"Sarge. How's the leg doing?"

His golden eyes swept downward as he looked at his feet. "I am so, so sorry I tried to kill you, Breena. You have to believe me. And I won't stand in the way of you and Corb getting together. I—"

I put a hand up. "Sarge, stop it. That spell wreaked havoc on everyone, not just you." Also I didn't know what to say to him about Corb. No. That wasn't true. I did have something to say. "Besides, I know Corb was just getting close to me to use me—Davin said so himself. None of it was real." I winked up at Sarge. "We're all good, okay?" A sigh of relief slid out of him, and I patted his massive bicep as I strode past him. "But you owe me."

He grunted as if I'd punched him in the belly. "That's it?"

I shrugged and kept walking. "That's it."

In the shadow world, favors were as good a currency as money or gold. And a favor from a werewolf couldn't be a bad thing as far as I was concerned.

I made my way to the gate, Robert swaying to my left. He collapsed at my feet, and I scooped up the finger bone and tucked it between my boobs.

Might as well give some man a thrill, even if he was a skeleton.

Corb caught up with me just as I reached the gate. I saw him from the corner of my eye and slipped through the iron rods so we had that between us.

He put his hands on the bars. "Hey. Are we still on for tomorrow?"

I shook my head, snorting. "No, I don't think so. I ran into Davin earlier, and he let spill that you've been using me. I think I'll pass on anything else with you beyond professional courtesy."

He cursed and then leaned his head against the rusty bars. "I know it looks bad, Bree, but I can explain. It's what I wanted to talk to you about."

"Yup, here's the explanation." I crossed my arms. "You've lied to me twice now. And I suspect there's something supernatural curling under your skin. Something you don't want to tell me. It's one more thing you haven't been honest about."

He swallowed hard, and I found myself glowering into his eyes while keeping up whatever mental protections I could. Because I was no fool. Something about him drew me, and whatever supernatural sauce he had, he'd been using it to get close to me. In that, he wasn't a lot different than Crash. He closed his eyes again. "I'm as much of a bastard as my cousin. Just in a different way."

"You introduced him to Davin," I said, that piece of information reminding me that he—Corb—had done more damage than he'd probably ever intended. "Davin helped him screw me over. And it looks like Davin wants me out of Savannah. Why?"

Corb opened his eyes and frowned. "What? Davin helped him? I didn't know that. I swear, I didn't!"

I didn't even know if I could trust that small bit of surprise. I took a step back. "Thanks for letting me stay with you, Corb. That was a good thing you did. And for cleaning my clothes that one night. And for kissing me to make Alan jealous. All good things. Honest. But that's where it ends. I'm done with liars."

I turned my back on him and walked down the street. The gates creaked open, and then a hand on my arm spun me around.

"I didn't kiss you to make him jealous," he said, moving toward me. I didn't expect what was coming next, honest.

Because suddenly that cheeky bugger was kissing me again. Only, it wasn't a casual kiss that felt nice and had a little spice behind it, or even the panty-melting kiss he'd planted on me in front of Alan.

This kiss felt like the ocean crashing over me, drowning me in salt water that slid under my flesh, caressing every inch of me with this man's touch and his taste, making my skin shiver in anticipation. This kiss had an oomph that I'd previously felt only with Crash, except instead of fire, it filled me with night air and the pull of the ocean tide. I dug my hands into his hair and held him tightly, feeling like there was something just outside the edge of my reach if I could only find it. I might have groaned. I'm not really sure, or maybe it was him.

His mouth slid off mine before I could grasp that elusive something, and it was then that I realized we were all tangled around each other—my arms around his neck, his arms around my back, one of his hands in my long hair and the other firmly grabbing my ass. To top it off, my legs were wrapped around his waist, which meant I could tell all too clearly just how happy he was to have me plastered over him.

Corb's breath came in gasps as if he too wasn't sure what had happened there. "Sorry. I'm sorry. But please don't push me away. I haven't felt like this about anyone for a long time, and I can't just let you walk away. I don't see you as someone to use. I don't. No matter what other people might say. Even if yes, that was the original job. It changed very quickly, Bree. You have to believe me."

I unwrapped myself from him, getting myself back onto solid ground. Robert's finger bone dropped to the ground, and he appeared once more at my side and let out a growl, which helped pull me back from the brink of forgetting that Corb had been lying all along.

"How can I trust you?" I said, hating how breathy my voice was with all those hormones rippling through me. Hot damn, that kiss had been something else and every part in me was tingling with a desire I couldn't shake.

He smoothed a hand through his hair. "We start again. You be honest with me, and I'll be honest with you."

I quirked both eyebrows up. "Just what have I lied about?"

"Nothing." He held up both hands. "It was a figure of speech. Please let me take you out tomorrow. We can talk then. I'll tell you anything you want to know."

Well, *that* was interesting. I still wasn't sure I wanted to get closer to him—my body's reaction was way too strong and that made me stupid—but I had nothing planned for the next night and my brain and hormones were scrambled badly, which meant that I wasn't really thinking about saying no. "Fine. One dinner."

And that was how I ended up going on my first real date in almost twenty years with a man younger than me, who held a wallop of power he'd been keeping hidden, and seemed determined to gain my interest back.

Yup, just call me a cougar.

9

The walk back to my gran's house helped shut off all the wild hormones, the pulsing of blood in my veins that called me back to Corb's arms. But not even the coolness of a Savannah night could burn off everything he had awakened in my body.

Which only left me feeling more confused. If you'd asked me after my kiss with Crash that morning, I would have told you that nothing could be hotter and there was no one I'd rather roll around naked with for hours on a plastic sheet with a heck of a lot of oil.

But the kiss with Corb had been just as strong, in a different way, and at a certain moment I'd wanted to just…I couldn't even find the words, but the closest I could come to was press myself into him. To sink under his skin. To let him wash over me.

I'd gone from being married and having zero sex to having two smoking hot guys kissing me in one day. Younger me would have been horrified. Older me was somewhat fascinated that this was even happening. And just kind of running with it. I mean, I didn't really have to choose between them, and I still didn't feel like it. Even if Crash had basically told me we'd be terrible together and Corb had lied to me.

"Weird, this is too weird," I whispered to myself.

Robert grunted and I glanced at my companion. "Robert, you don't like Corb?"

He gave a rolling shrug as he swayed along but said nothing. So I tried again. "What about Crash?"

Another rolling shrug and I burst out laughing. "Robert, you don't like either of them?"

"Friend," he said softly. And held out a hand.

"Ah, Robert. It really sucks when the sweet guy is the dead guy." I put my hand in his and his skeletal fingers tightened over my mine.

That's how I ended up walking all the way home holding hands with a skeleton. See? I told you Robert wasn't the worst date I'd ever been on.

I left Robert under the sprawling oak tree in the front yard, Spanish moss hanging low off the branches, swaying only slightly in the breeze. Kinkly gave me a wave from a branch partway up the tree, turned her back to me, and wrapped her wings around herself.

Up the front stairs I went, pausing on the threshold of the door.

Above my head was the distinct sound of furniture bumping rhythmically around.

"Seriously? Are you still going at it?" I muttered. I mean, don't get me wrong. I was happy Suzy and Eric were obviously getting along and getting to know each other in the biblical sense, but this was a bit ridiculous. Didn't they need to sleep too? It was after midnight.

I let myself into the dark house. "Gran?"

She flickered to life for just a second in front of me, gave me a look of irritation, and then disappeared in a puff.

I frowned. "Hey, I didn't deserve that. I didn't make them get busy, be mad at them. Can I talk to you please? It's about a new job." I wanted her take on all the strangeness that had unfolded at the Marshall House. "Gran, I could really use your help."

I waited, but there was nothing from her, not even another glimmer. Damn it.

She'd been moody ever since I'd gotten the yellow manila envelope that held information about her death and my parents' deaths. I mean, I knew she wanted to know what had happened to her—I did too. But I also knew it would entail opening another pathway of mysteries. I just couldn't do it all at once.

Apparently tonight she'd decided she was going to give me the cold shoulder to prove whatever point she was trying to make. The only other time she'd done that was when she'd caught me smoking weed as a teenager. I'd tried to tell her I was using it to enlighten my brain so I could connect more deeply with the shadow world. Surprisingly enough, she hadn't bought my reasoning. She'd pointed out that if I wanted to enlighten my brain, I would need something stronger than weed.

"Moody old lady," I muttered. She'd come out of her funk eventually. If I knew anything about Gran, it was that she refused to be hurried. "At this rate, I'll be dead too before you talk to me," I threw out to the open air.

A snort from the kitchen but otherwise no answer.

Adjusting my bag on my hip, I headed up the stairs, avoiding the ones that creaked. All I wanted was to drag my body into bed, pop a couple Advil, and close my eyes to the world for a few hours.

The morning was coming soon enough to deal with the stuff I'd gathered from Grimm. To pin Gran down. And to find a necromancer who could talk to me—

A loud bang rippled from Suzy's room. No, I wasn't putting up with that all night.

"Well, that's enough of that shit." I changed directions and headed straight for Suzy's room. I rapped a knuckle on it. "I know you two are having fun, but seriously, go to sleep. Or go to Eric's house or something."

I turned away and another loud thump sounded, this time accompanied by a muffled sound that could have been words in a pillow. Or something shouted into a gag. A tremor of unease slid up my spine. I stood there in front of the door as Feish stepped out of her bedroom, wrapped in a bright red silk kimono, yawning wide and showing off gills at the back of her throat.

"They still banging boots? Been all damn night, thumping and bumping. Like furniture being tossed." She wrapped her arms around her middle.

What if they weren't banging boots, as Feish had so delicately put it? What if something was wrong?

I put my hand on the door. "I'm coming in, cover up!" I yelled, gave them a beat of ten seconds, and twisted the door handle.

It didn't turn, but instead went ice cold and froze over. "Ah crap!" I stepped back, lifted a foot, and booted the door. Now let me tell you something, this was not my first attempt to kick a door down. The first time, I'd ended up bouncing backward and landing on my ass. I was hoping I'd gained some skill. I also held back a little, just in case.

I aimed for just to the left of the knob, and the door rattled but didn't splinter. "Feish, go get Crash!" I yelled as I kicked the door again. Nothing. I put my hand on the knob, and if possible, it was even colder than before.

Suzy and Eric were in there and someone was hurting them. I yanked both knives from the sheaths on my thighs and drove one straight into the keyhole of the door. The old metal cracked and groaned as I wrenched the knife left and right, shattering the metal as though it were glass.

The door was still stuck, and nothing happened when I shoved against it, pushing with all I had.

Crash raced up the stairs in naught but a pair of jeans, and then he was next to me, his shoulder against the door. "What the hell happened?"

"Ducked if I know! I was out of the house, and I figured they were having fun." I pulled back and shoved on the door again, the hinges groaning with our combined efforts.

"Again," Crash growled and a tingle of something rolled off him as we hit the door, his magic weaving with our bodies. The wood exploded and we fell into the room. Only it no longer looked like my gran's house.

I slopped forward through what could only be called swampland, the water up to my mid-shins. Vegetation better suited to the deepest jungles than the inside of a house covered every inch of the room, and that included the two figures tied to a couple of back-to-back chairs with thick vines. Eric's glasses were all I could see, and his eyes had never been wider.

I lurched through the water to his side and used my knife to cut the vines off his face first.

"Suzy, help Suzy!" he breathed out. "They did this to her."

"Shit, shit, shit!" I grabbed the vine-mummified Suzy and started slashing at the climbers, cutting them loose and yanking them off. Behind me, Crash helped Eric get fully free, and then they were helping me with Suze. Which was good because as soon as we cut through a runner, another applied itself to her. The water around us sloshed, and the impossibility of this situation—this room—was not lost on me.

"Why the hell didn't Gran warn me?" My anger wasn't really at Gran, but at myself for not having noticed something was wrong. For not checking on these two sooner.

"They spelled Celia, I think," Eric said. "She did warn us, but they did something to make her not herself."

I finally got the vines off Suzy's face, four layers of thick vegetation, and her eyes fluttered open. "Suze, we got you!"

"'Bout time," she whispered.

Ten more minutes passed as we fought the vines, finally freeing her.

"Out in the hall," Crash said.

Feish put out a blanket, and we laid Suzy on it as we got the last of the remaining vines off. "She needs another siren to help her," Feish whispered. "Someone strong enough to get her through this."

"What is 'this'?" I scooped up Suzy's hand. Her skin was deathly cold and clammy as if there were no hot blood pumping through her. "What is happening to her?"

"I think someone triggered her siren side, thinking she'd do harm to Eric." Feish stroked Suzy's pale face. "A half-breed siren with no control would have drained Eric of life. But she managed to fight off the urge, most likely because she's falling in love with the bigfoot." Eric startled, but Feish just plowed on. "And this—" she motioned to the swamp in the room, which was somehow not dripping out past the doorway—"is what happened."

Other than Suzy, I didn't know any sirens, half-breed or otherwise. "Her mom?" I offered.

Feish shook her head and Suzy grabbed my hand. "No. Not her."

I looked at Crash. "You know any sirens?"

He blinked down at me. "Call Corb. He brought her into the Hollows. He should know what to do."

Eric ran to get his phone, and he handed it to me while I gripped Suzy's hand. "Suze, we're calling Corb. Can he help you?"

"Yes," she whispered, her eyes scrunched tightly. "I'm sorry about the room, Bree. Please send Eric out."

"Don't worry about anything. We'll get the room cleaned up in no time." I squeezed her fingers, fear clutching my heart. Losing Suze was not an option. I dialed Corb. He didn't pick up, and I left a frantic message that I followed up with an equally urgent text: *9-1-1 Gran's house!!*

Eric shook his head. "No, I'm staying with you."

A tear slipped from under one of her eyelids. "You have to go. I can't control this much longer."

"I'm not leaving you." He went to his knees and scooped up her hand. "I'm not." Only she didn't answer, her body limp and unconscious.

I looked at Crash for help. He stood back at the top of the stairs, his upper body slick with water from the swamp, his jeans wet almost to his thighs.

As lovely as all that was to look at, it was his face that I locked onto and, more specifically, the uncharacteristic worry I saw there. I mouthed one word. *Bad?*

He gave me a slow nod and mouthed back *I'm sorry.*

I tightened my hold on Suzy's hand. "Is there nothing we can do to help?"

Feish stroked Suzy's hair. "If she'd drained Eric's life, she would have survived."

"Wait, are you saying she might not survive even with help now?" The words tumbled out of me as I tightened my grip on Suzy's hand. "Are you serious?"

"Even a siren of full power might not be able to help her at this point," Feish whispered. "It has been too long since it was opened in her, I think. I'm sorry, I should have known something was wrong."

My thoughts were racing as I tried to come up with a solution that would keep both Suzy and Eric with us. "Suze, hang on," I whispered as I gave her hand to Feish. "Yell if she changes."

I stood too quickly and my knees protested, but I ignored them and forced my legs to hurry to my bedroom, my arm reaching out to grab Crash along the way. He followed me willingly as I flipped my bag off my neck and onto the bed. "Explain to me quickly what is happening, please."

He stood across the bed from me as I yanked Gran's spell book out. I'd relinquished the hand-tooled leather cover (for a good cause), and the pages were now enclosed in the cover for *Spells for Beginners*. I flipped it open, searching for the section on sirens. I knew there was one because I'd looked for it after meeting Suzy, and also because Gran was nothing if not thorough.

"When a half-breed siren gets close to their fiftieth year and the change comes on them," Crash said, "they either stay weak and able to do only minor manipulation of emotions, or they come into their family powers." He took a pause, and I knew the next part would be bad. "If they have a victim on hand and can drain that victim's life, then their powers will be solidified, and they will be able to fully control their powers from there on out. But if not..."

I found the section I was looking for, held my hand there, and looked up at Crash, seeing the sorrow in his eyes. "If not?"

"Then the siren will die, and her last gasps of magic will turn the place of her death into a breeding ground for more sirens. It's sort of a circle of life for them. And in her case, since she is a swamp siren—"

"Her death will create a permanent swamp here in Gran's house."

You know, because it wasn't enough that the house was haunted and home to a bunch of shadow world supernaturals.

I put my hands on the book and read the words I'd been hoping I'd remembered correctly. Words that could maybe be the tipping point for Suzy.

"Not if I can help it."

10

I left the book of Gran's spells on my bed and hurried out to the second-floor landing. "We are going to save Suzy." I crouched beside her head and her eyes flicked open, flooding with tears. I smiled down at her and stroked her hair. "We are all in this together, and my gran's book says it's possible."

"How?" Suzy whispered, her lips blue. A trickle of water crept toward us, leaking out from around her and puddling on the floor as if she were dissolving in front of us.

"You're going to take energy from each of us. Not enough to kill us, but enough to get you through this. Okay?" I tightened my hand on her. I looked to Eric, already knowing his answer.

He nodded. "Of course."

Feish bobbed her head. "Of course."

I smiled down at Suzy. "See? You've got family, and love will see us through this. Just don't grab my boob, okay? I don't swing that way."

Her smile was subtle, but I was relieved to see it. "Eric, you go first. When you pass out, Feish, you'll take her hand next. I'll go last."

I glanced at Crash and understanding flowed between us. He would get us out if this didn't work. The fact that he didn't argue with me, didn't try to stop me when we both knew this was a crap shoot, meant everything to me.

That man was so getting into my pants.

I let go of Suzy and Feish sat back on her heels, her red kimono spilling around her like a big skirt. Eric scooped up both of Suzy's hands in his own, engulfing them. "You can do this, Suzy."

Nothing happened. There was no change in the air around us, no flicker of discomfort on Eric's face.

"You have to kiss me," Suzy whispered, her lips darkening farther to a blue so deep, they were nearly black.

"Oh." Eric swallowed hard, but he didn't hesitate. He leaned forward and pressed his mouth to hers. Her body arched under his mouth, and he clung to her hands, his body shaking. The air around us went from cool and damp to hot and humid like a jungle in the dead of summer blended with the peak of rainy season. Eric shivered despite the humid heat and his body slumped sideways after only a minute.

Crash grabbed him by the shoulders and pulled him off Suzy.

Feish didn't hesitate—she leaned over and put her lips to Suzy's. The air changed again, and Suzy's body shook once more as the air around us seemed to turn liquid. I found myself holding my breath as if we were underwater. I didn't dare take a breath as Suzy drew from Feish, her throat working as if she were indeed gulping the river maid down.

Feish held out longer than Eric, but even so, it wasn't long before her shoulders sagged and Crash pulled her off.

Suzy still had her eyes closed, but her skin had pinked a little and her lips were less blue.

Crash stepped around her and put a hand on my shoulder. "Be careful."

I squeezed his fingers. "Just pull me off when I can't hold out any longer. And it will be enough." It had to be.

I leaned over Suzy and put my mouth to hers, pressing our lips together. I closed my eyes, waiting for the pain, or whatever was coming for me. Instead, I blinked and found myself amid a swamp. Suzy lay in front of me on a bed of lily pads, pale pink and white flowers blooming all around her as if she were Sleeping Beauty.

"We really have to stop meeting like this."

I twisted around and found myself grinning. "Robert. You just couldn't wait to hold my hand again, huh?"

His icy blue eyes glittered as he laughed at me. "Your friend is dying."

"Yes, I've noticed."

"The energy the others have given her is not enough. It will only keep her alive for a while—it will not revive her. But you can pull her out, like you did for yourself." Robert slogged through the swamp, his black pants and shirt clinging to his frame. He stopped next to her feet. "You will need to give her more energy than the others did. I'll keep Crash from pulling you off her."

I looked at him and held out a hand. "You are a good friend, Robert. I don't know why you chose to talk to me on the first night we met, but I'm glad for it."

He looked down at my hand and then took it in his own, linking our fingers for just a moment before he released me. "One day I'll tell you why. And to be clear, I don't think either of them is good enough for you."

I grinned as I stepped beside Suzy. "I'll keep that in mind." I took a breath. "So I just give her my energy?"

"Yes, and you have to pull her through this swamp to the land of the living. This swamp is a place of the dead." Robert's voice petered out as he faded from view. Well, that explained why he could stand here with me.

I felt a dip in my own energy, enough so that I wanted to lie down beside her and take a nap, but I took a deep breath, then said, "Okay, Suze, time to go."

I grabbed her hand and tugged on her. She didn't move. "Shit. Please don't tell me I have to carry you."

I tried pushing her off the lily pads, which didn't work, and yanking her to the side, which was equally ineffective. "Suzy. You're lucky I love you, girl."

A pulse of energy blasted between us, and she opened her eyes, turned her head, and looked at me. "Hey."

"Okay, that was weird, but let's go." I held my hand out to her and she took it. I locked my fingers around her hand and started to walk forward. Ahead of us was a doorway that looked suspiciously like the doorway to her bedroom. She staggered to a stop behind me, and it was like tugging on Artax in the middle of the swamps of sadness in *The Neverending Story*.

Not an analogy I appreciated in that moment. The horse died.

"I don't think I can make it," Suzy whispered. "My feet are stuck."

I took both her hands and tugged harder. Nothing. "Let's try piggyback. I can't carry you in a fireman hold like Feish can."

I sloshed toward her and turned. Her arms went around my neck and I was able to get her feet out of the water.

But the minute I did, the swamp changed, the water around my legs shifting from lukewarm to so cold that my skin felt as though it were being jammed with a million little needles. "Duck, that's cold!"

Yup, still managing autocorrect.

Suzy clung to my back as I stumbled forward through the water. With each step, the door drew closer, yet it still seemed so far away. I was breathing hard, and I heard yelling in the distance on the other side of the closed door.

"She's draining her!" Crash roared, and Robert yelled right back, "FRIENDS!"

I started to laugh. I couldn't help it. "Hold him off, Robert, we're almost there!" The idea of the skeleton fighting off a man of Crash's size and power was too much for my quirky sense of humor.

The doorframe was within reach. I grabbed the knob, turned it and yanked the door open. I stumbled to my knees, throwing Suzy forward off my back and through the doorway.

"She did it," Crash said in wonder.

Suzy groaned. "She's still in there."

I struggled to stand, using the doorframe to pull me to my feet as water sloshed over me. A big splash behind me. I dared to look over my shoulder to see something reptilian looking at me with unblinking, bright yellow eyes. Its mottled skin was a color that would have camouflaged it anywhere in the jungle. Ears that should not have been on a reptile stuck out the sides of its head, giving it a goofy look even though the rest of it was terrifyingly awful.

"Just leaving." I took a step but was unable to look away from those canny eyes. "So you stay there, okay?" Because that's the way to make monsters behave—you offer a rational argument and hope for the best.

Yeah, I didn't think so either.

The reptile shot forward through the water, and I screamed as I fell through the doorway.

Something tangled around my arms. Eyes scrunched closed, I bucked and kicked, my body running on fumes but empowered by my fierce urge to live.

"You're back, you're back." Crash's voice rumbled through me, and I immediately eased off. I opened one eye and peeked around. Suzy was sitting against the far wall, Eric holding her carefully while Feish stood with one hand on Suzy's shoulder, and they were all watching me with wide eyes.

"I didn't die again, did I?" I whispered.

Crash's arms tightened around me. "No, you did not."

A sigh slid out of me. "Okay. Well, that's a step up from last time. There was a giant yellow-eyed snake in there."

Crash stiffened. "What?"

"A snake. Or at least it looked like one. It was huge with scales in all different greens and big buttery eyes," I said. "He almost had me at the end."

We all sat there on the sopping wet floor, the swamp from Suzy's room leaking a little, but mostly self-contained. The swamp had not left. Minutes ticked by and no one said anything. Maybe it was here for good?

"Anyone else want tea?" I said, and Eric startled like I'd shot off a gun into his ass cheek. "I mean, it's obvious no one's going to sleep well after this."

Despite the bone-deep, aching fatigue that tugged at me, I didn't think I could close my eyes any time soon.

"Tea would be good," Feish said.

I pointed a finger at her. "Not *that* tea."

Her wide mouth curled into a smile. "Oh fine. Regular tea then."

There was no chance she'd have given us the tea that turned your bowels into liquid fire, but it was just the joke needed to break the quiet.

Eric and Suzy stood carefully and he helped her down the stairs, not taking a hand off her once. He was as wobbly as she appeared to be.

I didn't try to move out of Crash's arms. "Corb kissed me tonight."

"Used his magic, did he?" Crash's chuckle vibrated through his chest, against my back. "He's pulling out the big guns. I'm not surprised."

I tipped my head back and looked at him. "How did you know that?"

"You've never said anything about him kissing you before, and I know he has. Which tells me he's amped up his game." Crash let out a big breath, not a sigh so much as exhaustion flowing through him. "If Robert hadn't stopped me, Suzy wouldn't have survived."

"Where is Robert?"

"I threw him out the window," Crash said.

A cool breeze from across the landing shifted my attention to the upper windows. One of them had shattered. We'd have to fix that in the morning. "Damn it."

"He'll be fine," Crash said. "He's a skeleton."

A skeleton with pretty blue eyes. That thought sunk into me as shockingly as anything else. I shook my head. "Yes, I know, but he's saved my butt more than once."

"He's a good friend to you," Crash said, pulling himself to his feet and taking me with him. "I don't think anyone should sleep alone tonight. Everyone should hunker down in the living room."

I took a step, winced at the pain in my legs but forced myself to keep moving, using the banister to help me get down the stairs. "Yes, that's a good idea. Like a sleepover gone terribly wrong."

He grunted. "I've never been to a sleepover like this one."

"I don't think any of us have had a sleepover like this either."

I reached the bottom of the stairs and headed straight for the bright lights of the kitchen, the smell of warming pastries, and the sound of a tea kettle boiling. "Gran, you coming?" I paused in the doorway, fully expecting her to come out to talk to me right then.

She appeared in the kitchen and looked us over, her eyes at half-mast as though she were sleepy. "What happened?"

Crash stood just out of her way. "Someone triggered Suzy's siren."

Gran put a hand to her head. "I feel like my brain is full of cotton. Who did this?"

"I don't know," Eric said. "No one was up there. But I could smell something, or someone. I didn't put it together right away."

Gran slowly paced the kitchen, one hand to her head, one hand on her hip. "This is ridiculous, I feel like I'm…fading."

My head snapped around so I could stare at her. "You aren't though? You just feel off?"

"Very," she said. "Very off. Whoever did this has an ability with the dead. They stuffed me in a corner, I think, so I wouldn't see them, then…did they leave something, Eric?"

I grabbed a chair and slid into it, stifling a groan. Everything hurt—every muscle, every limb—and I didn't have the energy to pretend otherwise.

Eric engulfed one of the mugs with his hands. "There was a beautiful box on her bed, carved from wood with metal hinges and a latch that had an engraving on it."

I really didn't want to get out of the chair. "Is the box still there?"

Eric pursed his lips. "Yes, I think so. It held the spell that triggered Suzy's siren."

With difficulty, I made myself get up and go back up the stairs. No one followed, and I didn't blame them.

Into Suzy's room I went, not caring that the water was still there because I was already soaked. I slogged to where her bed had been, and sure enough, a nondescript box sat in the middle of what was now a bundle of vines.

I pulled one of my knives and pushed the box over using the tip. There was no hiss of magic or anything else so I dared to pick up the box. The spell had been used; there was nothing left in it as far as I could tell.

Rolling the box over in my hands, I looked for something that would give a hint as to who had ambushed Suzy.

I shut the lid and looked at the hinged pieces that clipped it shut, and my breath caught in my throat.

Pulling my hip bag around, I dug around inside until I found the coin that belonged to Grimm. I held it up next to the box. The same etched design of feathers spread out around the edges, along with the lines of Goblinese.

This was no coincidence.

I backed out of the room and headed downstairs. I wanted to tell them what I knew. But Crash was still here.

And Grimm…he'd been adamant that Crash be kept in the dark.

At the kitchen table, I took my tea without a word.

I put far too much sugar into mine, plus enough milk to make it look less like tea and more like pale chocolate milk. I took a sip and added two more teaspoons of sugar. I didn't care if I rotted my teeth out. I just wanted to let my brain numb for a bit.

Crash sat beside me and slid a hand under the table and over my thigh, giving me a squeeze. I dropped my hand on top of his.

I put my tea down, leaving my other hand in Crash's grip. I didn't want to pull away. He turned his hand over, linking his fingers with mine as if it were the most natural thing in the world, and that simple gesture warmed me more than anything he could have done right then. "Suzy, will you be okay now?"

Her big blue eyes blinked up from her teacup. "I think so. Honestly, I don't know. No one ever expected me to amount to more than a middling siren with very basic abilities. Corb himself told me that after he found me trying to use my powers in the swamp. He said I wouldn't get much more out of my skill set so I needed to put effort into doing what I could and learn everything possible from the Hollows." She shrugged. "And we know how that went."

Yeah, we all knew how that went.

"Who did this?" Suzy asked. "I mean, I get that it was coming anyway, but why would they want to hurt Eric?"

Eric shrugged. "Hattie's crew might be gone, but my cousin was still killed in New Orleans. Could someone else want a bigfoot dead? Or maybe someone has taken up their mission?"

The thing was we didn't really know the answer to that. All the trails that led from Hattie had dead ended. Something told me this attack wasn't directed at Eric. Their love affair was hours old at best. Not even a day.

"Before today, who has Suzy been spending the most time with?" I said. Of course, I already knew the answer.

Everyone looked at me.

Yeah, that was my thought too. The hit hadn't been aimed at Eric at all, but at yours truly.

I wrapped my hands around my cup and took a sip. Damn it, I was too old for this shit.

11

After midnight, fresh out of a fight for our lives, the realization that the attack on Suzy and Eric had been meant for me just left me feeling tired. I couldn't even be that upset, not really.

Just too damn tired to care. Maybe in the morning I'd feel differently. Feish opened her mouth, and I gave her a subtle headshake, even frowned at her, trying to convey that we should say nothing about the Marshall House.

Feish, despite her best efforts at reading my face, couldn't seem to help herself. "Bree, do you think it's because of the goblin?"

"Goblin?" Crash was the one to echo the word. "What are you doing messing with goblins?"

Feish shot a look at me and made a face. Like oops, maybe I shouldn't have said that.

At least I knew better than to throw her under the bus.

"Jinx gave me a lead on a job," I said. "Feish and I went to check it out at the Marshall House. We got there about nine, I would say. We bumped into a goblin." I yawned to cover any weird vibes I might be throwing off. I wasn't a good liar at the best of times, and I didn't like lying, so this was a tough spot.

Eric and Suzy shared a look. "That was about when we went upstairs to talk."

Sure…*talk*. I'm sure that was what they'd planned on doing. A slight buzzing like an oversized mosquito filled the air, and Kinkly landed in the middle of the table. "What's going on? Robert came flying through the window and woke me up when he crashed down through the oak tree. And he was pissed. Growling and snapping his teeth."

Eric gave her a quick rundown of what had happened. And he didn't blush once. I think that Kinkly noticed the change in him too. Her eyes drifted over him and Suzy sitting hip to hip, his arm across her shoulders.

I drew a slow breath and looked at Crash. "Would you mind giving us a few minutes? The information I need to share with my team is for them alone."

Again, I thought he'd be pissed, but he just stood. "I'll go check on Robert and make my apologies." He stood and left the room. As soon as the front door shut, I leaned forward.

"The job I took was with a goblin named Grimm. What do you know about goblins, Kink? Aren't they fae?"

She fluttered above the table. "The goblins are Unseelie. But they have their own leader who considers himself a king. For the most part, they keep to the west of the city and I don't bother with them. No one from the Seelie court does. They are aggressive on a good day, so it works out better for them to stay in their own territory. That one of them was in downtown Savannah is interesting to say the least, although it's not unheard of. Sometimes they get booted out for one reason or another."

I kept my voice down and they all leaned in close to listen while I spoke. "While we were there, he gave me something to protect. He said it was a family heirloom someone else was trying to steal. After he handed it over, Feish, Robert, and I slipped through his window, and then Davin, Roderick, and Bruce busted into his room and trashed it. They had another goblin with them earlier, all dapper-like but I didn't hear another voice during the break-in. No idea where Grimm went. Only that he wasn't with them when they cornered me later."

I gave them all the rundown on what had happened next, from sending Robert and Feish away to finding the ghosts hiding in that room and…"Vampire. That's the word the Silver Lady mouthed to me."

Eric blew out a low whistle. "That is not a good sign, not for this town."

Kinkly nodded. "I agree. I think you should hide whatever it was that Grimm gave you."

"It's basically a family tree," I said, remembering what Grimm had said. "But I don't think that's the important part. There's a silver coin. It matches the etchings on the box upstairs."

Eric groaned and we all looked at him. He pulled Suzy under his arm and held her tightly. "That's the family crest of the current king of the goblins. I recognized it after we opened the box." I nodded, motioning for him to hurry up, and he went on. "It means you're on their hit list. Maybe because you're helping Grimm."

My palms went clammy, and I was suddenly doubly glad that Crash wasn't there holding my hand. "What has that got to do with a vampire, though? That part doesn't make sense."

"What's so important about those pages? Or is it that the coin is important?" Kinkly asked.

I rubbed a finger around the lip of my teacup. "It could be either. I didn't find the silver coin until we were in that room below Grimm's. The ghost found us soon after that."

Kinkly frowned. "I could pay a visit to the goblins' leader, see if he'll talk to me. If one of his goblins is acting up, he might help. I could say that I'm there on Karissa's behalf. He's always trying to cozy up to her."

"No, that would tell them we know they're gunning for Bree," Suzy said softly. "I say we take extra precautions. I'll need to work with these new abilities, but the truth is we are stronger now with me like this. I'll be able to manipulate water in all forms, and I should be able to shift to a new form once I get my strength back. And my ability to charm people will be seriously amplified." She was frowning as she spoke even though the abilities sounded like an amazing addition. "I mean, if you want me to stay."

"Don't be ridiculous. You're part of the team. Taking more precautions is a good idea. We'll stick together in pairs, at the least, and figure the rest out tomorrow." I lifted my teacup, Kinkly scooped up a thimble we'd set out for her and grabbed some tea, and we all clinked our glasses together.

I stood with a quiet groan, my muscles seizing hard, and went to the front door. I opened it to find Crash sitting on the top step. "We're all done."

He turned just his head. "Do you want me to leave?"

The way he asked it made it clear he didn't just mean for the night. I didn't like it for so many reasons. But the vulnerability in him was what tugged at me. How many people had turned him away over the years? Too many, even if no one else saw it.

"No. I want you to stay. But my team and their safety have priority."

He smiled as he turned and held out his hand to me again. I took it and let him lead me into the main living room.

We pushed all the furniture to the sides, threw couch cushions onto the floor, pulled blankets and pillows into the living room, and made a big plush bed. There was just enough room for us all to sleep with our heads clustered together in the center of the room and our feet sticking out like a giant pinwheel.

Suzy was to my left, and Crash to my right.

I looked over at Crash. "This is not how I saw our first night together."

He burst out laughing. "Nor did I."

Suzy giggled. "I don't know, I might have imagined a giant orgy or two."

A ripple of laughter flowed through the room, contagious in the way it always was for the overtired. I laughed until tears tracked down my cheeks, and kept laughing until those tears dried and I finally managed to rein it in.

Next to me, Crash offered me an arm, and I rolled into his hold, using his bicep as a pillow. He pulled a blanket up and over us, and his warmth sunk through me, my nose pressed to his chest, close enough to smell the fire and smoke that was so uniquely Crash.

"Sleep. You've more than earned it," he whispered into my ear. "I'll keep watch over you tonight." I didn't think he meant over just me either.

I yawned and snuggled against him, not caring if this was real or not. Not caring if he was only attracted to me because I was a little bit fae. Of the two men in my orbit, Crash was the one I trusted more with my life, if not with my heart. If he said he'd keep me safe, I believed him.

Sometime later, when everyone was sleeping deeply, the shuffle of feet on the wooden floor tipped my head up. Robert stood in the big arched opening between the living room and the entryway. I lifted a hand, reminded that there was one other man who would keep me safe no matter what it cost him. "Thank you."

He lifted a hand back. "Friend."

I closed my eyes, knowing without a doubt that for at least a few hours we were all safe.

And that was all I needed to finally let myself sink fully into a sleep that dragged me down into oblivion.

I woke not with a start, but a lazy stretch that made every bone, joint, and muscle in my body tingle—and not in a good way. More like a hey-you-forgot-your-Advil-last-night kind of way.

"Sore?" Crash asked quietly.

"Everywhere," I whispered back.

He sat up, taking the blanket with him. It pooled around his waist, reminding me of one of the first times I'd met him. He'd been draped in nothing but a sheet. I missed those ignorant days. Back then, I'd had no real idea what I was stepping into—what kind of life-or-death stakes I would be asked to accept, again and again.

The tattoo on his ribs made much more sense now, the flames roaring up the side of his abdomen. I mean, when I'd first seen them, I had suspected it was because he was a blacksmith. But maybe it had more to do with his magic, and the way his kisses set my body on fire.

"Like what you see?" He winked at me, catching me staring.

I winked right back. "Checking out that tattoo. Thinking about the first time I saw it."

His smile was slow and deadly for my rapidly beating heart. "You mean when I was naked?"

I patted his cheek—the cheek on his face, I mean, I'm not quite that brassy. "You had a sheet on."

A sudden pounding on the door rolled me to my feet, knives in my hands. I barely remembered reaching for them. Apparently, the training was finally catching up to my reflexes, or maybe it was the other way around?

The door burst open and Corb stood there, eyes wide, a gun in one hand and a knife in the other, his eyes finding me first. "Bree, are you okay?"

I tucked my own knives back into their sheaths. "A little late, man. You missed the party *and* the after party."

Corb slowly lowered his weapons, and although I couldn't see where he'd put them, or even where he could have put them, they disappeared. "Everyone's okay?"

Crash brushed past me and headed for the kitchen. "I'll make breakfast. And you talk in your sleep, Bree."

Oh, that last shot was definitely for Corb, but he just breathed a sigh of what I could only assume was relief. "What happened?"

I turned as Suzy stood, her long hair braided back from her head in a bunch of braids that told me Kinkly had been at work while she was sleeping. I touched my own head and found the same look had been woven into my own hair.

"Someone set my powers loose," Suzy said softly, totally not her usual self, but it wasn't like she'd lost confidence. More like her own near-death experience had made her more mature overnight. "They did it so I would kill whoever I was with." I noticed that she didn't say it was about me, which I was grateful for.

We had to keep our cards close to our chests.

I turned back to Corb. "We figured you might be able to help her. Seeing as you brought her into the Hollows and all."

Corb's eyes were locked on Suzy. "How long did you have to fend off the urge? Twenty minutes?"

Suzy looked at me. "Four hours."

Corb sucked in a sharp breath. "That's impossible. You…Suzy, how did you survive?"

She didn't look away from me. "It's not my story to tell, not really. I just hung on, and Eric, Feish, and Bree, they threw me the lifeline that pulled me out." She shrugged and then grinned. "I will say that they are all excellent kissers."

I laughed and Feish giggled a funny warbling laugh that only made me grin wider. The smell of bacon tugged at me and I limped toward the kitchen. Every step reminded me that not only had yesterday been one of my longest nights in a long time, but it had also ended up with all of us sleeping on the floor.

"Why didn't you answer the phone sooner?" I asked as I stepped up next to Crash and shooed him from the frying pan. "You chop the stuff for omelets."

Corb moved to stand across from me and Crash as we prepped breakfast. "The phone was off. I was on a job that couldn't be disturbed."

"Delicate," I said. "You don't get many of those. Or was this something for Davin?" I wasn't intentionally poking at him. But I wasn't going to avoid the subject either. Crash's muscles flicked like a fly had landed on him, and then he relaxed as if I'd said nothing.

"It was a job, pertaining to the O'Seans and the mess they left behind," Corb said. "And the remainder of the details are confidential."

Crash shot him a look. "Their sister causing grief?"

Corb's jaw ticked. "Something like that."

"Be careful, she's quick with a gun," Crash said.

Damn it, they both knew? And I couldn't know, of course, not. Jerks.

I nodded. "My new job is like that too, delicate and confidential." I couldn't help but lock eyes with him. Because yesterday he'd been all about honesty and transparency, but here we were, less than twelve hours later, and he refused to be honest with me about a stupid job. Okay, maybe that wasn't fair. Work was work, but in the shadow world, work had a nasty habit of showing up at home and trying to kill you.

And no, I did not feel bad for not telling him about the whole goblin situation.

Clearing his throat, Corb offered with a motion of his hand to take over the eggs, as if that would win him points. Well, it would, but not enough. I let him take my spot, stepping back with a flourish that would have made Vanna White proud. "Go right ahead. Far be it from me to say no to two gorgeous men cooking me breakfast. But maybe you should take your shirt off, too, so I can really compare." Laughing, I turned my back on them as Suzy and Eric stepped into the kitchen. Kinkly fluttered in above Eric's head and then she shot down to me.

"Do you like the braids?"

"They're great, thanks." I put a hand to them, already knowing that getting all the miniscule braids out was going to be a massive pain in the ass. But I wasn't going to burst Kinkly's bubble. Feish was the last to enter the room, and she was still giggling, whispering under her breath, "I'm a good kisser."

When I turned around, it was my turn to catch my breath.

Corb had stripped off his shirt and tucked it into his back pocket.

Both men were naked from the waist up, and I wasn't sure if I could breathe anymore. Kinkly shot forward and plastered herself to Corb's back. "I call dibs on this one."

He jumped and looked over his shoulder. "You're a bit tiny for me."

She bobbed her head. "Yes, agreed. If Bree is your type, you like 'em big."

I sunk into a chair and lowered my head to the table, mostly because I wasn't sure I could look without drooling. And I definitely couldn't look away.

Suzy sat next to me. "You did tell him to take his shirt off."

"I was joking. I mean, kind of." I lifted my head, grinning wide and not blushing a bit. "Maybe I should have a harem."

Crash twisted around first, but Corb was right behind him. Corb looked at Crash. "I could share. But I don't think you could."

Crash shook his head. "Not the way she means."

The sound of skeletal feet on the wooden floors turned me around again. Robert shuffled in, and when his head swung toward the two shirtless guys making breakfast, he growled.

"Oh, Robert, you'll always be my favorite," I said, and for just a moment the swaying slowed, and I saw him as he had been when he was alive. Icy blue eyes that locked onto mine. But the image faded and he was just Robert again, swaying.

The two guys served up a big breakfast, and amid much ribbing, laughter, and side eyes around the table, we were…happy. That was the only word for it. In that moment, contentment filled my heart, and I felt more at home than I ever had before.

Because I was with the family who'd chosen me, and I'd chosen them.

Unexpected tears pricked at my eyes and I stood. "I'm going to shower."

My plate was only half empty and I knew the others might wonder if something was up, but I didn't care. I didn't want to try to explain out loud how I was feeling.

"Don't want to jinx myself," I said as I pulled myself up the stairs to the second floor.

"You called?"

My eyes shot up to the oversized black spider waiting for me on the landing. "What in the hairy legs of hell now?"

12

Jinx the trickster spider stood on my second-floor landing, rubbing her long hairy legs against one another, a nervous tic if I ever saw one. "So is the boss here?" She shuffled forward, and I put a hand up stopping her.

"You told me about Grimm down at the Marshall House," I said softly as I hurried up the last few steps, which effectively pushed her back. "What do you know about his situation? The goblins are up to something, aren't they?"

"Grimm isn't there anymore." She rubbed a back leg against another back leg and squirted out a bit of webbing. Her many eyes all blinked closed at once. "That's embarrassing."

"Getting old, huh?"

"You have no idea," she whispered.

"I have a pretty good idea," I said. "I pee when I laugh too hard. Now tell me what is going on."

She did a funny little tap with all her legs at once, like she was drumming on the hardwood. "I can see the goblins were here already. I came to warn you that they were talking about paying you a visit. They passed under me and didn't see me. Grimm does not want Crash to know."

"Why would they come after me? You're the only one who knew I was going to see Grimm." I found my hand dropping to the handle of the knife strapped to my right thigh. "What did you tell them, Jinx?"

"Nothing, I swear it! Please don't kick me in the lady bits!" She hunkered low to the ground, like a dog cowering. "I watched them come down Factors Row, and they sniffed around and then started talking about you. They didn't even see me."

I crouched so that we were eye to eyes. "Anything else?"

"They want to kill you, I think. They said something about setting the siren loose on you," she whispered, then her eyes flicked to look at someone behind me. "Boss, I really came here to warn you."

Crash stepped onto the landing with us. I was impressed that he hadn't made a sound on the steps. "I believe you, Jinx. I also think you probably took your time as you tend to do."

She lifted two front legs in what could only be called a shrug. "But I still came. I didn't want to interrupt those two goons—they looked almost human. And they were wearing all black." Her eyes did this rapid blinking thing that reminded me of a crowd doing the wave at a baseball game, and it really made my stomach roll.

"You can guard the front yard," Crash said. "Stay in the oak tree out of sight. Don't bother the fairy that lives there."

She scuttled forward, ducking past me with a cringe that about pinned her to the wall—strike that, she climbed the wall and ran across it to the window Crash had broken with Robert.

She let out a *weeee* as she leapt through the open space, spitting a bit of web out of her ass as she flew.

"Corb left, and he took Suzy and Eric with him. He wants to see if he can help Suzy with her new abilities, and Eric doesn't seem inclined to leave her side," Crash said. "Feish and Kinkly are headed to Death Row to see if they can suss up any information. Feish has apparently decided she is a flirting fool."

I thought about the romance books she'd bought. "Well, maybe she's lonely." I paused. "Thank you for everything, but I really do need to shower."

He reached out and took my hand. "You look like you're about ready to fall down, Bree. Even with that bit of sleep."

I shrugged. "I took some Advil with breakfast and a hot shower will do wonders."

"I can help with that," Crash said, and gawd in heaven, the man blushed.

Crash blushed and that only made me go all hot, my own skin answering with a flash of heat so strong, I wondered why it didn't light my clothes on fire and burn them right off into a pile of ashes.

Now, just a warning, this is a moment where those of you with prudish tendencies might want to flip ahead a few pages. In fact, it might be best if you mosey along to the next chapter.

I'll wait for you to go.

Go.

Seriously.

Okay, I assume those who are still reading are all in for this next bit.

I tightened my hand on his and took a step back, drawing him with me. "Why are you blushing, Crash? Worried I won't be impressed with what I see? 'Cause let me remind you, I've seen it all."

He chuckled. "You make me feel young again, Bree. Like I haven't seen centuries pass, like I've never been with a woman before. Like I've never been hurt. I can't explain it."

I kept backing, walking through the open door to my bedroom heading toward the ensuite bathroom. With every step, my heart pounded a little harder. Should I have been trying to figure out what was happening with Grimm and hiding what he'd given me?

Yes.

Or making myself open the contents of that envelope with the information about what had happened to Gran and my parents?

Also yes.

Or figuring out how to stay safe from the goblins that were now gunning for me?

You bet.

But not right then. Not when Crash's finger was sliding around the bottom of my shirt and tugging it upward. Yeah, any thought of responsibilities, of what could have been, of what *should* have been fled my mind.

I looked down at the old, worn out, and stained with sweat bra I was wearing. "As you can see, I wasn't expecting to put on a show."

Crash's hands slid up my forearms to my shoulders and across to my neck. He stepped closer then, one hand sliding down my back to the clasp of my bra as the other dipped down to cup one breast. "I think I can manage," he murmured. Blue, gold-flecked eyes bored into mine and the heat flared between us so hard and fast that I thought we might both combust with that single touch.

"I really need to shower," I managed to say. "Like, I'm filthy."

His mouth tipped upward in a grin. "I can help with that too." I took note that he was repeating himself. Hell, we both were. Was it possible he was as flustered as I was? That only added to the flutters in my belly, because if he was flustered...maybe that meant this was something more than just a fling.

His fingers worked the back clasp of my bra, then he slid it off, one shoulder strap at a time. I could feel the weight of the girls' downward trajectory as they were released. Crash stepped back, and I looked up at the ceiling as if the peeling paint there was suddenly all I could think about.

"You are beautiful, Breena," he said, and the Irish accent that sometimes popped up lay heavy on his words. "Don't let anyone, including yourself, tell you otherwise."

I did look at him then. "I'm—"

"You don't see what others see. It took me a long time to understand that. But maybe that was the best thing your gran could do for you. It made you…a better person." He paused before adding, "I don't think you see what most fae want you to see either."

That caught my interest. Like seeing Grimm as a bat-eared goblin instead of as a handsome pretty boy?

"I see you," I said.

"I know. It surprised me even on that first day," he said. "Most see only the darkness that is wrapped around me. Few see through it."

I reached for his hand and tugged him forward. "Enough talking." He stepped closer, and I looked up at him as our bare chests pressed together. He lowered his head to mine, and the same fire rose between us when our lips touched—a low burning in the center of my belly that spread outward in pulses of sweet decadence. A promise of what was coming if I let this go too far.

Yeah, I was going to let it go too far, maybe even push the whole situation right off the cliff.

We stumbled backward into the bathroom, and I almost fell over my own feet. Crash caught me and our mouths parted. I giggled, and he laughed with me.

"Don't fall," he whispered.

"Too late," I said and his eyes sobered, the laughter fading, leaving behind only the heat that flared once more.

His big hands, rough with work, slid carefully over my body as we flicked the shower on, his touch as light as could be despite his years of working with his hands. He unbuttoned his jeans and slid them over his slim hips to the floor. The man had been going commando, there wasn't a brief in sight. The flames of his tattoo curled downward over his hip to a pile of black coal that settled on his upper thigh. I let my fingers trace the design, reveling in the way his skin trembled under my touch.

I shivered and his hands slowed, lowering to circle my waist, and then he lifted me into the shower. "Where's the soap?" he asked as he followed me.

Oh, Jaysus help me, the fire had gotten so hot I worried I might spontaneously combust, and that was with the water flowing over our very naked bodies.

Holy Christmas toast, I was naked with Crash.

Naked.

I backed up against the shower wall and he followed, a loofah sponge in one hand and a quizzical look on his face. "What the hell is this?"

His question broke the tension and I took the loofah from him. "Here." I poured liquid soap into it and got the bubbles going, then ran it over his chest, following the path of the sponge with my free hand.

His eyes widened. "Clever."

I lifted it and smooshed it into his face, leaving him covered in bubbles. He wiped his hand over his face and growled. "Oh, you'll regret that."

I squealed as he pinned both arms above my head and took the loofah from me. He ran it over my body, indeed getting me clean. I was groaning as he made a second pass with his free hand, sliding through the bubbles, smoothing them away. "Crash."

"Bree," he growled my name as his mouth dropped to my wet nipple and pulled it into his mouth. I cried out and arched against him, all thoughts of playing gone in a flash. His hand slid down from my other breast to my hip, then lower, to the V between my legs, effortlessly caressing the sensitive skin there.

He groaned as he pulled more of my breast into his mouth, then shifted with a trail of kisses across my chest to the other.

Fingers slid into me, tentative and careful at first as though he was gauging my comfort level. I wriggled, trying to open myself up to him, wanting the heat radiating off his body. Wanting everything he had and more.

He still had my hands pinned above my head, which meant all I could do was squirm under his touch, moaning his name over and over as again his fingers slid over my lips, finding that sweet spot that Alan couldn't have found with a compass, map, and detailed set of directions.

Crash's fingers pulsed in and out of me, slow and rhythmic, while his thumb rubbed at the center of every hot need he'd set off in my body.

He moved his fingers and mouth leisurely in an exquisite kind of torture, sliding over and in me, increasing the pressure a little more each time, and always easing off before I was ready. Yes, this was torture, this was the best kind that I wasn't sure I'd survive, and I didn't much care if I died right there. My legs shook, and all those muscles that had been tense and complaining just ten minutes before were more than happy to shake for a different reason.

The heat of his mouth on my breasts brought me up onto my tiptoes, and the pressure from his fingers cut through any lingering worry I had that this might be a bad idea.

I wanted to touch him, but he kept me pinned to the bathroom wall, the cool of the tiles on my back giving me the only sense of reality to standing there with him, his dark head bowed over my body, the curl of pleasure rippling outward, pulsing with the fire he stoked in me, the water dancing across his back and sliding over his bare skin.

A gasp escaped me, and he groaned, that deep rumble vibrating from his mouth and over my nipple. I thought he'd pull away, I thought he'd push himself into me and lift me onto his hips to finish the job in the most mind-blowing shower sex I'd ever experienced.

Hell, I'd need a hand hold for that, maybe some footrests. Maybe he'd put some in?

Crash let go of my hands as he went to his knees, and I might have squeaked in anticipation, my muscles clenching even harder at the thought of what he was about to do. Where his magic mouth was about to go.

A brief thought was simple and to the point: *Gawd in heaven, don't let me fart.*

And just like that, I could do nothing but stand there and think about not farting. About not letting something squeak out through the bands of muscles that had been ravaged by years of not being fit. I found myself pulling back, even though it was the very last thing I wanted to do.

Crash looked up at me, one eyebrow raised, but said nothing. He simply leaned forward and placed a kiss right below my belly button. He sucked the skin in, leaving a slight mark, and whatever fear I had dissipated in a rush of new heat that pooled wherever his mouth went, marking me.

Kiss after kiss, he made his way lower and I dropped my hands to the top of his head, sliding them through his wet strands, relishing every strand on his full head of hair.

He settled his mouth on that magic spot, and damn, it was like a direct line to every nerve in my body.

For a moment—although admittedly a brief one—I wondered again if this was a bad idea. What we were doing would surely tie me closer to Crash, but he was maybe not as bad as I'd first thought. He'd helped me reclaim my gran's house, and I genuinely believed he'd do anything to protect me. I leaned my head back as he growled, and the vibration sent me over the edge, waves of desire pulsing in increasing intensity with each flick of his tongue, with each stroke of his fingers, until I wasn't sure I'd be able to survive him and his mouth.

A last flick of his tongue, a last curl of his mouth, and all that heat…I couldn't help crying out his name as I found myself spiraling upward, unable to think straight as I hung there, pleasure pinning me against the wall as my hips bucked against his mouth, my body clenching out every last ounce of pleasure.

The shower water sprayed over us and I blinked a few times, trying to think straight and failing.

Hands under my ass held me up as I slumped against the wall, my body nothing but a bundle of Jell-O barely held together by bones and skin. Crash stood, a rather self-satisfied grin on his face as he grabbed the loofah and tugged me close to him. Pressed up against a warm, wet, grinning Crash was all it took for my libido to remind me that we weren't done.

He soaped me up, turned me around and scrubbed my back, all the way down my ass and the backs of my legs. "Beautiful," he murmured.

I tried to turn around to face him, but he kept me facing the wall as he started in on my hair, pulling out each of the braids Kinkly had put in, then scrubbing it. Helping me rinse it out. All very sweet, but while the heat between us hadn't cooled exactly, it was no longer the frantic need that had consumed us both.

"Crash?"

"Hmm." He put his mouth to that place where neck meets shoulder and pressed his lips hard against my skin.

"You…are you not…" Damn it, spit it out, girl! "Are we not having sex?"

He turned me around and kissed me. "When you've made your choice. Corb is right—I don't share well. It's why Karissa and I parted ways. She wanted a true harem." He paused, his eyes drifting up and down my body. "If I'm not enough on my own, then I'm not the right one."

I blinked up at him, the water splashing droplets all over my face. "You know I was teasing about the harem thing earlier."

"I know you were. But Corb doesn't. And his kind are more than able to share." He bent his head and kissed me again, lazy, deep, and the fire rekindled between us, hotter even than before, and once more he was pushing me against the wall. I hooked a leg over his hip, welcoming him to come just that last little bit closer.

I think he might have taken me right there, his body was poised to do just that, and I wiggled to get my legs around his hips, to draw him in. I could have made my decision right there and been happy as a pig in shit for the rest of however long I had Crash.

But, of course, that's when someone just had to knock from the bedroom.

"Breena, I know you're in there."

My ex-husband was at the fricking door.

13

For those who skipped the rest of the last chapter, here's the recap: Crash and I were getting busy, and we were about to seal the deal when someone knocked on the door.

Anyone would have been upset by that kind of interruption.

But did it really have to be my ex-husband banging on the door? Yelling at me to get my fat ass out of there?

"Who the hell let you in?" I yelled back as I slid down Crash's body, feeling every inch of him as I went. I whimpered at the loss of what that moment had almost been. He flicked off the shower, bent, and kissed me on the cheek.

"Rain check."

Rain check indeed. I swatted his ass as he stepped out ahead of me.

Alan banged on the door again. "I have a key. Get out here. What did you say to Corb? I caught him snooping around my place!"

Now, part of me was impressed, because the last time Alan had been here, he'd been stealing my gran's spell book and the talisman that I wore around my neck. I'd caught him and threatened to make his twig and berries shrivel up and fall off if he ever came back. Not to mention he'd peed himself because Eric had literally scared the piss out of him.

Yet here he was, being a pain in my ass again. That was dedication, I'd give him that. He banged on the door, rattling it hard. "What the hell? Why am I even here? I don't want to be here!" he yelled.

I blinked and looked at Crash. "Did he just say what I think he said?"

Crash tossed me a towel and wrapped one around his waist. I bundled up and opened the door to see Alan pacing my bedroom, grabbing at his mostly bald head. He wore the same outfit he'd worn to the auction the week before, and he had his hat in his hand. My mouth dropped open. Because…well, not because he was there, which was bad enough.

But because he was a damn ghost. "Alan."

"You did this to me, didn't you?" He spun and pointed an accusatory finger at me, but my gaze was fixed on the gaping wounds in his neck, like an animal had chewed on him and torn his throat out.

I put a hand to my mouth. Blood dripped down Alan's body, and while it didn't leave a mark on the floor, I kept glancing at the floor, waiting for it to happen.

"He doesn't know." Crash stepped up beside me. "I can only see him a little, but I can tell he doesn't know."

Alan pointed a finger at Crash. "Who the hell is this? Are you seriously banging a freak like that?"

I gave my head a little shake as I tried to catch up with this sudden and shocking reality. But a distant part of me wondered what Alan saw in Crash. What did he mean about him being a freak?

But that seemed like a minor question in light of the fact that Alan was in my room, dead. Hating Alan as I did, I didn't feel terrible about the fact that he'd died, let alone in an obviously shitty way. But it was a problem that he was here. My gran usually didn't let other ghosts intrude on her territory. "Gran, can you help me out?"

Oh, she'd get a kick out of seeing Crash in nothing but a towel. Almost as if he knew he was in for teasing and a tongue lashing, Crash stepped back into the bathroom. "I'm going to get dressed."

"You do that," Alan snapped. "This is ridiculous, you shouldn't lower yourself to—"

"Shut your piehole." I snapped my fingers at Alan and his mouth clamped shut, to both of our surprises.

I strode to my dresser and yanked clean clothes out while I waited for Gran to make her appearance.

Alan stalked in front of me, hands waving, mouth not moving, blood everywhere. I mean, not real blood, but still. "Alan. Go stand over by the window and don't move," I growled.

He backed up quickly, anger flashing on every part of his face. It was strange to think that at one point I'd loved this man enough to give up my gran, to give up my life here in Savannah. I shook my head. "I was a fool."

Crash stepped out of the bathroom, jeans on, but the way his eyes heated as he looked over my chest, still topless, told me he'd prefer to have them off. "Do you want me to stay here, while you…interview him?"

Alan couldn't seem to take it anymore. "Interview me? Interview me? What the hell is going on?"

That was a question I wanted answered too. I pulled on my bra and shirt and buttoned my jeans, amazed at how loose they were in the waist and thighs. I'd been so busy the last few weeks, I hadn't bothered to put on anything but the special leathers Gerry had made for me. Leathers that magically adjusted to my body as my musculature and weight changed.

"Alan, what happened to you?" I turned to face him, motioning for Crash to stay with me.

Alan huffed for a minute. "Well, I was at my rental place working on the computer." I think he blushed, although it was a little harder to tell with a ghost.

"You mean you were looking at porn," I drawled. "I caught you more than once, you nincompoop. So you were playing around with yourself and your fake girlfriends. And then what?"

He glared at me. "I do not look at porn. I don't need it. I have plenty of women who want me."

I rolled my eyes to the ceiling. What was it about the ceilings in this house that just begged me to stare at them when I couldn't find the right words? "Look, you were on the computer, and then what?"

"I don't know," he said, and there was nothing more pitiful than those three words. "I woke up and everyone acted like they couldn't see me, including Corb, so I…well, I didn't choose to come here. But I figured you put a spell on me, like you threatened. Because I was just here, and now I can't leave!"

I shook my head. "No spell, Alan. Can you see yourself in the mirror over the dresser there?" I pointed at the piece of furniture. Alan stayed put.

"I don't want to see myself."

"Because?" I wasn't sure how this was going to go, counseling my now-dead ex-husband into realizing that he was indeed dead.

Crash sighed. "He can't see through the glamor I put on to keep people at bay. People, not spirits. Which means he hasn't accepted his current situation. Until he does, he's going to be stuck here."

I looked over my shoulder at Crash, thinking if I just squinted my eyes, I'd see what it was he made others see, then decided not to. I liked him as he really was. "Can't I just tell him?"

"No good. He'll only hear what he wants to," he said quietly. "And because you and I can see him, what do you want to bet that he's not leaving anytime soon?"

I bowed my head and covered my eyes as I started to laugh. The hysterical, *this can't be happening to me* kind of laughter. It took me a minute to pull myself together. "Okay, okay. Alan, you can stay here until we figure this out."

He crunched in on himself, hunching his shoulders. "I don't want to see you with anyone else."

"Tough shit, I'm dating three men right now," I snapped, wanting desperately to bring Alan back to life, just so I could kill him myself.

"Three?" Crash gave me a look, and I winked at him.

"Robert counts, doesn't he?"

Crash rolled his eyes, but there was humor in it. "Right, for some reason I always forget Robert."

As if on cue, Robert scuttled up the stairs, swaying and bobbing with each step. "Friend."

Alan peered around me to look at Robert. "What is that?"

"Who," I corrected him. "That's Robert. Don't piss him off, he bites."

Robert stepped closer and tapped a skeletal finger on the yellow envelope that held all the information on Gran and my parents. Damn it. "I'll get to it, Robert, I promise."

"I'll just stay here," Alan said, slumping down to sit under the window, the gaping wound in his neck almost not noticeable. You could believe he was alive if you didn't know better.

"Don't leave my room." I turned my back on him and left. "Gran, I could seriously use some help here!" I shouted into the house only to get a flicker of her form across from me, in front of her room. There and gone.

"He can stay for now," she called out. "But tell him to stay in your room. I don't like him."

"Nobody likes him," I muttered, then shouted, "Don't come out of my room, Alan!"

I headed down the stairs, the envelope under my arm, and my bag bouncing on my hip. I opened it and stuffed the envelope inside, then checked to make sure I still had both knives, Gran's spell book, and Grimm's stuff.

Speaking of…I needed a place to stash Grimm's stuff, so it wasn't on me in case I got taken by the goblins. Because yes, despite the fact that obviously this job was far more dangerous than I had originally thought, I intended to see it through. But I also needed a hiding place that was not in the house.

A place where no one would ever think to look.

"You know, this is all happening because of the O'Seans and Hattie." Crash pulled me from my thoughts as we went through the kitchen to the back door of the house. He held it open for me and I stepped into the bright sunshine of a Savannah day. The smells of growing things and pollen were heavy on the air, and I was glad I didn't suffer from hay fever.

"What do you mean?" I asked. What connection had I missed?

"Whatever job you are on now," he said. "The people who hired you probably knew the job would take you up against someone they didn't like—and knowing your reputation, they're assuming you'll fight hard. Maybe even kill the person coming at you."

Oh, so he didn't think they were actually connected. I scrunched my face. "My reputation?"

"There are whispers that you're known as one who kills first and asks questions later," he said. "Not a bad rep to have in the shadow world, but in this case, it might have worked against you." He took my hand, lifted it to his mouth, and turned it over so he could kiss the underside of my wrist. He opened his mouth just enough that the tip of his tongue laved that sensitive spot, reminding where his tongue had been not that long ago, which sent another rush of fire coursing through me. "Let me know if you need me. And try to stay out of trouble." He paused. "And stay away from any goblins."

"I'm—"

He held up his hands, stopping me. "I know, the job isn't with a goblin, but be careful. If they are out and about…they are trouble. Okay?"

"I'm not promising anything." The defiant words slipped out of me, and he let out a growl that made me shiver and my fingers itch to tangle their way back into his hair. "But in this case, I'll mosey off by myself." Well, that wasn't entirely true. Robert would be with me. "Come on, Robert. We can go on another date. Then I'm not all by myself as per our agreement to not go out alone."

Robert swayed around the side of the house, making his way to my side.

Crash's laughter followed us as we left the yard. I took note that the Sorrel-Weed house was exceptionally quiet. Good. I didn't want anything to do with Matilda's monstrous boyfriend. I shivered and picked up my pace. Robert kept next to me easily.

"We need to find a hiding place where nobody would think to look," I said, considering my options. There weren't many, off the top of my head. We could try burying the stuff like we'd buried the fake fairy cross, but I doubted that would work again.

Who could help me think of a place? Only one person came to mind. I swung back around the side of the house and found my feet heading to the front door.

I let myself in and stood in the entry way and called up the stairs. "Gran, I need to ask you a question."

"Quiet, I'm trying to sleep!" Alan shouted from my room. Duck me, that man was going to make me pull my hair out!

I snapped my fingers multiple times, hoping it worked at a distance.

A sigh rippled through the air. Gran appeared at the top of the stairs, her image wavering. She seemed thinner than before. Could ghosts lose weight? "What do you need?" she asked, her voice faint.

Her eyes locked on me, and I found myself fidgeting with the bag on my hip. "I need to hide… something for a job." Why wasn't I just telling her that it was the goblin's stuff? No idea, but I found my mouth unable to speak. "But I need to be able to keep an eye on it. In case someone comes for it. I don't want to leave it here in the house, I feel like that's just asking for another kick in the ass. Same thing with keeping it on me. If someone's really coming after me, then I can't have the stuff on me."

Another sigh and she flickered to life at the top of the stairs, just a quick image of her in one of her old-school dresses. There and gone. "The Sorrel-Weed house. Hide it in the room that Matilda haunts. You can put whatever it is in the desk."

Bile rose up my throat. "Yeah, but I'd have to go into the house then. I don't want to go in that house." Sure, I sounded like I was ten years old again, so sue me. That place freaked me right out of my big girl panties.

"Yes." Her words were soft and sorrowful, which cut right through me. "Yes, but whatever it is that you hide would be safe there. The darkness would keep any goblin out—they're afraid of it."

Safe.

I wasn't sure that safe was a word I'd put together with the Sorrel-Weed house, but darkness, I'd agree with that. "You sure? I mean, you don't have another suggestion?"

Please, please, please, please.

Gran didn't answer and didn't even attempt to reappear. I sighed. "Okay, thanks, Gran. I'll talk to you later. Love you."

A whispered "love you too" floated back and I smiled as I turned and left the house again.

"I hate you!" Alan shouted.

"DITTO!" I roared back and slammed the door behind me.

14

I sighed as I let myself out of the house and down the steps. Gran's suggestion that I hide Grimm's stuff in the Sorrel-Weed house next door made my skin try to crawl right off my body and run down the street. As plans went, it was a logical one: goblins did hate the dark, and the Sorrel-Weed house was about as dark as they came. But I hated that I was going to have to go *into* the house that terrified me so.

Robert waited for me on the stone path that led to the gate, swaying side to side. So lost in my own self-pity and fear, I didn't see Charlotte, our neighbor's daughter, until she shouted to me from across the street.

"Hi! Breena. I said hi twice, didn't you hear me?"

Her call startled me, and I turned to see her waving from the top step of their house. "I'm going to New Orleans with my auntie and uncle now!" Her smile was missing just one tooth which made her all the more cuter. She was a sweetheart and seeing her always made me wish for things that would never be.

I waved back, forcing a smile to my cold lips. "Did you get cookies from Eric yesterday?"

"Yes, he sent me off with bags of them. See you in a few weeks, I hope." She hurried down the steps, ponytail bobbing, and I watched as she slid into the backseat of a dark blue SUV.

They pulled away from the curb, and she waved at me as she went by, both hands going as hard as she could. I grinned and waved both hands back at her. "Nice kid."

Swaying beside me, Robert lifted a hand and pointed at the small figure tucked into the side of the brick house that Charlotte and her mom lived in. The shape reminded me strongly of Grimm. Was it another goblin? Maybe one that could help?

"Good call, Robert," I whispered. And checking out the goblin gave us an excellent reason for not going straight to the Sorrel-Weed house.

Of course, I was procrastinating—who wouldn't when the task they'd assigned themselves was to enter a house of ghostly darkness that was freaky as hell? Besides, it was important to deal with the goblin situation head on. Suzy and I had been inseparable prior to her powwow with Eric yesterday, and there was no doubt in my mind that she'd been triggered in an attempt to take me out.

I hurried out of our yard and across the street toward our goblin neighbor. "Hi, have you lived here long? Bridgette, right?" Wasn't that what Charlotte had said her ghost was named?

The goblin startled and pinned herself against the wall, blending almost perfectly with the bricks. "You can see me?"

"Why do people keep asking me that?" I muttered.

"Well, it's not usual to be able to see goblins when we are trying to stay hidden." She ran long spindly fingers through her short shorn black hair as if she could tuck it behind her larger than life ears. Interesting that she was flying so far under the radar that Charlotte thought they had a ghost, but Grimm had been staying in a hotel. Maybe he hadn't been trying to hide as much as Bridgette? "But…yes, I've been here a few years. Just over ten."

I stepped a little closer and she gave me some side-eye. "Do goblins live in the city often?"

Her shoulders slumped. "No, I was removed from the hive. I didn't conform well."

My eyebrows shot up. "Didn't like getting told what to do?"

She tipped her face and gave me that side-eye again. "Maybe."

I crouched, then gave up and lowered my butt to the ground so I could lean against the brick front of the house. "My name is—"

"Breena O'Rylee. I know. I'm Bridgette." She held out a hand and I shook it. "The shadow world here in Savannah is all in a twist because of what you've done the last few weeks. Like you woke everyone up to the badness that's still out there. Reminded them it's not all cookies and ice cream."

I blinked a few times. "I'm trying to help."

"I know. Most of us do." She smoothed her long fingers over her clothing. The cloth shifted color depending on where she stood, giving her an even better camouflage. Cool. I'd have to ask Gerry if she had that kind of material for a second set of work clothes for me.

I thought about asking Bridgette to read Grimm's pages, but I didn't know her well enough. But I could ask her about goblins in general and maybe get a read on whether Grimm was on the up and up. "Are there many disputes between goblins about family heirlooms and such?"

"Oh, shit, all the time." She sat in front of me, crossing her legs under her. "It's a pecking order, so someone is always trying to move up the ladder to the top. Mostly with the men, but it happens with the women, too, from time to time."

Interesting. So that part of Grimm's story checked out. "In the past, did goblins have much to do with—" I paused and whispered the word, "—vampires?"

Her eyes went wide enough that it was all I could see when I looked at her face. "Are you serious?"

"Yes." There might not be a connection, but a lot of things had started happening at once, and I had to chase all the angles. Plus, if there was a vampire at the Marshall House, it could have had something to do with Grimm, or the council members' interest in him.

My thoughts shot straight to the no-face council member, Bruce. Yeah, he was my first pick for secret vampire. That guy gave me the damn heebie-jeebies.

She shook her head. "No one has anything to do with the fanged ones. They nearly wiped out Savannah, you know. The goblins were as against them as everyone else. You could ask the court bard if you ever meet him, he knows all the stories."

I nodded. I did know, now, that the yellow fever plague hadn't been a disease at all, but an influx of new vampires that had killed off humans and supernaturals alike. The problem had been squashed by the rest of the shadow world, but not before many lives were lost. So why the hell would anyone want a redo?

Tapping my bag, I debated showing her the coin and, in the end, pulled it out. "Any idea why this might be important..."

She pulled back from it. "The stamp is that of the royal line. How did you get it?"

Well, that confirmed what Eric had told me at any rate.

"I can't tell you," I said. "Is it dangerous to have one?"

Bridgette put her hand out and waved it over the coin in my palm. "Dangerous? I don't know about that. But they are...they aren't just coins." Her eyes lifted to mine. "It's made with a specific type of magic, Breena O'Rylee. One that can be malleable. Unseelie magic flows through this coin. I can't tell you anything more than that." She shrugged and tucked her hands into her armpits.

I put the silver coin back into my bag.

"Thank you. I don't know if what you've told me will help, but I appreciate it." I paused, thinking about the timetable Grimm had given me for hiding the pages. "Is there something special happening in the next day or two? Like a goblin event?"

She blinked a few times. "Tomorrow night is the call of the silver moon."

Silver moon. Where the hell had I heard that lately? I frowned. "So it's a big deal?"

"Yes, it's a big deal especially to the king. A new king can only be crowned on the night of the silver moon. It only comes once in a generation." She tipped her head to one side. "What are you thinking?"

I didn't know exactly what I was thinking, but at least I knew this was almost over. Tomorrow would be day three, and my commitment would be at an end. "Do you think this coin can be tracked with magic?"

Because the council members, along with their goblin guide, had easily found Grimm, not that he'd put much effort into hiding. They hadn't shown up at the house last night or this morning, but then again, they likely knew we were all on high alert after the attack yesterday.

They clearly knew it hadn't worked; otherwise they'd have come along to pluck the coin. Which should probably have made me wary of the goblin that lived across the street and could potentially be a spy, but my intuition told me Bridgette wasn't one of them. With the remarkable exception of Alan, it hadn't let me down yet.

She blinked a few times. "Magic could possibly trace it."

Possibly. But it could just as easily be the pages that Grimm gave me, seeing as they were all in Goblinese, there was no way to know exactly what was on them, and I just didn't know Bridgette well enough to ask. My gut feeling was to stash them both away and play it safe in that regards. Because the reality was, if it could be used to find me, then I couldn't keep carrying it around in my purse. Damn it, Gran was right about putting it in the Sorrel-Weed house, much as I'd been hoping she'd be wrong. "One more question, are goblins really afraid of the dark?"

Again, she tipped her head. It struck me that she was probably surprised I'd essentially asked her about one of her own weaknesses, but she didn't hesitate to answer. "Yes. But more the darkest dark. Our greatest fear is the darkness of demons and devils." She shuddered and rubbed her arms.

I reached over and touched her shoulder. "Let me know if you ever get lonely. We have big meals at my gran's place, and it's kind of loud, but—"

"I'd love to," she said in an undertone, casting a glance at the house, "but are you sure the fae king wouldn't mind? He doesn't like goblins."

Now that was interesting, and it seemed to fit with what Crash had told me earlier. "He doesn't?"

She shook her head. "No. In fact, he really, really doesn't like us."

"Well, it's not just his house. So come on by, maybe this weekend."

She grinned, showing off blunt teeth. "Thank you, Breena O'Rylee."

I gave her a wink, pulled myself up off the ground with only a small groan, and headed back across the street. Robert stepped in beside me once I was on our side.

"Robert, that was a good call. She's a nice goblin."

"Friend," he said.

I offered my fist up to him for a knuckle bump, and he slowly raised his own hand, clenching his skeletal fingers into a fist and gently bumping them against mine. "Boom, we make a good team."

He swayed but said nothing else. I drew a deep breath and looked at the hulking house next door. To the outside world, the bricks appeared bright and clean, but I could see stains of darkness climbing up them like choking vines.

I didn't want to do this.

But I also trusted Gran, and she'd told me this was the way to go. I trusted she was right about this house, and my conversation with Bridgette had only convinced me it was a good hiding place. Darkest of darks and all that. I just had to put on my big girl panties and get it done.

Okay, maybe medium-sized panties. Surely I could squeeze my butt into those by now.

"Maybe a stretchy pair," I whispered. Yes, I was talking to myself. I was scared.

I mean, really, the Sorrel-Weed house would be an easy place to monitor given it was literally next door.

I wasn't going to be running all over town again. I wasn't twenty anymore, thank you very much. We needed a *work smarter, not harder* plan.

"We can do this," I whispered, trying to psych myself up.

But my feet slowed as we drew closer.

The Sorrel-Weed house was a tourist attraction extraordinaire. Lots of people went in and out. In theory, that would make it easier for someone to sneak in and out unnoticed. But it sounded like no goblin would step foot in there. Plus, if the council members had tracked the coin to Grimm's room, they'd failed to sense that it had been moved to the one below—whatever tracking mojo (assuming it had any) it had wasn't infallible. If it led them here, they'd probably assume it was tucked into Gran's house.

Ugh. That wasn't any better. It meant we all had to be out of Gran's house for the next day and a half. But we could do that. In fact, it was probably a good idea anyway, given we'd already been attacked there once. I'd leave a note for the others in case I missed them.

The square that lay kitty corner to the Sorrel-Weed house and Gran's place would work for a place to sit and watch. We could run shifts, me and the others, to keep an eye on the two places, and still stay tucked out of sight. I nodded to myself, satisfied with the decision. It would work.

As long as the weather didn't turn cold and start snowing—highly unlikely—then we'd be fine watching from there.

I looked at Robert, knowing all my stalling was up. "Ready to go on a tour?"

"Friend," he whispered.

I forced my feet to step onto the property, my knees knocking and my skin clammy. I had to pause a moment and clench my Kegels to keep it all in. You know what I mean.

Shit, none of this was good. I wanted to go back and talk to Gran again, to see if she'd thought of some plan B or C, but I didn't.

"Robert, we have to be careful," I whispered, and my voice seemed to pull the attention of everything in the house. The orange stone in the exterior walls darkened wherever those nonexistent vines ran, turning a deeper red until it looked as close to black as I'd ever seen. A black that swallowed the life around it and made the light of day dim.

My teeth clamped together with a pulse of fear that I struggled to swallow. Fear in a place like this would only make me more vulnerable to darkness. Gran had always told me that fear could weaken you as well as warn you.

Suddenly the fatigue that had been chasing me since I'd moved back into Gran's house made more sense—sure, I'd been working hard and training lots, but this was bigger than that. Getting a good night's sleep was nearly impossible with a house like this next door.

I paused on the top step. Maybe it wasn't the goblin intruder who'd hurt Gran. What if she was fading because the Sorrel-Weed house was affecting both of us? In the shadow world, almost anything was possible, and it seemed as likely an explanation as any other.

I closed the distance to the front door before I could turn and run the other way. Knocked once, and the door swung open on its own, with no one behind it. Yeah, I don't think that happened to everyone who came here either.

Beside me, Robert growled and I kind of wanted to do the same. Instead, I pulled a knife out of my bag, wishing that I'd strapped them over my jeans instead of tucking them away. I didn't shout out "hello." I knew better—I knew how the horror movies went.

Because more than likely someone who was *not* alive would answer me.

If not for Gran's certainty that this was the best place to hide Grimm's stuff, and for Bridgette backing her up, I'd already have been out of the house and running the other way.

"Matilda," I whispered her name, hoping the lady of the house would show herself and help me.

The floorboards creaked under my feet, and I wrinkled my nose in self-disgust. I mean, I didn't know the house well enough to avoid its creaking patterns, but still—I absolutely did not want to attract that dark creature's attention if I could avoid it.

I let my feet go where they wanted, following some instinct that I wasn't sure I wanted to acknowledge. Robert slid one hand into mine and I clamped down on his skeletal fingers, never more grateful for him than I was then.

Voices circled up to us from an open doorway. I found myself letting us into another room to stay hidden. Which turned out to be small but with a writing desk in it, a single chair, and a handful of fake coins piled in the center of the desk.

The sounds of running feet snapped my eyes back to the doorway I'd left open just a crack. A moment later, a group of tourists burst out of the door across from the main entrance. Stumbling over one another in their haste to leave, more than one of them had wide eyes, pale skin, and a sweat-covered face. I'd love to say it was from the heat, but I doubted it very much, which made own sweat glands turn on the faucet.

Fear had never looked so real, and it had never looked me so straight in the face.

The tour guide lifted her hands above her head, her dark skin pale with what could only be the same shock the others clearly felt. "Please, everyone be calm. Let's make sure we're all here."

The group huddled together as the tour guide counted, nodding as she got to the end. "Okay, I think that's enough for today. There are times that the ghosts of the Sorrel-Weed house are more…active than others, and it looks like it was your lucky day."

"Lucky?" An oversized man with a bright shiny head ringed with brown hair stepped toward the tour guide. "That thing down there attacked us!"

The tour guide swallowed hard. "As I said, some days are better than others in terms of—"

"I want my money back," he snapped and his hands clenched into fists.

For a moment, I saw them not as they were, but as the house saw them, and its perception fed into a story older than any of the living people who were there.

The large, overbearing white master, his clothing expensive and his attitude beyond shitty, beyond inhuman. Cruel. Unjust. And the diminutive black enslaved girl unsure if she should run or stay, trying to figure out the best way to protect herself since no one else ever had.

How many times had the house seen this moment played out in slightly different variations? Too many, far too many.

My eyes pricked with angry tears as I stepped out of hiding and entered the foyer. I found myself stomping on the floorboards with the heel of my boot without even thinking. Three times, drawing all the attention to me despite what I suspected it would mean. That the entity here would know I was inside.

Those three strikes reverberated through the room and, from there, through the house. Everyone in the group turned to look at me. I don't know what they saw besides a forty-one-year-old woman with a knife in her hand, but that alone seemed to make enough of an impression.

"Everyone get the duck out." I snapped the words and they seemed to lash at the tourists, driving them into action. They scrambled out the door in a pushing, shoving flash. Fat boy was at the front, shoving two women out of his way.

The tour guide was the last to leave. "Who are you?"

"A neighbor who specializes in stuff like this." I waved my hand to encompass the house. Because I wasn't sure how else to describe what I did for a living and why I was there uninvited. "What happened?"

Her eyes closed and then opened wide. "Don't go into the basement. Certainly not today. The demon down there is…he is wide awake today and angry. He cut a few of them, and he cut me too." She held out her arms to show me long scratches running from the crook of her elbows to her wrists. Three strikes on each arm, six total.

"Demon?" It was my turn for wide eyes. Sure, I'd killed demons before, but I'd never set out to fight one. The first two had been accidental. "Did you say *demon*?"

She frowned and shuddered, rubbing her arms. "Yeah, I did. But you specialize in this, so you're like a demon hunter then?"

I stared at her, horror flickering through me, shrugged and then nodded. "Yeah, sure, why not."

"Be careful then," she whispered.

And she left me there, alone in the house with a gawd-in-heaven, lawdy Jaysus demon.

15

Here's the thing," I whispered to Robert as we crept upstairs onto the second level of the Sorrel-Weed house. "We need to hide this stuff here because Gran said it would be safe. And I gotta agree—if goblins are afraid of the dark, this place is the damn darkest."

The plan was as simple as could be. Stash the stuff from Grimm in the desk in the room across from Gran's. So, perfect, simple.

That was if I could make it all the way to the second floor without peeing my pants. Now that my anger was gone, fear ate at me like worms burrowing in deeply under my skin. I kept one hand on Robert, unable to let him go. He swayed along next to me, quiet as he'd ever been.

The tour guide's words were still banging away in my head, which was my main problem.

She'd said there was a demon in the house.

I'd faced two demons before, killed them both. So you would've thought I'd be good with whatever I might've run into.

The thing was, I'd read up on demons after my encounters last week. The demons I'd faced were lower level, barely conscious balls of negative energy created for a single purpose and without any real thought behind them. As bad as they were—and they were bad, don't get me wrong—they weren't the worst of the bunch.

There were three levels of demons, it turned out, and each level had different subcategories of strength.

Initiate—the kind I'd faced and managed to kill. Even if I hadn't killed them, they would have faded as the power used to bring them forward ran out.

Medial—temporary demons on this plane of existence. Stronger than the initiates and born of powerful magic that could keep them around for weeks, and even months.

Blood-born—the worst kind of demons to possibly deal with. Why, you ask? Because they weren't created; they weren't called forward; they were *born*. Born of a witch and given life so they could torture and kill, so they could drive fear and darkness into the world. They had a mind like any creature, but they could be solid or they could be incorporeal, which made them deadly as all get-out.

The only good thing was that the blood-born demons tended to be tied to a single place. Tethered like junkyard dogs. The demon in the Hanging Tree downtown was one of them; it couldn't leave.

And I was pretty sure the same was true of the demon in the Sorrel-Weed house—which meant it was a blood-born demon too. It could bark at us and be as angry as it pleased, but it was stuck. And unless someone was dumb enough to go into his space, they were good.

Yet here I was, dumb as could be.

"Duck, duck, duck," I whispered under my breath and Robert's hand tightened on mine. My energy spiked, and I unintentionally pushed it into Robert. He groaned and tugged me sideways.

"Friend," he said, and clacked his teeth together. The energy pulsed around and between us, suddenly darker than before, and it was as if I were drowning in water that was deep and cold. I didn't let go of Robert, just gasped his name, and he tugged me upward out of the cold and into his arms.

Arms. Not bones.

I blinked up at him to see those icy blue eyes staring down at me. "Hey, Robert."

"What are you doing wasting your energy to make me solid for a few minutes?" He helped me stand, his long dark hair pulled back from his face which allowed me to see the lines of his jaw and the concern in his eyes. I didn't know why he'd suddenly become solid—as in, not just a skeleton—but the wild guess that wanted to come to the front of my mind was not one I liked. So I pushed it away.

"Well, I thought we could go on a tour, you know, like a date." I grinned, knowing the grin was giddy with fear. "What a lovely house, don't you think?"

Robert's eyes slid past me to take the space in. "The house is lovely, but you need to work on your destination dates. This is terrible."

I laughed, and the laugh was eaten up by the house, the positive energy sucked up like chocolate milk, but I didn't care. "I just need to tuck this stuff"—I tapped my hand on my bag—"somewhere up in that room across from Gran's."

Robert blew out a breath and tugged me forward. "Quick then, in and out. Let's go."

We hurried upward—Robert doing as much pushing and pulling as I was doing walking—trying doors until we found the right one. The one that Matilda liked to stand in and mock Gran.

I half expected Matilda to be there, but she wasn't. The room was empty. A small writing table was pressed against the wall, just to the side of the window, like Gran had said. Only…it wasn't visible from Gran's window. How had she known it was there? That thought caught me off guard, there and gone in a flash.

I pointed at the desk. "There, we can move that under the window." It was my turn to drag Robert across the room, and he helped me lift the simple desk and position it just under the windowsill.

I dug around in my bag and pulled out the yellow envelope holding the pages written in Goblinese and the silver coin. Folding it in half, I tucked it into the desk drawer. "There. Nice and safe. Just another day and a half and—"

"Breena," Robert said my name softly, "you need to turn around."

As I gazed out the window, the skin on my back prickled as if I'd been touched with electricity. The glass reflected something behind me in the doorway of the room that should not have been possible. I mean, obviously it was because it was there, but I didn't like it. "Maybe I don't want to."

"I don't much want to look either, but here I am, looking," he said.

I forced myself to glance over my shoulder. A mass of darkness filled the doorway, moving like smoke, only thicker. Way thicker than smoke.

"Oh, no, I don't like that," I said.

Robert backed up so that we were side by side, still holding hands. "I never much liked demons either."

The darkness let out a low rumbling laugh that sounded less human and more animal. "*Fools to come to me.*"

I nodded, so beyond fear that my mouth took over when I probably shouldn't let it. "Fools, yes, for sure. We should just go now. Robert, what do you think?"

"Going would be good." He cleared his throat. "I mean, unless you want to stay for tea and biscuits?"

I looked at him, and I think I might have managed a single eyebrow quirk. Maybe it took bowel-twisting fear to give me that ability. "Tea and biscuits."

"With honey?" He shrugged. "I mean, if we're staying, we might as well be comfortable."

"*You will not stay. I will devour you!*"

Oh, I got what Robert was doing. I winked at him. "You know, that bedroom on the first floor would be perfect for my office. I could put a giant Jesus picture right in the middle of the wall. Maybe throw in a few statues of Saint Michael."

The demon hissed and spread out in front of us. "*Insolent.*"

I laughed. I couldn't help it even though my legs were jelly and I was pretty sure I'd never been so afraid in my life. "Not the first time I've heard that."

"No, it's really not. I was there," Robert confirmed. He grinned at me, laughing, and those icy blue eyes glittered with humor. "It's a family trait, I think."

The room went from bright and airy with sunlight spilling through the window to a darkness so complete, I couldn't see in front of me.

"Oh shit." I stumbled, barely able to keep my feet under me. All around me was darkness, death, despair. It crawled into me and reminded me of my lack of worth.

I was past my best before date.

I hadn't even been able to conceive a child.

I was out of my league with Crash. Corb was using me.

This job wasn't meant for me. I was going to get my friends killed.

No good.

Too old.

Out of shape.

Useless. Beneath notice. A joke.

Scared.

I was so scared that everything around me was a lie. That everything I was, or thought I was, was some fantasy I'd built on a stack of beliefs that weren't even real. My heart slowed as tendrils of darkness wrapped around it and squeezed. Tears leaked from my eyes.

One less of your kind.

Sadness crushed me, and I bowed under the weight of the darkness and the truths it spoke to my heart. Truths I'd been trying to ignore, trying to re-write.

Glass shattered behind me, and a warm breath of spring air spooled in around me, cutting through the black weight that had taken hold of me. An arm wrapped around my waist, and then I was falling through the air, floating. Maybe I was dying. You saw a bright light when you died, from what I understood, and bright light burned my eyes…except I'd almost died just a week ago, and I'd seen nothing of the sort then.

This light…it encompassed everything. I couldn't see anything outside of it, but I sure as hell felt the ground as I landed flat on my back, all the air rushing out of me, showing me that I was indeed still alive. At least for the moment.

I lay there, waiting for my lungs to kick back in, knowing they would but not sure how long it would take. To my left, Robert swayed, his long hair hanging forward over his face once more, his skeletal body rattling with what could only be fear.

He had saved me. Again.

I lay there and stared up at the shattered window and the shadow arms that clung to the edges. When you looked into darkness like that, and it looked back, there was only one thing to do.

My body was moving, running on instinct before I could think it through, before I could even get a real breath of air. I ran, hobbling, sucking wind hard until I hit the front yard of Gran's house. I hurtled over the small fence and crawled across the grass until I was under the oak tree. Robert hurried after me.

"That was a terrible idea," I said.

"Bad," he rumbled. He didn't have a big vocabulary in this form, so I suspected the effort it had taken him to come out with *bad* meant it was maybe even worse than I'd thought.

I stayed there under the oak tree, cold and shaking, for a long time—hours was what it felt like, but I couldn't be sure. My mind was torn up, freaking out about what I'd seen and felt, about falling from a second-story window. Robert crouched beside me, unmoving, a silent companion. Or mostly silent.

"Whiskey," he finally said.

"That's a ducking excellent idea." I pushed to my feet, my legs tingling from the stress of...everything. I let myself into the house, went straight for the liquor cabinet, and grabbed the full bottle of whiskey and a single glass.

Maybe I could have gone to Crash and warmed myself with his heat. I could have called Corb or any of my other friends to be with me. But something had happened in that house with the blood-born demon that shook me to my core and made my old wounds raw again.

I wasn't sure I could face anyone. That I was worth facing anyone.

Back out under the oak tree partially hidden by the hanging Spanish moss, I poured Robert a drink of whiskey first. He knocked it back like a pro, the golden liquid sliding down his spine and puddling under his butt bone.

I put the bottle to my lips and tipped it back, drawing more than a shot or two, the firewater burning its way through me, driving out the cold. Lowering it, I drew a shaky breath and poured Robert another drink.

Drink, pour, repeat. That became the mantra. The bottle was more than half empty by the time the sun starting going down. Bridgette came over at one point and asked me a question. I'm not sure what, but I saluted her with the whiskey bottle and mumbled, "Every house will whisper its secrets to you, if you listen."

She backed away, understandably, and I think she might have told me to sleep it off. I slumped against the oak tree, wondering where in the hell that had come from. No, that's not true, I'd seen that saying somewhere. I fumbled with my bag and pulled out the old spell book. Or I pulled *a* spell book out. The kraft brown paper crinkled under my fingers as I cracked it open, looking for that line.

I couldn't find the passage I wanted, though—my drunken fingers unable to even separate pages properly, never mind find the right book. The sun was gone and with it the light, and I knew I had to be in Gran's room, that I had to watch the house next door.

I had to tell my friends to not come home. I dug around in my bag until I found the cell phone Suzy had insisted on. Managed to put together a group text, telling everyone to stay away from the house until things had settled.

> **Stay away my friends, I love you so mmmmmuch, oh gawd, I'd feeling so ducking bad if something happened to, so you need to go sleep off somewhere else.**

"Too many things," I whispered. I scrubbed my hands over my face, which meant I rubbed one side with the phone, and then looked at the book in my lap. I'd flipped all the way to the back looking for a silly saying about houses. The top edge of the back page curled ever so slightly, separated at the corner like…it was glued together?

I picked at the edge with a fingernail, still drunk as a skunk but pleased to have a distraction from everything. The paper crackled as I pulled at it, and it slowly gave way under my persistence.

A slip of paper fluttered out, hidden in that pocket between the pages. I picked it up and stared at the words, not really understanding what I was seeing. Of course, I read it out loud.

"Of death and power, of magic and pain,
That which comes shall find those slain,
Raised anew and given life,
A warning alone, this call is strife."

I frowned at the paper, turned it over to see nothing but a number on it. Three. What the hell did a three have to do with whatever it was I'd just read?

I folded the paper, tucked it back into the pocket, and squeezed the edges shut. They stuck, not well, but they stuck. Good enough for me. I leaned my head back and looked up into the underside of the oak tree's leaves.

Feeling like shit. Not because I was drunk, but because the darkness in the Sorrel-Weed house had pricked holes into every piece of self-confidence I'd been building since Alan and I had split. Every fear, every worry that I was going to duck up this new life of mine, ate at me once more. The sound of footsteps turned my head to a man in a long black trench coat marching up my gran's walkway to the steps leading up to the front door.

I recognized him.

"My plate spilleth the duck over," I muttered to myself, doing that stage whisper the drunken do. You know the one.

Roderick paused on the path and then bent over to look under the hanging moss and stare at me sitting under the oak tree, a half empty whiskey bottle in hand, skeletal buddy passed out beside me and snoring ever so slightly.

I held up the bottle, forgetting for a moment that he was a council guy that I probably shouldn't like at all. "Wanna drink?"

16

Roderick turned out not to be too bad in terms of the other douche-tastic council members. Okay, the only other ones I knew were Davin and No Face Bruce, but they'd both made an impression—neither good. Roderick may have forced magic on me in the hotel, but now he helped me to my feet and hustled me inside my gran's house to the kitchen.

He paused and tipped his head to the side as if listening to something, and then went to the counter nearest the sink.

"Let's get some coffee into you," he said. "Where are your friends?"

"Out." I laid my head on the table, not liking the way the room spun and my stomach pretending it had never had whiskey before. Had I had that much of the amber drink?

"Out? On jobs?" Before I knew it, he set a cup of coffee close enough that I could smell it and feel the warmth against the back of my hand.

My stomach rolled, and I lurched out of the chair, barely making it to the kitchen sink. I heaved until my belly was empty, not sure if it was the whiskey or the residual darkness from the house next door that had sunk into my skin. I blinked and stared at the black bits and pieces that floated in the whiskey.

Yeah, that couldn't be good.

"Bad mojo," I whispered. I ran the water, rinsed my mouth, and a cold cloth was placed over the back of my neck.

Slumping by the sink, I clung to the edge.

Roderick cleared his throat. "The council would, of course, like to see you tonight."

"Of course they would," I mumbled. "When?"

"As soon as I can get you moving. They are waiting on us."

"Maybe I'll just lie down on the floor then." I slumped farther as if to make my point. He tucked a hand under my armpits and pulled me upward.

Back on my feet once more, I had to admit, if only to myself, I was feeling much better already with an empty belly. The whiskey must have bounced around with whatever bad mojo I'd picked up from the Sorrel-Weed house and bounced it right back out.

"You have until that coffee cup is empty, and then I'm taking you in." Roderick leaned against the counter and folded his arms over his chest. "And while you drink, I'm curious as to just what all that"—he motioned at the sink and the last few flecks of darkness that clung to the ceramic white basin—"was about. What exactly did you get into that you probably shouldn't have?"

I made my way carefully to the chair I'd apparently flipped over and stood it back upright so I could lower myself into it. "I went into a place where a blood-born demon resides. I don't recommend it. He is a rather large nasty ass." I sipped at the coffee and grimaced. My preference was tea, but coffee was warranted in this situation. I dumped a bunch of sugar into it and stirred it around, finally lifting my eyes to see Roderick watching me closely.

"What are you exactly?" he asked.

"A mature, seasoned woman, who is all out of ducks to give," I said and took another sip of the now overly sweetened coffee. I grimaced, not sure that the sugar had helped at all. But at least it was hitting my bloodstream quickly enough to perk me up.

"Yes, I can see that part," he said, not moving from his spot but I had the feeling he was tensing. "I can speculate there is a little fae blood in you, based on your grandmother's dalliances with them."

My eyebrows shot up. "Them? What do you mean by *them*?"

He chuckled. "Celia has always wielded a great deal of power in Savannah. The strongest witch our town has seen in two hundred years, from a long line of powerful witches unique for coming into their power late in life. Her daughter died before anyone knew if she carried the power, and her granddaughter"—he dipped his head toward me—"was, for all intents and purposes, a dud in terms of witching magic. Yet you came back to Savannah and the shadow world in this town is suddenly ramping up as if preparing for a war."

I took a sip of coffee. "You digress. You said *them* in reference to my gran's lovers."

Holy shit, Gran's lovers. As in plural.

Roderick gave a wry grin. "Hard to think about your parents or grandparents getting busy between the sheets, isn't it?"

I grimaced and it had nothing to do with the horrid drink in my hand. I held onto it for the warmth and because it helped dispel some of the cold that still clung to me. "Spit it out."

He tipped his head toward me. "She liked the fae. Their magic meshed well with hers. While she did settle down with one in particular, your grandfather to be exact, there was a time when she…hosted several in her home." His grin was altogether too ducking cheeky for this conversation. I shivered with what it could mean. He didn't appear to be fae, but was he one of those she'd hosted?

Jaysus, Gran, you could have warned me. No wonder she was making herself scarce. She wouldn't want me to know how wild she had been in her prime. Certainly not in front of a council member.

"Awesome. So my gran had a bit of a cat house going on," I said.

He shrugged. "She always did as she pleased, before and after the council was created. Once your grandfather won her heart, though, she was all in from what I remember. She was a loyal woman in many areas." He frowned and looked down, shook his head. "I hear rumors you might be following in her footsteps. Trying out the variety of dishes offered to you?"

I blew a raspberry, feeling much restored after a big puke and a little horridly sweet coffee. And I surely was not going to discuss my mess of a relationship status with this guy. "I'm dating casually. That's what you do after a shitty breakup. You don't jump into another relationship as a fix."

His smile said he didn't believe me for one second. Hell, I didn't believe me, but I was trying. I took another sip of the coffee. I might as well get this council meeting over with. I didn't doubt they would send someone else to get me if I refused.

Besides, it wasn't like the goblins would take a shot at me while I was with a council member, right?

But maybe No Face Bruce who might just be a vampire would. I shuddered and pushed the coffee cup away from me.

"Look, I have to get a few things. Can you wait outside and then I'll come along like a good little girl?" I stood and scooted my chair back.

His eyes tracked me as I got to my feet, and he smiled. "That's a lie if ever I heard one. But I'll wait outside. You have five minutes before I come in and get you."

I waved a hand at him and made my way through the house to the stairs. Up I went, one at a time, feeling a little unlike myself. I got to the top of the stairs and quickly checked the other bedrooms. Suzy's was still a quietly brewing swamp, and Feish's and Eric's rooms were both empty.

I checked my phone and saw some laughing faces in response to my drunken text, but everyone had seen it, with the exception of Crash. The others would all stay away then. That was good.

I turned and caught a glimmer of Gran's skirts in her room. I followed the movement in, but she ducked into her bathroom.

I sighed. "Look, Gran, I don't care if you took half of Savannah to bed. I really don't. But I…" I was going to tell her I wanted her help, that I needed her, but I found myself backpedaling. "I have to go out. Will you keep an eye on that window across the way for me? Please? Just tell me if anyone comes in, especially a goblin. I don't think they will, not with that demon watching over things, but still…"

It was the best I was going to be able to do, given that there was no one else in the house I could ask. Even as I glanced at the room opposite Gran's, a shadow moved. I frowned.

The window in the Sorrel-Weed house that Robert had pulled me through in order to save my life was somehow fully intact, no longer broken. This despite the sound of shattering glass and the impossible logistics of how we'd gotten through it. I swallowed hard and backed out of the room, feeling the weight of those eyes watching me from the darkness as surely as if they were laser pointers. The demon grinned at me, showing all shining silver teeth in the pitch black of that house.

I backed all the way into my room and shut the door, leaning my head against it.

"About damn time!" Alan barked and I spun with a shriek.

"Jaysus Christmas!" I yelled at him. "What the hell are you doing sneaking up on me like that?"

He glared at me from his spot under the window. "I don't want to stay here."

"Well, I don't much want you around either," I replied as I pulled out my leather pants and boots. I quickly changed into my work clothes. I didn't know what Gerry had done when she made them, but it was like they never really needed cleaning. They never even smelled bad. It was basically the dream outfit. I really needed another set, though, maybe one with that camouflaging effect I wanted.

"You've lost a lot of weight," Alan said.

"That's what happens when you're not eating your emotions anymore," I grumbled as I strapped the sheaths that held my two knives to my upper thighs and slid my bag over my shoulder.

"Can I come with you?" he asked quietly.

I looked at him, really looked at him, and saw just how afraid he was, and I tried not to feel bad for him, I really did. But I'd been with him a long time, and I knew him inside and out and could read him like a book. Damn it, he was pitiful.

And even if he did deserve to suffer, I wasn't the kind of person to deliberately hurt someone who was in pain already. I sighed. "You can come with me, but you need to stay out of my way."

He stood and put the hat on his balding head. "Maybe I can pick up some stuff from my place after?"

"Yeah, sure," I answered without really thinking about it. Not like he could actually pick anything up.

I hurried down the stairs and out the front door, Alan on my heels. I checked on Robert first, much to Roderick's amusement.

"What are you looking for? A heartbeat?" he asked. "He's already dead."

"Oh, nothing," I said as I listened to Robert snorting in his sleep, a rattling of teeth and gurgling of throat that was not really there. "He usually comes with me, though."

"Anything else before we go?" Roderick asked with only a slight dose of sarcasm. His eyes flicked to Alan. "What about this one?"

"I'm stuck with him for now, so he's coming along," I muttered.

Alan snorted. "I was stuck with you for years."

Oh, I would've strangled him right then if I could've.

I pursed my lips. "How far is this council place?"

"Ten miles."

Both my eyebrows shot up. "And we're walking?"

"That is the general rule of thumb in Savannah."

I snorted. "Maybe for you." I tapped the ground with my foot. "Skel, I need a ride." The skeleton horse Robert had introduced me to pulled himself (I'd decided I would go with a boy, seeing as all identifying parts were pretty much gone) out of the ground one hoof at a time.

Roderick stumbled back a few steps and swallowed hard. "Is that…is that what I think it is?"

"A quasi-skeleton horse, yes." I patted Skel's neck, pleased to see that it had fleshed out more since I'd ridden him last. I paused before getting up in the saddle. "One more thing."

"Of course there is," Roderick said. "There is always one more thing with you women."

"Watch it. Keep talking like that, and one of those women is likely to throw a knife at you," I said, half laughing. I mean, I didn't want to like Roderick, but he seemed exceptionally relaxed considering my interactions with Davin.

Davin the dipshit.

Davin the deceiver.

Davin the…demon?

I shuddered on that last one, even if it was just wordplay.

"This one's easy. Just wait here for a second with my friend Skel. I need to check something." I said it over my shoulder as I rounded the side of the house, not giving Roderick much choice. Ignoring the Sorrel-Weed house and whatever demon lurked in there, I hurried to the door that led into the basement and Crash's forge. I had to make sure he'd stay away. Not only so he wouldn't get hurt, but also because he didn't know that I was dealing with a goblin problem.

Down the steps and through the door I went, shutting it behind me. "Crash?"

There was no sound—no hammering of steel, no whoosh of the forge going. No smell of burning coal.

I made my way through the basement space until I found his work bench. A single sheet of paper lay on the wooden table. I should have left right then, but I couldn't help but take a peek at it.

Flowing script. A very obvious feminine hand had written the words that blurred a little as my eyes watered.

It wasn't even hot in there, at least not much. It was as though the words didn't want me to read them, as strange as that may sound. I squinted. Maybe it was just runny old eyes. I blew out a raspberry and picked the paper up.

Meet me at the fountain. I must speak with you right away. I miss you.

K.

K. Karissa? Most likely. I didn't think Kinkly could write words that big, even if she had a pen she could hold. Nor did I think Kinkly would say she missed Crash.

What in the world was the fairy queen up to now? I pushed away the old fear that I wasn't good enough, that he'd taken one look at my less than perfect body and run the other way.

I flipped the paper over and scribbled my own message to Crash. *Stay away from the house a few days. My job is getting dicey and could bring more trouble. B.*

Not so flowing, not so nice. But the block letters would be hard to miss.

I left the note and strode out of his basement shop, around the house (with a hand raised to block my line of sight to next door), and into the front yard.

I looked at Roderick and snapped my fingers. "Now I'm ready to go."

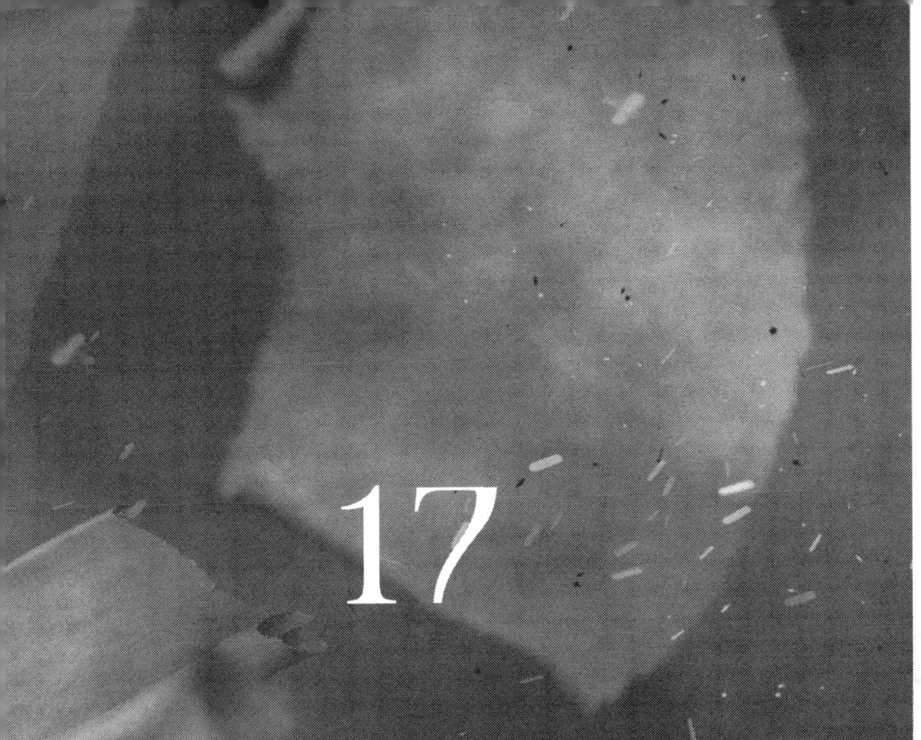

17

Getting to the council was interesting. Let's start with my dead ex-husband. That was truly my favorite part.

Alan paced beside the horse and I patted my bag. "Get in."

"I won't fit, are you crazy?" He stared at me like I'd lost my mind, and it was annoying enough that I barely noticed that he was still dripping blood from his neck. Real or not, that probably should have bothered me more.

I opened the bag with one hand, reached over, and grabbed his ear with the other. Let me tell you, stuffing my dead ex into a bag was truly the highlight of my day. Especially the last bit where I had to put a little more effort into it, and he complained that my bag stunk like funk and seawater.

That done, I turned and pulled myself onto my horse.

Roderick said nothing, just raised both eyebrows. "That's your ex-husband?"

"You bet." I grinned up at him.

Roderick's mouth quirked. "Remind me not to piss you off."

"I didn't kill him," I said. "Not that I was ever offered the chance."

He mounted behind me on Skel, and handed me a blindfold.

I rolled my eyes. "What, now we're in *Mission Impossible*?"

"They don't trust easily. There are those in the shadow world who would wipe out the council and the SCE if they could. The more people who can find us, the weaker we become," he said.

Sighing, I put the blindfold on. "You realize that a blindfolded ten-mile walk is totally ridiculous? What would have happened if I didn't have the horse? Is this your typical way of bringing people in?"

"Not my idea. No, it's not typical, and yes, it would have been ridiculous, but even if I agree with you, this is how they wanted it done," he said.

"Let me guess, Davin's idea?" I muttered.

His grunt confirmed it. Davin really was a dick.

The ride took just over half an hour with Skel going at top speed. Roderick was quiet, not a word spoken the entire time, and the longer we were galloping along, the more worry pricked at the back of my mind. I knew that Roderick was a council member; I'd seen that for myself.

But what if he was working for the goblins? What if I'd just let a bad guy kidnap me and use my own skeletal horse to transport me? Jaysus Christmas, what had I gotten myself into?

By the time I'd come to the conclusion that I might have to fight my way out of this situation, Skel started slowing to a stop. Roderick hopped off first and took my hand, helping me down.

"Don't take the blindfold off," he said. He led me along, and I did all the mental gymnastics I could to figure out where we were.

My feet were on old-school paving stones, the irregularity of them obvious with each step. The smell was sweet and sugary like candy with a hint of briny water. The river wasn't far either, I could hear a boat blow its horn. If I hadn't known better, I'd say were about to go into Death Row, the location of the supernatural market. That wasn't ten miles away. If I was right, we'd just been riding in circles to pass the time. Tricky buggers.

I kept my thoughts to myself, and Roderick led me by the wrist through a narrow squeeze of cement walls on either side of me, the rough material scratching at my bare arms and pulling at the leather. Next came a set of wide, slick stairs from the feel of them. I stumbled twice going down, and Roderick caught me both times.

"Hey, here's an idea," I said as we made our way down the stairs. "Why don't you all use your magic to make a damn elevator?" Stairs going this far down meant stairs going this far up.

Stairs, why did it have to be stairs?

My legs and knees were already hurting just at the thought of having to climb up.

"Because we are trying to remain hidden," he said. "And flying under the radar means forgoing a few conveniences. Including using human electricians to make an elevator. Memory wipes are never one hundred percent. The mind and the heart are more powerful than any magic, and so taking a memory is not a sure way to keep things a secret. Threats are far better."

I bit back my smart-ass comment that if they wanted to remain hidden, they should do so somewhere other than Death Row. But I said nothing. Look at me go, managing to bite my tongue.

A door creaked open followed by the sound of squeaking hinges and what had to be a heavy wooden frame dragging across the stone floor, and then I was finally allowed to take the blindfold off.

I blinked a few times and just stared at the room in front of me.

The floor was a patterned carpet, green with black and white lilies woven throughout it. There was a desk to my left and one to my right, both made with a dark wood that had been heavily and elaborately carved. I stared at the one on my left, seeing skulls and bones, tombstones, and moons, and the same feathers etched into the coin Grimm had given me. That did not assuage any of my fears. The desk to my right was decorated with animals and trees, climbing vines and sunbursts—a much more cheery scene, all in all.

"When you step between the desks, any glamor or spells you are using will be stripped from you. You can only appear in front of the council naked of any magic." Roderick stepped between the two desks, and his body shimmered, sparkles flickering over him and wrapping around his hands, which he spread wide as if to show me it didn't hurt.

He didn't change—he didn't suddenly get shorter and turn into a goblin or get taller and sprout wings. He seemed to have more magic curling around him from the left side, from the desk made up of skulls and such. Interesting, but I didn't know quite what to do with that information. His magic was intense, and after experiencing it at the Marshall House, I knew it was far from light and fluffy.

"Your turn," he said. "Any spell that is on you will be returned to you when you leave."

I cleared my throat and stepped forward. The magic between the two desks swept up and around me, bright, pretty sparkles reaching out to me from the right while shadows swirled out from the left.

I watched as the magic spun around me, circling me as if they didn't quite know what to do. My bag shook, and Alan was expelled as if the bag puked him up.

"Where are we?" He clutched at his hat as he turned around. "I don't like this place."

I ignored him and spoke to Roderick. "Maybe I don't fit into either category."

Roderick shook his head. "This isn't about having one kind of magic. It's about stripping you of anything you'd hide from us."

Well, that explained why Alan had been barfed out of my bag.

I spread my hands wide and the magic circled around them, settling into my palms before dispersing back to the desks.

Roderick just stared at me. "You look a little different, but not much. The glamor was slight, and it was old. A spell from a long time ago. Perhaps from Celia?"

I shrugged. "Don't ask me. I didn't do anything to hide from anyone."

He turned his back on me and snapped his fingers. The air in front of him shimmered and the room opened as if a curtain had been lifted.

Thirteen desks circled a room much larger than it had looked, and a male in a long dark cloak sat behind each one. Not a single woman on the council, but really, was that any surprise?

"Bunch of peeping Toms," I said, not caring they could hear me.

Roderick left me there and went to sit where an open desk awaited him. Six to the left, six to the right, and one smack dab in the center, facing me from across the room.

I kept my eyes on that one. Long gray hair flowed down over his shoulders, offsetting the dark robe.

He had a long white beard that was braided into two pieces, bright bits of jewels and metal woven into those strands. His eyes were dark, and I don't mean dark brown. I mean dark as in black, bottomless eyes.

"At least they aren't pink," I muttered, and I felt the room stiffen around me. "Oh, get over yourselves. You know I dealt with the O'Seans. Which, by the way, you're welcome for."

To my right, closer to the thirteenth seat, sat Davin smirking at me, though his face was paler than usual. A glimmer in the air behind him materialized into the Silver Lady, who tipped her head toward me.

I couldn't help giving her a wave. She dropped a hand onto his shoulder and his smirk faded as his skin color turned a sickly green, and then she sunk back into him. Interesting that she hadn't been kicked out of him by those spells at the entrance. Or maybe she had been, and she'd gone back?

Alan left my side and hurried to stand beside Davin.

"Davin, you have to help me. I've been stuck with her all day. I think that last spell didn't work so well." Alan leaned in close to touch Davin on the shoulder.

One of the council members to my left shifted in his seat, his eyes going from Alan to Davin and then to me. I gave him a tight nod. So that had to be one of the necromancers.

I pointed a finger at the green-faced, baggy-eyed Davin. "You and I are going to have a chat after this, boy."

Again, muttering and stiffening. Gawd save me from misogynistic men standing on empty formalities in an attempt to put me in my place. "Look, you all brought me here, made me walk between your magic desks so you could see that I am not the devil…" A series of gasps went up as if they were scandalized Victorians clutching at their fake pearls. "What exactly do you want from me?"

The man at the center desk slowly stood. His eyes flicked over me as if inspecting a newly discovered creature. "You have left the Hollows Group, correct?"

"Well, to be fair, they kicked me out." I smiled as they muttered to each other. They clearly hadn't known that little tidbit.

Oh, I was going to make the best of this. Maybe it was the residual whiskey in my veins, maybe it was the fact that these boys didn't know who they were playing with, but I was almost having fun. What a bunch of grumpy old fuddy-duddies.

Alan shook his head. "I know that look. Don't start a fight, Bree."

"You shut your mouth." I pointed at him, but it looked like I was pointing at Davin. Fine by me.

Davin growled and the necromancer to my left cleared his throat. "She has a ghost with her who is standing near Davin, that's who she is speaking with."

A chorus of grunts went through the room.

The old guy in the center raised his hand, and they all went silent. "You carry a ghost with you?"

"And an animated skeleton usually, but Robert is currently passed out under the oak tree. We were drinking together, and you know how it goes with whiskey." I shrugged and made a glug-glug motion with my thumb to my mouth and pinky finger in the air.

Roderick looked as though he was fighting a smile. He was the only one. The necromancer watched me closely. "Why is it that you need to speak with Davin alone?"

All I could think was…game on. I did a slow turn toward the necromancer. "You can see my ex-husband?"

He nodded. "I can."

"And could you make him tell the truth if he tried to lie?" Based on Gran's book, that was the deal with necros. They could manipulate the dead fully, forcing them to speak. I'd never had such luck—just look at Gran's silent treatment of late—which meant no necromancer abilities for me, despite my affinity with Robert and other ghosts. Despite whatever connection my father had with the dead. And I'd never seen Louis, the Hollows teacher, do more than say he could talk to the dead.

"You think the ghost would lie?" the necromancer asked.

I grinned. "Like a ducking snake."

Alan spluttered. "I'm a lawyer. I uphold—"

The necromancer waved a hand at him. I turned in time to see Alan's jaw snap shut. Oh, this was going to be fun.

If it was possible, Davin looked paler than before, and he swallowed hard before speaking. "I don't think we should let her talk. How do we know *she* won't lie? She fought Roderick when he tried to force her to tell us what she was doing in the Marshall House."

All the members of the council looked to Roderick, and I took a deep breath in that moment of respite.

"She is part fae," Roderick said softly, placing his hands on his desk, palms down. "You have but to bind her to her word for the duration of this meeting, and she will not be able to lie."

I spread my hands out to my sides. "I'm game. But let's be *very* honest before we start—some of you aren't going to like what I have to say. Especially Davin. I mean, I'm assuming you have rules about how you can use your magic as council members?" That was a guess, but by the series of nods that went around the room, I'd hit the nail on the head.

Damn it, I should have asked for a meeting with the council sooner.

I put my hands to my mouth and blew Davin a double kiss. He jumped up, red-faced. But Roderick was already moving toward me, his hands glowing with the same magic that had pinned me down in the Marshall House. Damn it, I should have thought this through. That had been uncomfortable at best.

"If you don't fight it, then it won't hurt," he said, no doubt seeing me tense.

I nodded. "Sure thing, Rod."

The necromancer's mouth quirked up on one side. "She is very much like Celia in some ways."

I tipped my head toward him. "Thank you."

"But very different in others. She has strengths Celia did not," Roderick chimed in as his magic swept around me, stealing my breath.

The necromancer stood. "My name is Jacob. What is it that you wished to speak with Davin about?"

The words were already there, eager to come out, but I worked them into the best order I could. "Davin helped my ex-husband manipulate the human court system so that Alan—that's the ghost over there—could foist all the accrued family debt and then some onto me, take both our house in Seattle and my gran's house, and leave me penniless and alone. But"—I held up a finger—"Davin and Alan didn't count on me figuring out their little connection. Then Alan over there broke into my house and tried to steal not only my gran's amazing spell book that everybody and their dog wants to get their hands on, but also a talisman that my gran left me.

"And now, as you can see, poor Alan over there had his throat ripped out by an animal. Which I highly doubt was a real animal—more likely it was a shifter, or maybe a goblin, but I don't doubt it was directly due to his connection to Davin." I drew in a big breath, Roderick's magic in me humming along. "But again, let's be honest here, gentlemen, Alan couldn't see a good thing if it kicked him in the ass.

I mean, he threw me away like I was nothing but a piece of garbage. Like I was worthless."

"You *are* worthless," Alan yelled across the room. "A worthless, no good—"

Jacob snapped his fingers, and Alan's mouth snapped shut. I really didn't want to like any of these councilmen, but Jacob was moving up the ranks in that department. "I did not give you permission to speak, ex-husband of Breena."

Alan's face twisted with a fury I knew all too well. Whenever I'd disagreed with him or proven him wrong in a public setting (no matter how politely), he would lose his marbles on me as soon as we got home. Tell me that I was undermining him and making him look bad—something he would never do to me in front of others.

Not that he hesitated to do it the moment we were alone. Although what was there to badmouth? I'd cooked and cleaned for him; I'd made the money that had paid our bills while he went to school. I'd been more than happy to have sex with him whenever he wanted. All of that, and I still hadn't been good enough for him.

That old wound in me cracked open a little, and I hated the insecurity that leaked through it.

"Is there anything else that you'd like to say?" Jacob asked. It struck me that he had taken charge, not the man in the center of the room, whom I'd assumed was the head honcho.

I lifted my head, barely realizing that I'd lowered it. "Well, did you know that Davin had Sarge and Corb from the Hollows Group playing double agents with Hattie's crew? Or that the O'Seans were only one of five groups trying to take over Savannah? Or how about that Missy is still a royal pain in my ass? That the goblins are acting up? That there is a damn demon in the house next door to my gran's?" I shuddered, feeling the urge to spill the beans about Crash. That one wasn't necessary, but my lips quirked upward anyway. "You want to hear about my sex life too?"

Alan shot forward. "I saw you with that man, and that is entirely ridiculous. He looks like a troll! It's embarrassing to me that you would lower yourself by carrying on with such a freakshow." He blinked and shook his head, staring hard at me. "You aren't this pretty. Did you get work done?"

I stared at him, not sure where to start with all that.

Roderick cleared his throat. "She had a glamor on her, likely one that her gran put on her when she left Savannah to keep her safe. It dulled her sparkle, if you will."

Holy shit. Gran had kept me from being…too pretty? Was that what Crash had meant when he'd said I didn't see myself as others did? And what was this troll business? Crash was gorgeous by any person's terms. He'd mentioned that most didn't see the real him.

Alan shook his head again as if his ears couldn't believe it. "You could've modeled."

I almost thanked him.

"If you hadn't been so chubby."

Oh, he did not go there.

This time I snapped my fingers at him, grabbed his ear, and yanked him toward my bag while he caterwauled. I stuffed him into the bag while he squealed, not caring who saw me manhandle him. Flipping the bag closed, I turned back to Jacob who was staring at me with new interest.

"She is not a necromancer," he said softly. "But she has some power over the dead."

"Interesting," the others all murmured, and a soft discussion began that I couldn't hear.

They'd blocked my ears to talk about me in front of me.

Of course, that's when I noticed that Davin, that slippery little duck, had snuck out.

18

Excuse me." I held up my hand, stopping the flow of conversation between the council members. Roderick noticed me first. I pointed to where Davin had been sitting.

The council members burst into a flurry of movement that impressed even me. Half of them took off running, and the other half circled around Jacob. The only person who didn't move was the old guy sitting at the center of the council. He beckoned me forward.

I walked over to him and crouched beside his desk so he didn't have to look up and crane his neck. "They pretty much ignore you, huh?"

"Perceptive. They think age has rendered me useless, and they have given me this seat only out of respect for the past. My age has given me great wisdom, as yours has done for you." He tapped his fingers on the desk. "They won't ask me…but I know what you are, young lady. And I know how much you are needed in Savannah." His kindly smile made me think of a grandfather I'd never met, of a father who'd died when I was too young.

Now, before you get any ideas, I'm not implying he was related to me—not at all—just that he had a kind of fatherly air to him. Like he'd give good counsel if asked.

I smiled at him, already catching on to his game. "You aren't going to tell me or them, are you?"

His smile broadened, lifting the loose skin around his eyes, his lips not truly visible beneath all that beard he had going on. "No, I'm not. You will figure it out. And you'll be better off for having learned the truth yourself. That is the way of the shadow world. Those who must fight for distinction earn all that they accomplish. Those who are given everything, like Davin, do not appreciate their power. They do not use it wisely."

"I think I'd like to call you Obi-Wan," I said.

He waved a hand at me. "I never much liked *Star Wars*."

I laughed and he clapped a hand on my shoulder. "They are done with you. Davin has sealed his fate by running. You were right that he should not have used his abilities and connections within the council to help your ex-husband sabotage you. Most likely he did it in order to get his hands on that spell book of your grandmother's. Before you ask, they will not amend the situation for you—whatever debt you have is yours. You must deal with it on your own, or force Davin to do it for you."

Damn it, that had been my next question. "How deep do his connections go?"

Obi-Wan sighed. "He is like a spider, weaving his web for years. I have no doubt he has many people who would help him, and some who would kill for him."

He let his eyes flutter shut for a moment. "The rumor is that Missy has the book now, that you traded it to her for information. But they say she is having trouble cracking the spell you and your gran placed on it."

I blinked up at him, trying to keep a straight face. "The…spell? Yes, of course, she asked me about that." I couldn't help it, I winked at him to bring him in on my little secret. That Missy's ego was keeping her from seeing what should have been obvious.

She'd been duped.

Again the skin around his eyes wrinkled upward. "Ah, so there is no spell on it, blocking her from seeing the pages?"

I lifted my hands, palms upward in an exaggerated shrug. "I guess not."

The old man chuckled. "She is so busy being clever she can't see the simple switch you did. Well done."

His praise was something unexpected and lovely. Like a beam of sunlight breaking through the clouds to warm my face.

"Thank you. I don't trust her."

He snorted. "Few do or should. She is dangerous still."

Movement to my side drew my eyes. Roderick stood there. "I should take you back now."

I stood and lifted both eyebrows. "Everyone is satisfied with me?"

"They realize you mean no harm. Your new group promises to be more effective than the Hollows, if a bit unorthodox. We can accept that. They might call you in from time to time in the future." Roderick gave a short bow.

"Did you ask him what he thought?" I pointed a thumb at my new friend.

"Stark is an old man, and while he brings much wisdom, he rarely talks anymore," Roderick said.

I looked down at the old guy, Stark, and saw that he was smiling ever so slightly. I gave him a wink. "You know what? You're right. But Stark, let me be clear that you are always welcome for tea at my gran's house." I offered him my hand and he took it, sandwiching it between his two dry-as-autumn-leaves palms.

"I accept."

Roderick watched this back and forth and then put out his elbow for me to take. I looped my arm through it as if we were going on a date. Which was a funny notion—it would mean that I'd had a date with a fae king, an animated skeleton, and now a mage, all in the space of about twenty-four hours.

And Corb.

"Oh shit. I have a date waiting for me!" I yelped and started to drag Roderick forward. I wasn't as desperate as it sounded—I was mostly concerned about keeping Corb waiting. Plus, I needed to tell him to lie low like everyone else, and I kind of wanted to grill him for some answers. "Let's go!"

Roderick trailed behind me as I bolted between the two desks that had stripped me of whatever glamor I'd had going in.

"Stop, you won't be able to get through!" Roderick yelled, but it was too late. I was between the desks, the magic putting the glamor back onto me with a bit of a sting. I shook it off. No worse than a quick wax job.

Roderick was on my heels as I raced up the stairs. "Stop!" he yelled, and my legs froze, locking at the knees. "Stop," he said in a softer voice. "You can't know where we are."

"You mean y'all still don't trust me?" I teetered on the edges of two stairs, my legs unwilling to move against Roderick's command. But that wasn't entirely true. A tingling sensation rolled up through me, and I pulled on that feeling of energy until it popped my feet free. I took a couple of steps and looked back at Roderick.

He shook his head. "It's against the rules here." He paused and stared at my now moving feet. "Full of surprises, aren't you?"

I shrugged. "I'm a woman. Of course I'm full of surprises. How are you just learning that now?"

Roderick did a slow blink. "You have a point."

"Of course I do." I shook my head and pointed at the scrap of material he'd retrieved from his pocket. "If you put the blindfold on me, then you have to carry me up the stairs. As you heard my ex say"—I smacked my bag on my hip earning a grunt from Alan—"I'm on the chubby side."

Roderick lifted the blindfold, paused, and let out a sigh and lowered it. "Don't tell anyone."

I grinned and hurried up the stairs. Well, hurried as best as I could. Somewhere around what felt like stair two hundred the burning in my legs reminded me that I still hadn't reached peak physical fitness.

Nor did my knees like these stairs. "Kill me now," I whispered somewhere around stair three hundred.

Roderick grunted. "Don't say things like that. It's the best way to end up dead in an alley."

I leaned against the wall and looked back at him. "At least if I were dead in an alley, I'd be lying flat on my back. This is terrible."

The slog up the last hundred or so steps left me sweating and shaking by the time we reached the top. I felt no shame as I fell forward onto my hands and knees in a perfect yoga tabletop—a move that Suzy had been drilling into me over the last week. Roderick offered me a hand, and wobbled as I used him to drag myself into an upright position. I leaned into him. "You know, you should probably hold your council meetings somewhere that's not so close to Death Row."

He startled. "How the hell did you know?"

"I could smell the candy and hear the river. I grew up here—this place is in my blood." I wiped a hand over my face, taking the sweat off, but a fresh layer quickly replaced it. Those stairs were freaking murder.

Roderick led the way out through a tunnel that did indeed end up funneling into the far end of Death Row.

I could tell we weren't far from Oster Boon's bookshop. Only Death Row was completely silent without a single vendor in sight.

"Where is everyone?" I asked.

Roderick held his hand out and the air in front of us shimmered as if a sheet of water were flowing down from above, kind of like the curtain that had kept me from seeing all the council while they watched me come through the magic desks. On the other side of the clear curtain, the Death Row I knew was bustling. Vendors were yelling across the space to one another as a few shoppers picked out their items.

I lifted a hand and Roderick smacked it down. "No, don't touch it. Who knows what your magic might do? You are totally unpredictable."

I snorted. "That's just the hormones."

He took me by the wrist and pulled me sideways, behind the vendors. The magic worked like a one-way mirror.

"Holy shit, you can spy on everyone?" I gasped, realizing the implications.

I could look at every vendor, but they couldn't see us. They didn't even blink twice.

He seemed unrepentant. "People tend to gossip when they shop. Rumors are often woven through with threads of truth at some point. We were the ones to create Death Row, for that very reason." He led me away from Death Row through a narrow bend of concrete shaped like an S, and then we were in the back of the candy shop. Not the part I'd passed through before to get in and out of Death Row, but near the ovens. No one seemed to see us.

"Your horse waits for you outside. The council will call on you if we have more questions." Roderick gave me a slight bow. "No human will see you leave. It will be as if you are a ghost yourself."

Good enough for me. And even better? I was supposed to meet Corb at Vic's Restaurant, which was just up the way from the candy shop.

I rubbed a hand over my face. "Roderick, what is going on in this town? Are the people of the shadow world really battling for control? Or is there more to it?" New Orleans came to mind, and whatever force had been summoned with the death of Eric's cousin.

Roderick's eyes never left my face. "They are. And we are…and it's happening fast. We're struggling to keep up with it." He stepped closer, not in an intimate, *I'm going to kiss you* way—more in a *you need to hear this secret* kind of way. "You are the first to slow the oncoming tidal wave, Breena O'Rylee. That makes you two things: dangerous and a target. Keep your friends close and your enemies within your sights. If you're not careful, I fear you may go the way of your grandmother."

He took a step back and bowed at the waist, disappearing as he slid back between the two ovens. It was as if the wall had just swallowed him whole.

I hurried out of the candy shop, using my temporary invisibility to my advantage and snagging a couple of bags of homemade pecan bark. Hey, my appetite was raging, and I'd never claimed to be a saint. "Keep my enemies in my sights." I snorted as I stepped out of the candy shop.

I bit into the first piece of pecan bark, and the caramel melted slowly against my tongue. Skel waited quietly outside, standing between two overpriced bright red sports cars. Probably they belong to some of the council members. I had an urge to egg them, just in case.

No, bad Breena, bad. I shook it off and kept moving.

I wondered what the hell was going to happen to Davin. Or if they'd managed to catch him.

"Wait here, Skel. I've got one more meeting."

Meeting, not date. I cringed as I realized I'd started thinking of it less as a date and more as a business transaction. Then again, that kiss…that kiss had awoken all sorts of things inside of me. But it had almost certainly been infused with his magic. Did that mean it wasn't real?

Why did it matter, anyway? I'd showered with Crash hours ago. Was my libido just that far out of whack that I wanted anyone who could make my blood sing? What about loyalty and connection? Things in common?

What about hotter than sin sex between satin sheets?

Maybe it was just too many years without attraction, without feeling wanted, without so many things that I was craving now that I'd finally awoken.

Maybe, just maybe, I wasn't ready to decide yet. Crash might have been right to hold off on me. I needed to figure out what the hell I was doing.

I blinked at my own thoughts.

"Jaysus, something is wrong with me."

"I doubt that."

Corb stepped out of the narrow doorway that led into the basement of Vic's Restaurant. Dressed in dark jeans and a tight dark green T-shirt that pulled up the color of his eyes, I noticed that he was freshly shaved and smelled amazing as always. He looked me over. "You're in your work clothes. Everything okay?"

"Long day," I said, still feeling a hint of the whiskey circling through me. "But a meal would help. And a good discussion. Also, we need a table with our back to the wall."

He held his hand out to me and I took it, letting him lead me upstairs like it was a real date. I didn't order the pomegranate mojito this time. Water would be plenty strong enough. I took note that the damage from the explosion had been cleaned up. Maybe Karissa had used smoke and mirrors to make the damage look worse than it was.

I gulped down two glasses of water before I slowed enough to see that Corb was staring hard at me.

"What? You're supposed to drink like ten gallons of water a day," I said.

"I think it's ten glasses." He smiled and I settled slowly into my chair, muscles in me sore and completely fatigued.

"Same difference, and I've not been keeping on it."

Corb chuckled, but he quickly sobered. "So you figured out that I'm not human."

"Hmm." I nodded and crossed my arms. "Go on."

"Alan and I, our moms are only half-sisters. They share the same father. My dad was from the shadow world, and my mom's mom was from the shadow world, and—"

I held up a hand, stopping him. While I fully intended to find out more about his magic and his background, we had more important matters to discuss. This would have to wait. "Doesn't matter what your family tree looks like, though I'm sure it's better than Alan's." He rumbled in my bag and I smacked it hard—twice for good measure—though that did earn a look from Corb.

I took a deep breath. "Alan is dead. He's a ghost and I stuffed him in my bag."

Corb sat very still, then reached for his whiskey and snapped it back. Tapped the rim, and when the waitress came over with the bottle, he took it from her.

"We're going to need this," he murmured. "I was in his apartment, but I didn't see his body."

I shook my head and put my hand over my empty glass before he could pour me anything. "I've already drunk most of a bottle today, thanks."

His eyebrows shot up. "Start from the beginning."

I looked at Corb, really looked at him. "Can I trust you? I mean really, truly trust you?"

That earned me a sad-eyed look like I'd just kicked a puppy dog. "Bree, I've never done anything to hurt you. I've tried to protect you as best I could, and given your ability to find trouble where there is none, that in itself is exhausting. I have ties to certain groups of people that force me to not always tell you stuff upfront."

"You find me exhausting?"

He paled. "That's not what I meant."

I grinned and winked. "Couldn't help it. You set yourself up for that one." I leaned back in my chair. "So you've signed something like a non-disclosure agreement?"

"With spells woven through it, yes. There are things I literally cannot say," he said softly.

The waitress showed up with food we hadn't ordered and I looked at Corb. He gave a nod. "I ordered ahead of time."

I didn't care. I dug into the food, realizing only then just how hungry I was, how much energy I'd burned in the last twenty-four hours. I cleaned my plate and looked up to see Corb with a fork partway to his mouth, his eyes wide.

I leaned back, letting the food settle. "Here's the deal. It started yesterday really." Had it only been yesterday? Jaysus lawdy, my life had turned upside down…"The minute I opened the envelope that holds all the information on my gran's and my parents' deaths." I breathed out the words, recalling the feeling of ants all over my body, biting me here and there. The sensation that my life was to go to shit the minute I peeled that envelope open.

"What was in it?" Corb laid down his fork.

"I don't know, I just…I didn't get a chance to look at all the stuff." I frowned, thinking about that. "I poured the contents out onto the bed and then…I got distracted," I said. In fact, even though I'd been in the bedroom again during the last twenty-four hours, I still hadn't looked at the contents of the envelope. I put a hand to my head, feeling those invisible ants crawling all over me again.

Corb frowned. "That sounds like a spell of some sort. Some of them are subtle, not necessarily made to kill, but to keep you…busy. As you said, stuff just kept happening, obstacles kept getting thrown in your way."

A spell would make sense.

Who would put a spell on my gran's death papers? The person who killed her. But did that person even know I was looking? Probably not. Which meant it had to be someone else. I knew it wasn't the human police officer who'd given them to me, Officer Burke. In fact, I suspect she'd put herself at risk to get the information to me.

Corb tapped the table with one hand. "We need to go back to the house and look at those papers. That's the only way to figure this out."

"You can tell if it's a spell?" I frowned, wondering again about what he was, supernaturally speaking. "What about Missy?"

Corb's eyebrows shot up. "What about her?"

"She is the most likely candidate, and she showed up at the house yesterday, pissed that she couldn't get Gran's spell book to work." But even as I said it, I found myself thinking about those desks I'd passed before entering the council meeting, the ones that stripped people of magic.

"I don't think it's a spell," I said. "I really don't." If the envelope had carried a spell, then it would have clung to me, right? The desks would have removed it, and Roderick would have noticed. He'd said there was only a glamor on me.

Corb stood and offered me a hand. "Just trust me, okay? We're going to go for a walk, and I'm going to show you around town. While we walk, I'm going to make a phone call. I think we'll need Tom on this one. I don't want to risk you being hurt, so let's just play it safe, okay?"

One look at him told me that he was genuinely concerned.

Besides, Tom was a good guy, I liked him, and hanging out with him was fine by me. Besides, as long as I kept moving, the goblins would have a harder time pinning me down.

In the back of my head, my own thoughts whispered the fear that Corb was indeed right. That the envelope was spelled and I'd unleashed its dark magic simply by opening it. I should have trusted my feelings all along and asked an expert to look at the envelope to figure out why it had upset me so.

It struck me that Robert had kept tapping at the envelope. A warning, damn it, had his tapping on it been a warning?

Corb led me out of the restaurant the way we'd come, sending a text one-handed as we went. I waved at Skel. "Go relax, I'm walking from here."

The skeletal horse snorted and flipped his mane once before turning and trotting up the street. I don't know if Corb even saw the horse, and if he did, he didn't so much as flinch.

"Tell me what you've been doing," Corb said as he slid an arm around my shoulders and tugged me close as he finished sending the text. "I know a bit from earlier but tell me in more detail."

I started slowly rehashing the last two days, everything from opening the envelope but not looking into it to getting information from Jinx, finding Grimm, coming back to find Suzy dying, seeing Alan's ghost in my room, putting Grimm's pages in the Sorrel-Weed house, getting drunk with Robert, and heading to the council with my new bestie Rod. "And now I'm here with you." Funnily enough, I skipped right over the shower scene with Crash.

Talking through the situation, it struck me that I didn't feel like I *couldn't* look at the papers. It was more like I had legit been too busy.

"Not a lot of time spent in your own room even, never mind the house," Corb said, and I ducked my head, again choosing to say nothing about that blip in my timeline with Crash.

"Are the papers still there, in the house?" he asked.

I paused, forcing him to stop. "They're in my bag." I put a hand to the bag on my hip and Corb stared at me, horror flickering through his eyes. "I've got them with me right now."

19

Corb took the bag from me, almost yanking it off, and opened it. Of course, the first thing that came flying out was Alan. What hair he had was all mussed and fluffed up in every direction, and his eyes were wild with rage.

He immediately started shouting at the top of his lungs. "How dare you stuff me in that bag," he shrieked. "I have every right to defend myself against your lies. In a court of law—"

I snapped my fingers at him, and his mouth clicked shut.

Corb didn't so much as flinch as he dug around in the bag. "Where is it?"

I turned my back on a freaked-out, mouth-flapping-but-no-sound-making Alan. We stood on River Street, tourists flowing around us, and we were going to pull out something that potentially carried a black magic spell. Probably not the best idea we'd ever had. I tugged Corb away from the flow of traffic and down a set of stone stairs that led to the river's edge.

You'd think there would be a lot of people there, but you'd be wrong. Most of the humans were up in the shops or eating their dinners, doing things that kept them busy enough not to pay any attention to a pair of people digging through a bag.

"Look at us, our first date and we're playing with a spell," I muttered.

"First implies that there will be second," Corb said as he put my bag down at our feet.

Alan shot between us, finding his voice again. "Don't you dare kiss him, Breena. Don't you dare."

"Not right now, Alan. Seriously." I snapped my fingers again and made a reach for his ear. He dodged me, stepping over the edge of the walkway, and floated out over the water. If he looked down, he might wonder just what was happening to him. Then again, he'd spent the last several hours in a bag that was far too small for his physical body, and still he didn't seem to understand his situation.

You know, that he'd been killed and was currently a ghostly pain in my ass.

Corb seemed perfectly unfussed that I was talking to his cousin, now a ghost; he crouched down. Likely he couldn't see him. I followed suit, my thigh muscles screaming at me. Forget that, I went to my knees, tucking my feet under my butt with a heavy sigh.

"Give it here." I took the bag from him, stuck my hand in, and pulled out the manila envelope. I opened it and dumped out the contents.

I blinked a few times, staring at the script that was scribbled all over the thick paper. It took me a moment or two of staring at the contents to realize what had happened.

"Oh shit," I whispered.

"What?"

"The envelopes got switched. How the hell did that happen?" I frowned, thinking of the moments in the second-story room of the Sorrel-Weed house. I'd been distracted. I'd grabbed the envelope I thought held all the papers…

Corb touched the paper. "This is all in Goblinese."

"It's Grimm's family history." I touched the pages again.

"No, I don't think that's it." Corb picked up one sheet. "I only have a little of that language under my belt, but this here is a stanza." He touched the middle of the paper, which looked no different to me than any of the other sections.

"Okay, and a stanza for what?"

"I think it's a spell. Something about a warning. Strife…no, I'm not sure if that's the right word. It's been years since I studied this language." He flipped through the pages. "Whatever it is, it's hidden within this family tree crap. I can't make it all out, though, it's been too long."

I closed my eyes, thinking. I could ask Bridgette. She'd said she'd help if she could. But I couldn't focus on that thought—my attention was on that word: strife. It had stirred something in me, but I couldn't pinpoint what or why.

"Are you okay?"

"Just give me a minute. There is something in here, something that my brain wants me to piece together." But it was like grasping at oil-covered straws. I couldn't for the life of me grab hold of the pieces and make them stick together.

Corb and I sat there across from each other. "Will you let me help you, Bree? I think this is bad. All of it stinks of dark magic and secrets that seem to want to put you in the path of some very bad people."

Alan snorted. "Magic isn't real."

Corb looked right at him. "Says the dead man walking on water."

Alan stared down at his feet—and kept right on staring. "Holy shit. I *did* die. I thought I was dreaming."

Apparently Corb could see him after all, but my mind was preoccupied by the fact that Alan still didn't believe in magic even after he'd used it to screw me over. It really said a lot about his mental state and inability to see what was happening right in front of him.

Corb grunted, stood, and handed me my bag, and he most definitely saw the look I was giving him. "I can't always see the dead, Bree, but yeah, I can see him. It's likely because he's related to me. I was hoping if I ignored him, he would go away. You can do that with ghosts."

I took my bag and slid it over my shoulder, choosing to shift the topic rather than to press him. "Where is Tom meeting us?"

"At your gran's place," Corb said.

Which really wasn't that far of a walk, but Corb had his high-powered Mustang waiting not that far away. He let me in, and Alan climbed over me into the backseat—a weird sensation since I could feel and see him pass through me, but there wasn't any weight to him.

"You aren't getting rid of me," he snarled. "I'm coming with you and you're going to fix this. I am not staying dead."

I didn't bother to look at him. "You'd think that dying would improve your attitude. Also, just so you know, no one can fix you, Alan. You are the epitome of asshole."

Corb gunned the engine and peeled out of his parking spot as only a younger man would do, not thinking about his engine, the rubber he was leaving behind from his tires, or the costs those things could incur. And yes, I thought about both.

"So are you going to tell me what you are?" I asked quietly. "Or why you tried so hard to stop me from joining the Hollows Group and returning to the shadow world? I'm assuming you knew all along that I actually had potential."

I leaned back in the leather seat, enjoying the fact that, for the moment, I wasn't running or climbing stairs. That my belly was full, and I was safe. I let my eyes close ever so slightly, watching him from just under my lashes.

Corb tightened his hands on the wheel, turning them this way and that. "Yes, I knew you had potential. I wasn't worried about your age, but I knew it could be a deterrent to the other mentors. Or I thought so anyway, and I played it up."

I watched him as he worked through his thoughts, noting that he still hadn't answered my first question.

"What are you?" I asked again. I had a few guesses, but I wondered if I was close to the mark.

His hands slid down the steering wheel. "I'm a siren."

Alan guffawed. "Siren? Like calling sailors to their deaths? Please."

Himself might not see it in his cousin, but the second Corb said *siren* I started nodding, feeling the truth of his words even though I'd never heard of a male siren. It made sense, though. That was why he'd brought Suzy into the Hollows—because she was like him and…

"So that's why there's all that lube in the bathroom!"

Corb groaned. "Actually, no. That was Sarge trying to tempt me. We had a…fling when we met years ago. Every once in a while he tries to get me back into the sack."

I could feel my jaw dropping. Maybe the heat in the car had cranked up, or it could have been the image of the two of them together—let's be honest, that's totally what it was—but suddenly I was flushing. I grabbed the envelope and started fanning myself. Hormones, they were going to be the death of me if this curse business wasn't.

I cleared my throat. "So you aren't really into me then, you prefer guys."

Corb swallowed hard. "I swing both ways, but I tend to lean toward women more. It's…being a siren is fluid in more ways than just the water we use to power our magic."

That made sense. "I could taste the ocean when I kissed you. Were you…using your magic on me? Was that even a real feeling between us?"

Corb was shaking his head before I finished. "No. No, you wouldn't have remembered much if I'd used my magic on you. It has a tendency to erase memories. But I let you in…if that makes sense."

I lowered the envelope to my lap. "You let me see your magic?"

"Something like that," he said softly, almost as if he were afraid of my reaction.

"This is stupid," Alan grumbled, and I twisted around in my seat to stare at him.

"You know what's stupid? You. You're stupid, Alan."

"I am not," he snapped back. "I passed my classes with an A- average."

I looked across at Corb. "How? How are you two related?"

He reached across the seat and carefully took my hand. "Really, we're not all that related if you think about it. We're, like, half cousins. Please don't hold it against me." He was grinning as he spoke, and I grinned back.

"I see now why you're the black sheep of the family. Full of sex magic and naughtiness. Not much of a fit with all those lawyers and doctors on Alan's side." I laughed and Corb joined me. Alan did not laugh, which only made me laugh harder.

We pulled up to the front of Gran's house less than a minute later. From the corner of my eye, the Sorrel-Weed house seemed to shimmer, the bricks turned dark once more. That was where Gran's and my parents' stuff was, along with the goblin coin. Damn it, I was going to have to get it back at some point. I let myself out of the car and scrambled forward into the front yard where I felt safe.

Robert stood swaying under the oak tree, his head hanging low. "Friend. Safe?"

"Hey, Robert. Yeah, I'm okay. You okay? That was a lot of whiskey."

He reached out and tapped a skeletal finger against the oak tree. "Friend."

I nodded, not sure what he was referring to exactly. That he'd had a good sleep under the tree? That he thought the tree was his friend?

"Anyone home?" I asked Robert, already knowing he couldn't answer me.

Alan strode past me and down the street. "I'm going to my room—Jesus, what is that?"

I twisted around to see him staring at the Sorrel-Weed house. "You mean the demon watching you from the windows?"

Alan squeaked and scuttled backward until he was partway up the stairs to Gran's house.

Corb stepped up next to me and Robert let out a grumble that could have been a laugh at Alan's expense, or irritation at how close Corb was to me. Corb didn't see him, though, so there was that. We both turned as the rumble of a familiar motorbike cut through the evening.

I stepped out from under the low-hanging Spanish moss first and saw Sarge getting off his bike. Tom had already climbed off and was heading for the small front gate.

"Trouble already?" Tom grinned. I smiled back.

"Are you allowed to help me? I mean, I don't want to get you in trouble right along with me."

Tom waved a hand in front of his face as if he smelled something bad. "I can see the spell attached to you from here. Easy to remove."

I blinked a few times. Something about there being a spell on me didn't sit right, didn't feel right and I couldn't put my finger on it. What was it?

"It is? Don't you need the envelope the spell came from?" I really didn't want to go into the Sorrel-Weed house anytime soon. Especially in the dark. I mean, it was important to know who'd killed my family, and Grimm would probably want his coin back, but I did not want a repeat with the blood-born demon.

"Well, no, you don't need the item that the spell came from." Tom paused, and his dark eyes held me in place. "It's a subtle spell—the kind of minor manipulation that the average person wouldn't notice." His dark eyes were serious as he drew close and dropped his hands onto my shoulders. A smell of burnt toast filled the air as he whispered words that made no sense, more like sounds than words, and his magic curled around me, sinking into my skin and sticking to the inside of my nose.

I sneezed and wiped at my face. "Okay, what now? Blood of a unicorn? Sacrifice a werewolf's hide?"

Sarge ignored the jab. He was too busy looking around the yard as if he wanted to pee on something. I opened my mouth to warn him off the oak tree and ended up sneezing again. A chunk of something dark flew through the air and splatted on the ground. For all I knew, it was leftovers from the Sorrel-Weed house encounter.

"What the hell is that?" I spat a few times, tasting burnt toast even though I hadn't eaten anything of the sort.

Tom winked and stepped back, pulling a small pouch from his pocket. He opened it up, pinched something between thumb and forefinger, then sprinkled black dust onto the gob of…whateverthehellit-was. "That's it. It truly wasn't a bad spell, just one that was meant to deter you. Which it was doing easily."

Only I wasn't fully convinced, still feeling weird about a spell being on me that wasn't really on me.

I looked at Tom, but he was already looking away from me. Not meeting my eyes, which was confusing. "Tom?"

"Look, you can owe the Hollows a favor for me helping you, how about that?" He smiled at me, but it was strained around the edges. As if he didn't want to say it.

My head was shaking of its own volition, mostly because I couldn't stop staring at what now looked like a slug shriveling up under some salt. That was in me? Gross. "But that makes no sense, does it? I mean, deterring me is one thing, but—"

Tom patted my shoulder. "You didn't really want to open the paperwork. Something about it worried or scared you?"

I gave a reluctant nod. "Yeah, something like that." Still, something wasn't adding up, but Tom talked right over my thoughts.

"Some spells aren't meant to be big and loud. Simple ones can be more effective than powerhouse curses or spells. Because you don't sense them, and they align with your own hidden thoughts and inclinations. I've seen people with spells on them for years without realizing it. Sometimes they think they're haunted, but they aren't. Just spelled." Tom gave my shoulder a squeeze when I shivered. "Trust me, this was not a bad one. Effective, but not bad."

The real question was why that paperwork would have a deterrent spell on it. Who was trying to keep me from finding out about Gran's and my parents' deaths?

"Any idea who did it?" I asked. "I mean, I assume it was someone who had something to do with their deaths, but a name would be great."

Tom sighed. "I can't trace magic like that. Sometimes the spell bears someone's signature style, and it's obvious, but not in this case. Though you could ask Missy. She's better at tracing spells than I am."

I wrinkled my nose. "I'll put that low on the priority list, thanks."

Corb, who'd stood quietly beside me the whole time, finally spoke up. "So she's okay? It really wasn't bad?"

Tom grinned and looked from Corb to me and back again. "She's fine, Corb."

Holy crap, was he that worried about me? I felt the tension in him slide away with Tom's words, and a terrible warm, fuzzy feeling suffused me. The spell hadn't been a big deal, but Corb hadn't known that. And that was why he'd gone out of his way to get Tom over here.

I squeezed his hand. "Thanks."

Corb didn't let me go. "I don't want to lose you, Bree."

The hum of power under his skin whispered to me, and the smell of the ocean tugged on me. I bit the inside of my lip and pulled my hand away. I wasn't sure what to think about the possibility of him and me…not when Crash was in the picture. Not when Alan was in the damn picture, for that matter.

Behind me, Robert grumbled. "Friend." I twisted around to him. He pointed at Sarge.

Sarge was across from us, sniffing the air, and I grimaced at the thought that he might be smelling Roderick. I couldn't say why, but I didn't feel like explaining my dealings with the council. "What are you smelling?" I asked.

"Goblins."

That one word from Sarge—goblins—was not unexpected. I shook my head, relief flowing through me. "I have a goblin neighbor, Bridgette. She came over here earlier." Or so I recalled from my drunken haze.

Sarge shook his head again, nostrils flaring and the muscles across his chest flexing with the deep breaths he was taking. "No, there were a lot of them—a full mob by the way it smells. Way more than should be anywhere this far into Savannah."

"A mob of goblins?" Tom asked. "There hasn't been anything like that in Savannah in years. New Orleans, yes, but that's a whole other ball of wax and trouble."

A niggling bite of fear had my feet moving toward the front door of the house. I'd warned everyone, but my friends could be stubborn. What if they'd come back anyway?

Just in case, I headed up the stairs and into the house, shouting, "Eric, Feish? Suzy? Kink?"

No answer.

My stomach rolled, although I wasn't sure why—if they hadn't come home, they wouldn't be there to answer, right? Still, something felt wrong.

I picked up speed, heading straight up the stairs to the bedrooms. "Gran, have you seen anyone?"

"No," she answered quietly. "No one has been here since they were taken. The spider did not stop them."

I skidded to a stop, grabbing at the banister railing on the second landing. "What did you say?"

Her image was wispy and faded in and out as she walked toward me. "They were taken."

Only…only this wasn't Gran as I knew her, but a younger version. Like she was aging in reverse and was now closer to fifty rather than a late seventy year old. Was that possible? What was happening to her?

Her image stuttered as if she were on a projection screen that had suddenly hit a rough patch. Her voice was soft, and she kept her eyes low. "They took them all, Bree, and you are the only one who can save them."

20

I wanted to grab the ghostly version of my now youthful Gran and shake her until her teeth rattled, but of course that was impossible. I settled for snapping my fingers at her, which had worked rather well with Alan's ghost. Her eyes flew upward so her gaze met mine, hard and flinty with a steel that age had mellowed in her.

"Took them all. *Who* is gone?"

"The bigfoot, siren, river maid, and fairy, your four friends. The goblins took them. The spider was here too, but they scared her away," she said, her words barely audible. As if all her energy were going into projecting this more youthful visage. Damn it, when did she get vain?

I raced downstairs to find Corb in the kitchen, leaning over a piece of butcher's paper. "Let me guess, ransom note?" I asked.

He stared hard at me. "How did you know?"

"Much as I'd love to pretend it was a good guess, Gran told me." I leaned over the paper myself and shook my head. "It's in that same Goblinese crap," I growled as I scooped it up.

"I was trying to decipher that," Corb said.

"I've got someone who can read it." I jogged out the front door, feeling the pull of time on my entire body.

Grimm had said I needed to protect the paperwork for three days, but I'd only made it two. If I got the pages and coin back to the people who wanted them, they could use them for whatever nefarious purpose they had. Something to do with the silver moon.

And if I didn't?

Well, I only knew I wouldn't let them hurt my friends.

I bolted across the street—okay, I was limping a little, but that was because of a muscle pull from earlier in the week—and ran up the steps of the brick house that Charlotte and her mother, Ryoko, lived in with their resident house goblin. I banged a fist on the door.

"Bridgette, tell me you're home!"

A scuffling came from inside and then the door cracked open. Bridgette's big round eyes stared up at me in surprise that didn't look feigned. "Breena? What's wrong?"

"Did you see a mob of goblins take my friends?" I bent onto one knee so we were at eye level. "They left this."

I held the butcher's paper out to her, and she took it gingerly, her eyes scanning the glyphs and letters that made no sense to me. Her eyes rose to meet mine. "They took them to Goblin Town. You have until midnight to bring the spell book to them."

I blinked a few times. "Spell book."

Holy shit, so they didn't want Grimm's paperwork at all?

That left two options. Either they wanted the black spell book that I'd found in the library, the one that Oster Boon had said I'd need to take. Or they wanted Gran's spell book. With everything that was happening, I was leaning toward the black spell book. I didn't really believe in coincidence, which meant I had it for a reason.

"Is that it? No other dire consequences?" I doubted that was the case, which was why I asked.

"If you don't deliver, your friends will be killed, fed to the pit monster." Her eyes closed and a tear slipped out. "And Savannah will be overrun by goblins."

"That it, huh?" I took the butcher paper back and folded it up, tucking it into my bag.

Bridgette's eyes popped open. "What do you mean, is that it? Isn't that enough?"

I shrugged. "I don't know, it seems rather un-original, don't you think?"

"I don't understand." She stared up at me. "Why aren't you afraid?"

I shrugged. "I *am* afraid. But if I've learned anything, it's that all fear does is slow you down and make you want to lie flat on your back, tits to the sky. I can't do that when my friends are in danger." I paused on the bottom step and looked back. "Thank you for your help."

She swallowed hard. "You can't take anyone from the Hollows with you. That's what it says on the paper."

Both of my eyebrows climbed up. "What's the exact wording?"

"You may bring no one who works for the Hollows or for the SCE," Bridgette said. "But I could come with you."

That gave me serious pause. "That would put you in danger, for people you barely know. Why would you do that?"

Her big eyes blinked rapidly and tears filled around the edges. "The king is a tyrant and he hurts anyone who stands against him. My family was one that did that, and…most were killed." Her round chin tipped upward. "And they threatened Savannah. This is my town, too, now and I'll protect it if I can. It's where Ryoko and Charlotte have made their home and…I love them even though they don't see me."

Oh man, right in the heart strings. Her words plucked at my emotions, and I found myself nodding and speaking around a rather tight throat. "Right. Okay."

Bridgette fell in behind me as I hurried back across the street. Tom, Corb, Sarge, and Robert stood in the front yard of Gran's house.

Gran watched us from the open door, still younger than before, closer to her forties and her image flickering in and out of stability.

"We have problems of rather unprecedented proportion," I said as I drew near. "The goblin mob took Kinkly, Eric, Suzy, and Feish to Goblin Town and are threatening their lives if I don't give them this." I pulled out the small paper-covered book from my hip bag. I handed it to Tom first. He flipped it open and then dropped it like it was hot.

"Bree, where in the seven hells did you find that?" His eyes shot to mine. "And why are you carrying it around with you?"

I grimaced. "Where would *you* put something like that, something you didn't want anyone else to get their hands on?"

Sarge scooped it up, flipped it open, and then literally threw the book at Corb, who caught it. He held it the longest of the three, though he paled. "The goblin king wants this?"

I waved a hand at Bridgette, who cleared her throat. "His ransom note says the spell book for the lives of your friends."

"No Hollows Group members can come with me. No one from the SCE either, not that it matters," I said. "That's part of the deal. Bridgette is going to come, and of course, Robert."

Sarge was the only one of the group who could see the animated skeleton, and his eyes shot to him. "It won't be enough, Bree. This is bigger than fighting the O'Seans, and it's a hell of a lot bigger than fighting an old lady in a graveyard. You're going to their home. This will be a fight all the way with more goblins than you can imagine. Someone might even challenge you to a duel."

"I can't leave them there," I said. "I won't."

Alan chose that moment to step out from under the tree. "You're an idiot. Your friends wouldn't fight for you, you know that, right? You were always the fool, running to save your friends. Even though they didn't deserve it."

"I've had about enough of you." I reached over, grabbed him by his ear once more, and stuffed him into my bag. "You can stay in there forever, for all I care."

I caught Corb looking at me as I finished with Alan. "You can't come with me—"

"I quit the Hollows Group," he said softly, and a tiny bell sounded in the air, like a gong going off. Tom groaned.

"Corb, this isn't a game. You quitting will cause all sorts of issues with—"

Corb's eyes never left mine. "I'm not letting her go in there without me."

Sarge sighed. "I quit the Hollows group too then."

Another little bell pealed through the air, and Tom all but whimpered. "You two idiots. Do you know how pissed Eammon is going to be?"

Eammon might be pissed, but I thought my ticker might burst from sheer emotion. I understood a little why Corb had put it all on the line for me. But Sarge?

"Sarge, are you sure?"

"While there was a minor rough patch last week," he drawled. Rough patch? He tried to ducking kill me. He continued, "I consider you a friend. More than that, I think you are a kick-ass bitch." He slung an arm across my shoulders. "And I owe you."

I put an arm around his waist and tipped my head up to him. He bent and kissed me—not in a sexy way, but a quick peck on the lips. "You're good people, Bree. I knew that from the moment I tangled with you in the graveyard."

"You mean when Robert ripped your ear off?"

Robert let out a growl and Sarge shivered. "Yeah, even then."

I pulled back from him and looked at the quickly assembled team. Tom shook his head when my eyes landed on him. "I am going to tell Eammon what you fools are up to."

"You aren't going to try to stop us?" I offered.

"You aren't children, none of you." He turned his back on us. "But try not to get killed, and don't give them the book."

There was a moment where we were all quiet.

"Okay"—Sarge clapped his mitts together—"let's go."

I shook my head. "We have six hours. Bridgette, how long will it take to get to Goblin Town?"

"About an hour, maybe two at most if there are blockades up," she said.

I nodded. "Then we prep first. If this is war, I'm not running in willy-nilly."

Corb nodded. "You have a plan?"

"Working on it. First, we need to visit Gerry."

The two guys frowned in unison, which tickled my funny bone. "Who the hell is Gerry?" Corb asked.

I grinned and crooked my finger for them to follow me. "My seamstress."

Death Row was bustling when we got there, almost shoulder to shoulder shoppers, which was the fullest I'd ever seen it.

I didn't pause anywhere but went straight to Geraldine's—Gerry's—stall. She saw me coming and gave me a once-over from head to toe and back again.

"Girl, did you get laid?"

Oh shit, was it that obvious I'd had an orgasm?

I stumbled, partially stunned, and Corb stumbled right into my backside. To keep us both upright, his arms shot around me and yeah, he got two handfuls of the girls.

We both froze for just a moment, and then he adjusted his grip and helped me up. I held both hands in the air. "I'm fine, I can walk on my own two feet, no need to use my handles."

"Didn't look that way to me." Gerry winked and then took a good long look at Corb. "And I don't blame you one bit for buckling to the pressure."

I put a hand to my head. "It's not like that. Look, I'm wondering if you can whip up some new clothes, for all three of us."

Gerry looked us over. "What kind are you thinking?"

I motioned for Bridgette to step forward. "Something that can camouflage us, like Bridgette here."

The goblin stepped close to Gerry. Gerry took a good look at her. "That cloth is expensive."

I grimaced and nodded. "How much?"

Gerry ducked under her table and pulled out a bolt of cloth that was mottled green and black. "This is all I have. Will probably take the whole amount to get three of you decked out."

"How much?" I repeated and watched as she caressed the fabric. Yeah, this was going to cost me.

"Three thousand," she said.

I started to nod, thinking that wasn't too bad.

"Each," Gerry clarified. "This fabric is hard to come by. The goblins don't give it up easily."

Corb tugged on my arm, dragging me back a few steps. "Not worth it."

I looked at him. "I'm not asking you to pay, Corb. I invited you to this party. I'll pick up the tab." I flipped open my bag and pulled out the money. Because, yes, I did just walk around with thousands of dollars in my handbag.

Of course not. I'd brought all my cash with me for our shopping trip.

"Gerry, we need these done right away." I plunked the cash down on the table but didn't take my hand off it. "How fast?"

She blew out a breath. "Two hours. That will be pushing it, but I can make it happen."

I took my hand off the cash and she tucked it away and set to work, her hands flying over the bolt of material with a pair of wicked shears that seemed like a better fit for cutting wool off a sheep than making clothes.

Corb put a hand on my shoulder and a cool wash of his power rolled down to my toes and back up again.

"What was that?" I asked.

He smiled. "A little extra protection. Should deflect anything for a little bit. Why don't you go see Annie, see if you can get any information out of her? Just be careful; like we said earlier she's been off. Not herself."

Annie being the psychic who pulled tarot cards for the Hollows Group's new recruits and had been the nicest to me when I'd first rejoined the shadow world.

I nodded. It wasn't a half bad idea, and now that he'd mentioned it, I did feel a pull to go talk to her. "You guys look around for anything else we might need," I said, stepping back from Corb and Sarge. Bridgette stayed close to my side. "We'll go on up to Annie."

The guys nodded and slid through the crowd toward the weapons vendors, the blond twins with the cheap wares. When would they learn?

I sighed and wove my way through the crowd to the stairs that led up to Madame Trebon's Tarot Readings, Annie's shop.

"Tell me what you can about Goblin Town," I said to Bridgette.

"There are multiple ways in, but the two main ones are west of Savannah. They are both heavily guarded. There are other ways, but they're harder to find. One is through the land of faerie. I think that the note said you're supposed to come to the main gate. That is where King Derek likes to hold his trials."

Great.

With one hand on the wall, I made myself go all the way up the stairs without stopping, which was, in and of itself, a freaking miracle. At the top I paused, breathing hard, my legs tingling horribly as my muscles seemed to scream for air. "Oh, that's going to hurt come tomorrow."

Bridgette nodded. "I hate stairs too."

Sometimes it was hard for me to remember that I'd only been at this gig, trying to keep up with the young ones, for about a month. Had I lost some weight? Yes. But I still had extra pounds on me, and I wasn't fit by the standards of those I'd been running with in the most literal of senses.

And yes, I knew I was only thinking about things like stairs and exercise to avoid letting my mind circle back to the fact that my friends had been kidnapped by a mob of goblins. I wasn't sure I'd be able to keep my cool if I let myself think about that. Because, no, I wasn't about to cry. I wasn't about to whimper and wish that someone would save me.

Gawd in heaven, help those goblins once I got my hands on their stringy little necks. I'd tie them in knots and use them for target practice.

Look at me go and look. There be my last duck, and it was completely on fire.

21

My breath came in sharp bursts as I stepped into Annie's back room and pushed through the hanging beads that delineated the front and back spaces. Bridgette hung back. "I don't want to go in."

I paused. "You okay?"

"I don't like the smell," she said.

The smell of sage and a sharper, darker incense filled the air. I couldn't put my finger on that one, but it was familiar and tugged at something in me, though it didn't bother me the way it was bugging Bridgette. Peering out of the shadows, I could see Annie at the cash register, helping a tourist by the looks of it.

"So this crystal, it will help stave off bad dreams?" The woman looked to be about my age, with dark hair and the brown fearful eyes of a deer in the headlights.

Annie laid a gentle hand on hers. "If it doesn't work, you come on back and I'll do a reading on you free of charge. But I think you'll be just fine with this." She wrapped up the crystal in tissue paper and tucked it into a silken bag before handing it back to the obviously very freaked-out woman. Fear rolled off her in waves.

"Thank you, I really hope it helps," she said softly, her hands clutching at the small bag as if it were her lifeline. "I can't go on like this much longer."

Annie patted her on the back and saw her to the door. "You're going to be just fine."

She closed the door after her customer and flipped the sign from open to closed.

"Well, I didn't expect to see you out this way again," Annie said without turning around.

"And why is that?" I leaned a hip against the doorway that led from the back room to the main area. "You know something I don't?"

Annie turned to look at me, but she didn't smile. "I work with the Hollows Group, not outsiders. You can show yourself out."

My eyes narrowed as I wondered just what the hell was going on now. "I'm just a customer here for a card reading. And I get on fine with the boys from the Hollows Group."

"Three hundred dollars," she said.

I knew she'd picked a figure intended to shock me and make me go away. But why? She'd been perfectly pleasant in our first interaction. If anything, she'd seemed to be concerned about my well-being. Something had obviously changed. Corb was right about that.

Was it just that I'd been fired from the Hollows Group?

Well, I had three hundred, and while it was maybe stupid, I felt compelled to make a solid point. Or two.

One, I wasn't going anywhere.

And two, she was not scaring me off with a high number.

"You want that in fifties or hundreds?" I reached into my bag and peeled off six fifties. "Never mind, here." I slapped the bills onto the counter next to me.

Annie's face was a thundercloud if ever I'd seen one, but she gathered up her tarot cards and sat at her small table with a heavy flop of her body. The table was set against the far wall, and my back would be to the glass door, but I felt better with it there, than my back to her. I could see just past her shoulder into the back room, and I was half hoping Bridgette would show herself. To our right was the chest-high counter with the cash register on it. Thickly made of old railroad ties, or maybe wood ballast off the ships from the river, that was more likely.

With a motion of her bejeweled and braceleted hand, Annie waved for me to sit across from her. I did, but I found myself putting a hand against the knife sheath on one thigh.

She shuffled the cards as she spoke. "You have caused some serious grief for me."

"Really, how so?" I didn't so much as twitch as I watched her shuffle the cards. "I've barely spent any time with you."

Having spread the cards across the table, she leaned back and folded her arms over her chest. With my left hand, I swept my fingers over the deck. It didn't take long for a single card to attach itself to me. I flipped it over and found myself staring at the Devil himself.

"Ego," Annie breathed. "It will be the death of you and your friends. Or the death of a relationship." Her eyes hooded slightly and her breathing hitched; her one hand resting on the table began to shake as she read the card for me. "For you, Breena O'Rylee, there is danger at every turn, in every aspect of your life. Danger and seduction, temptation and choices."

"Sounds fun," I muttered.

Her breathing hitched again. "Cage. I see a cage made of iron surrounding you, and the only way to break free is to destroy it." She blinked and looked straight at me. "Satisfied?"

I scooped up the devil card and stared at it, at the artistic lines and the style of the image, from the horns to the empty eyes staring at me. Something in me made me pull out the first card I'd drawn when I'd come back to Savannah, right here in Annie's place.

I laid the death card down first, then pulled out the second card I'd drawn, the moon card, and finally the devil card. The moon card I'd pulled from a deck down by the river, a deck belonging to the tarot card reader who'd been killed by Sean O'Sean.

"Quite the lay if you look at them together," I said, running my hands over them, seeing something beyond the cards. I scooped them up, fanning them to show her the faces. "But you know what stands out to me the most?"

Annie stared hard at me. I could feel the weight of her eyes. "What is that?"

I lifted my eyes finally and peered over the top of the cards. "That they are all from the same deck. How is that possible when two are from you, and one is from the deck that belonged to the tarot card reader O'Sean killed? Unless O'Sean had your deck for some reason?"

She stood, sending her chair scooting backward until it slammed into the wall behind her, her hand reaching for something at her side, hidden by her voluminous skirts.

I dropped the cards and threw myself to the side as the boom of a gun went off, rattling the air. The feeling of something zipping by me had me flattened to the ground, but I couldn't stay there.

Crash had said O'Sean's sister was quick with a gun.

Oh. Shit.

Guns had more than one bullet, the last I checked, and I'd taken a bullet to the leg a little over a week ago. Once a month was plenty in that department.

I scrambled around the back side of her counter. "Annie, you really going to kill me?"

"You killed Sean." The hitch in her voice made me grimace. Yeah, this was going to go badly.

"Well, to be fair…" I moved so I could peek around the edge of the counter. She had her back to the wall, and she saw me and pulled the trigger.

I yanked myself back, and the corner of the counter exploded in a shrapnel of splinters. "To be fair, he was trying to kill me."

"I don't care," she snarled. "But rather nice of you to come to me, rather than making me come to you."

How the hell was I going to get out of this pickle? I could throw a knife, but if I missed, I was down a weapon.

Unless I managed to get her to empty her gun. How many bullets in one round? Five? Six?

She'd shot twice already. I took a deep breath and forced myself to look around the corner again, pulling back even before she shot, which she did.

Three. That was three shots.

"Annie, this is not a good way to deal with things," I said. "Don't you know O'Sean was trying to take over Savannah?"

"I didn't agree with him," she said, her voice as strong as ever. "I told him that it would get him killed, but he didn't listen."

"Well, men rarely do until their balls are in a squeeze," I drawled as I dropped into a crouch. My hamstrings screamed at the tension, and then screamed a little more when I forced myself to pop up like a freaking groundhog.

Or maybe whack-a-mole. My head cleared the top of the counter and I was back down again as she shot not once, but twice. Five shots. Was there a sixth?

The scuff of a foot on the wooden plank floors told me she was coming in for the kill, in the most literal sense.

"Annie, don't do this. The O'Seans weren't the only ones dabbling with dark magic in this town. I'm trying to protect Savannah. You said it yourself, you told him not to do this." I shifted my weight on my heels at the sound of her shuffling around the side of the counter, crouched just out of sight, no doubt.

"Brothers rarely listen," she said.

I blew out a slow breath, understanding dawning. "Annie, I'm sorry he died. I am."

"That's not good enough."

"You have to believe me. I don't want you to have the same fate as him and your father."

"My father? What do you know about my father?"

Well, shit.

She whipped around the counter, gun raised, and I found myself staring into the barrel as I slowly stood, one knife in hand. Annie tipped the gun, motioning for me to step to the side. Maybe she figured she had me cornered and wanted to shoot me somewhere less messy. But as soon as the muzzle flicked away, I lunged forward, grabbed her wrist, and yanked her arm underneath mine so my back was to her chest, the gun pointing away from both of us.

She screamed and the gun boomed twice more. Man, I'd been seriously wrong about the number of bullets.

The door at the back of the shop rattled and Corb yelled my name. "The door is jammed!"

"Kinda busy in here!" I grunted and rolled with Annie through the shop, fighting for control of the weapon. Sure, she'd fired seven times at this point, but I hadn't heard any empty hammer clicks. For all I knew, there was some kind of magic on the gun, granting her extra bullets.

Annie jerked hard against me and I let her go, digging my nails into her hand, forcing her to release the gun. Heat raked down the sides of my face, and I realized she'd scratched me while we were wrestling for the weapon, her nails going for my eyes.

Her breath came in big gasps. "You killed my father too?"

My jaw ticked and I wrinkled my nose, because damn, that was not a great question for me to answer right then. "Yeah, same problem as your brother. He started it. And to be fair, he kinda killed me too."

Her eyes narrowed. "Now you are *mocking* me? When I grieve for them?"

Only she didn't look all that grief-stricken. Not really.

I shook my head, my chest heaving, and said, "You didn't even like them, did you?"

"That's not the point." She threw her hands into the air. "I'm going to finish what they started. You have to defend your family."

I leaned back against the counter. "No, actually you don't. Just because they're family doesn't mean they aren't also crazy and dangerous." I took the clip out of the gun and pulled the slide back a few times to make sure it was empty. "Even crazy people have family, Annie."

We didn't get any further than that.

The back door of the shop burst open, revealing Corb, gun already pointed at Annie. As if he'd known she would be the problem, and not some intruder. Bridgette stayed in the shadows, I could see just a glimmer of her eyes.

The front door rattled, glass burst in around us, and a squad of men dressed in black suits rushed in. Judging by the beeline they made for Annie, they weren't surprised she'd turned murderous either. She didn't fight them as they caught her by the wrists, cuffed her, gagged her, and dragged her out the way they'd come in, all in under thirty seconds. I noticed they didn't actually say what they were arresting her for and thought about asking, but then realized I had enough problems of my own. I didn't need to add Annie's problems to the list.

I tucked her gun into the back waistband of my pants, but nope, it tried to slide down my pant leg.

I yanked it out quickly, before I could lose it entirely. It distracted me, somewhat, from the tingle down my spine that said I needed to ask Corb if this was his latest job.

The crunch of glass turned me around. Roderick strode in, cravat in place. His blond hair was as immaculately swept back as the other times I'd seen him. His eyes slid over to me, and he arched a perfect brow, damn him, as if he hadn't seen me just hours before.

"Breena, why am I not surprised to see you here?"

"You know me, always where the fun happens," I drawled.

Roderick looked at Corb. "You did a good job of flushing her out. Annie never did like having a more powerful woman on her turf."

I flinched as if I'd been hit between the shoulder blades. What had Corb said down in Death Row?

"Why don't you go see Annie, see if you can get any information out of her?"

Damn it, he'd fooled me again. Even if he had put some sort of protection spell on me.

"Roderick"—I kept my back to Corb deliberately—"does Corb work for the Supernatural Council Enforcers?"

Roderick dipped his head. "He's one of our best investigators. Top of his class, which is even more of an accomplishment given his lineage. Not many people could pull off double duty between us and the Hollows Group, but he makes it look easy."

I nodded as if that, of course, made sense, but all I could think was that I'd been stupid enough to think I meant something to him. Again.

Jaysus lawdy, when was I going to learn?

I made my way across to the small table that had somehow stayed upright during the fight, scooping up my cards and the rest of the tarot deck, plus the three hundred dollars I'd slapped on the cash desk. Small payment for almost getting killed, and for helping Roderick and the council apprehend someone they'd apparently had their eyes on.

Hell, my curiosity got the better of me. "What did she do?"

Roderick tucked his hands into his coat pockets. "Nothing that needs to concern you. But her attacking you was enough of a final nail in her coffin to make the arrest."

I nodded and turned away from him.

The reality of my situation was suddenly in front of me again, weighing on me so heavily that my chest felt as though it were being crushed. Corb and Sarge's support had felt like a lifeline, but I couldn't rely on them. Not really. And I certainly couldn't expect them to keep me alive. There was a real chance that I'd die in Goblin Town tonight, and I had to be realistic about that.

"Liar, liar, pants on fire, hanging from a telephone wire…" I whispered to myself, knowing that Sarge at least would hear me. Turning back to Rod, I asked, "If I don't make it past midnight, would you mind seeing about the blood-born demon in the Sorrel-Weed house? The papers that show who killed my gran are in the second-floor desk, third room on the right. Maybe you could look into that."

Roderick blinked a few times. "And why wouldn't you make it past midnight?"

"Going to war," I said, then thumbed at Corb. "Mr. Trustworthy here is supposed to be my backup.

So you can understand why I might be concerned that I'm walking into a trap. Or, worse yet, being used as bait again." Here's the thing, I'd gotten rolling, and now I couldn't stop. "I mean, GAWD forbid I should be told the truth about anything. GAWD forbid my woman-sized pea brain could handle what's really going on. Lawdy, save my lily-white ass from having to take care of myself!" Yeah, I might have been shouting at that point.

Movement to my left, the sway of a body and long dark hair soothed me a little. "Robert's the only person left I can rely on. A skeleton, for duck's sake!"

Robert swayed a little faster. "Friend."

I blew out a slow breath, forcing myself to face Corb. At least he had the balls to meet my gaze.

"It wasn't like that, Bree," he said. "I didn't think she would attack you. I was weeks away from breaking this case with Annie. I didn't think she'd confess that she was going to continue their work to you. I meant only to get your cards read, to help you tonight. I put that extra layer of protection on you, just in case." His eyes pleaded with me to believe him. Maybe he believed himself even.

Sarge, who'd joined him, made the slightest of faces. Like he didn't believe Corb any more than I did.

Who could I trust? Who should I take with me to save my friends?

Because the clock was ticking, and if I chose wrong, we were all as good as dead and buried six feet under.

22

I stood in front of the fountain in Forsyth Park, the portal that led to the land of Faerie, and hopefully to Crash. Robert swayed behind me, and Skeletor pawed the water at our feet. I patted the horse's neck. Bridgette rode in front of me, quiet as a mouse. Sarge, who'd ridden over on his motorcycle, stood to my right.

"What about the time difference?" Sarge reminded me. "We won't know just how long you are in there; you could miss the midnight deadline completely."

I gave him a tight nod and grimaced. "I'm throwing all my cards in with Crash right now. He's here; if I can get to him in time, then he can help me get the others out. I don't see any other way, do you?"

We'd already been through this, but hell, why not one more time?

Sarge sighed. "Yeah, I know, but I'm worried is all."

"Me, too, but jabbering here is just wasting more time." I took a breath and looked them over. "Okay, here we go."

"Why again do I have to be here?" Jinx grumbled. She stood in her spider form to my left.

"Isn't Crash your boss?" I asked. "Shouldn't you try to help me find him, seeing as you buggered off when you were supposed to be guarding the house?"

"Finding him while he's boinking his ex is not part of my job description," she said. "He can jump on all the women he wants. My job is to keep him apprised of the goings-on in Factors Row." She rubbed two front legs together.

"Apprised is a big word. Did you learn it from the book I got you?" I asked.

Her beady eyes blinked up at me. "I did, actually."

"And you remember that another book is your payment for this?" I reminded her of the conversation when I'd gone to ask her for help. Come with me to find her boss, and another book on editing was hers.

A hand patted my leg. I glanced down at Sarge. "You good to wait for us here?"

He gave a quick nod, saying, "For what it's worth, I do think Corb cares for you." He sighed softly. "I just don't think he's good at real relationships. Very few sirens are, Bree."

"No shit," I muttered. "But you agree that I can't trust him. I saw your face in the shop. He was lying to me about Annie. He knew I'd draw her out, or at least that it was a potential outcome." Which Corb adding a protection spell of sorts on me only made more likely.

Sarge gave a reluctant nod and a sigh. "Yeah. I could smell it on him. But that doesn't mean he wanted things to go down that way. I know he wouldn't intentionally put you in danger."

I patted his hand. "You're a good friend, Sarge."

He shrugged. "So are you, Bree."

"Enough mush. Let's get this done. I want my book." Jinx splashed water at us.

Skel stomped his foot closest to her, sending a spray of water over her head. I rubbed his neck again and bumped my heels against his sides.

We trotted forward, under the fall of water, and through the fountain into the land of Faerie.

It looked different than it had the last time, but I wasn't here to study the scenery.

"We have to hurry," I said. "Skel, find Crash."

And just like that, the horse lunged into a flat-out gallop that had me bouncing on his back and hanging on for all I was worth with hands and legs. It didn't amount to much, apparently, because Bridgette and I started slipping sideways. I was not a natural horseback rider and the speed was not helping. I squeaked and tried to claw my way back upright.

Robert grabbed me by the back of my shirt and yanked us both back onto Skel's back.

"Thanks!" I yelped, and then we were skidding to a stop, a spray of flowers floating up around us as if they were dandelion fluff. I blinked and wiped a hand over my face, finally seeing the landscape. The ground was covered in a thick carpet of springtime moss and flowers, all in hues of pinks and creamy whites, like a teenage girl's bedroom. Ahead of us was a gazebo with a massive bower of woven flowers around it, a curtain of the same flowers hiding whatever—or whoever—was in that gazebo from my gaze.

But it didn't do a damn thing to muffle sounds that were definitely not sleeping.

I looked at Jinx, who blinked her beady eyes up at me. "You know he might not want to be interrupted."

"I need his help," I said. "And no matter who he might care for, I…I think I can trust him."

"Think? That's not the best word for this situation," Jinx said. "Ruminate might be better. Or ponder."

"I ponder that I can trust him?" I slid from Skel's back, and Robert followed, his bones clacking as he landed. "That's not good editorial advice."

"I think it's fabulous advice," she muttered.

"I'd stet it," I threw back as we walked toward the flowery bower.

I looked back at Skel and Bridgette waiting. She was staring around as if she couldn't believe what she was seeing. Then again, she might never have visited the Seelie side of Faerie before. I motioned for her to keep her eyes on us and she gave a quick nod.

The sounds from the bower seemed less sinful the closer we got, more like someone talking in their sleep. "I don't think they're getting it on," I whispered.

"Coitus. Humping. Banging. Roll in the hay. Bow-chick-a-wow-wow," Jinx said.

"Stop it," I hissed and took a swing at her, a back-handed swat.

"I'm showing off my skills with synonyms." She scuttled sideways.

I pointed at the bower. "You go up top, see what's going on."

She glowered at me. "You want me to look at the Boss porking his ex?"

I closed my eyes. "That is the worst synonym, don't…just go look, damn it!"

The spider scurried forward and I waited about ten feet away from the bower, staring at the curtain of flowers. Knowing that Crash was in there. I could just call to him. Maybe that was what I should do, but what if he was in trouble?

Part of me hoped he *was* in trouble. Because what if Crash was sleeping peacefully with her? What if it was obvious that they were…back together? Her note had said she missed him. What if he'd taken one look at my body, and gone running back to his ex-wife?

My ego wasn't quite ready for that blow.

Jinx's long legs took her up the side of the bower in a jiff, and she crept to the center and peeked through.

A wave of one feeler and I moved forward, pulling my knives. I motioned for Robert to stay outside. Just in case. Because gawd in heaven, my last encounter with Karissa, queen of the fae, here in her realm had gone just…okay. We'd parted on terms of reluctant understanding, but she'd seemed displeased with the thought that Crash might have any sort of interest in me.

Maybe he didn't.

I swallowed hard and lifted a knife to the flowers, cutting through them as if they weren't even there. I stepped through into the candle-lit room, if it could be called that. Karissa was in the middle of the bed, her young lover to the left of her, and Crash…Crash lay to her right, hands above his head under his pillow, a flash of his tats showing with the sheet just barely above his waist.

My heart did a funny stupid squeeze that made me wish for an aspirin, because it felt like a boa constrictor was tightening around me, preparing to swallow me whole. Damn it. Seeing him sleeping there with her hurt a hell of a lot more than I wanted to admit.

But I still needed his help.

He was the boss of the goblins. I should have come to him first. I should have ignored Grimm and asked Crash for his help right from the start.

Shoulda, coulda, woulda.

I crept to his side, tucked my knife away, poked him in the ribs with a finger, and backed up quickly.

I knew what happened to people who woke him unexpectedly. I recalled all too vividly being thrown across the room the first time I'd tried it.

He opened his eyes and stared at the ceiling of the flower bower. Jinx waved at him and pointed toward me.

His head barely rolled my way, just moving enough for him to see me, and the anguish in his eyes dropped me to my knees. "Get out, Bree."

The words were growled, but there was no real heat behind them. Karissa sat up beside him in bed and then draped her body across his, all of which I caught in my peripheral vision. Because I couldn't look away from Crash, and what I was seeing in his eyes was that none of this was his idea. She'd used her power to compel him, somehow.

"Oh, she did show up," Karissa purred. "You didn't go to save your friends then?"

Which meant she knew something about it. Because, of course she did. I stood and faced the fairy queen, pulling out the one card I had that she likely didn't know about. "Ah, well, you have something of mine."

She ran her fingers over Crash's chest. "You think he's yours? That's amusing."

A smile slid over my lips even though a small aching part of me still wasn't entirely sure he wasn't enjoying his time with her. "Here's the deal. I freed him from the slavery that tied him to the O'Seans. He willingly became a piece of my property at that point. I believe his words were, *I am yours*."

I snapped my fingers at her in a perfect zigzag pattern. It had been intended as a saucy gesture to show her just how little she bothered me, but light burst from my fingertips—teal blue sparkles flecked with black. They whipped around Crash, and Karissa squeaked and fell backward. I had no idea what I was doing—hell, I'd snapped my fingers for effect, not because I'd expected some sort of magic to pop out of me—but I tried to keep that out of my expression.

Karissa squeaked a second time as the sparkles danced over her, and she fully pulled away from Crash, who was able to sit up and stumble forward, the sheet sliding off him.

Both disappointment and elation filled me.

He had his jeans on.

I stepped forward and let him put an arm over my shoulders as he wobbled away from the bed. Damn. She'd done a number on him.

I helped him out of the bower, fully expecting her to follow. Robert swayed up to us, and I motioned for him to keep pace. Jinx scuttled down off the bower.

"Boss, she promised me another book to help, but I want one from you too." Jinx was in front of us, walking backward. Crash managed a nod, but that was it.

"Crash, how big of a fight is this going to be with her?" I asked.

"You won't see it coming." His Irish accent was heavy, his words slurry as if he were completely drunk. "She'll come at you when you least expect it."

"Ah, excellent. Just what I was hoping for." I helped him over to Skel. The horse went to one knee without being asked, and Crash managed to pull himself onto his back. I hopped up in front of him, Bridgette still sitting in front of me, as she had never gotten off Skel's back. I held out a hand to Robert.

"Come on, friend, we aren't done yet."

He put his hand in mine, and between one blink and the next, I held a finger bone in my hand. I tucked him back between my boobs. Crash leaned heavily on me, his head on my shoulder.

"Skel, back to the fountain," I said, and we were off and running.

It was not lost on me that this was the second time I'd taken a prisoner from Karissa, both times with very little fuss on her part.

Call me overcautious, but I was going to have to deal with her soon.

Sooner than I would've liked, for sure.

Crash's arms were around me, holding on for balance more than anything. Sprays of flowers floated up around us as we galloped through the land of Faerie, and I found myself pulling on Skel's mane. In the distance was a dark peak of a mountain, bright lights illuminating it as though I were staring at a modern-day Las Vegas in the middle of Faerie land.

"Goblins are Unseelie, a part of the fae," I said softly. "Bridgette, you said there is an entrance to Goblin Town here in Faerie?"

"Yes." She bobbed her head excitedly, her ears flicking. "You can see it too?"

"I've a little bit of fae blood in me. Enough to make trouble." I grinned at her and she grinned back.

"We can sneak in the back way," I went on. "Your outfit and mine will keep us from being seen and then there shouldn't be as big of a time difference." I touched the fabric that was currently clinging to my body. Gerry had had the suits ready in time, and mine fit like a glove, camouflage and all.

She was spot on. The goblins would be watching the front gate, the way we'd been told to come in. I pointed at Jinx. "You go with Sarge, head straight for Goblin Town. Keep their attention on the front gate. Don't engage them other than to taunt the shit out of them, okay? Tell them I'm hurrying as fast as I can, buy us time!"

Jinx grumbled as she shot toward the fountain exit. I turned Skel and asked for more speed as we raced across the land of Faerie toward Goblin Town, a passed-out fae king against my back, an ousted goblin riding in front, and a skeleton's finger bone tucked between my boobs.

How could anything possibly go wrong?

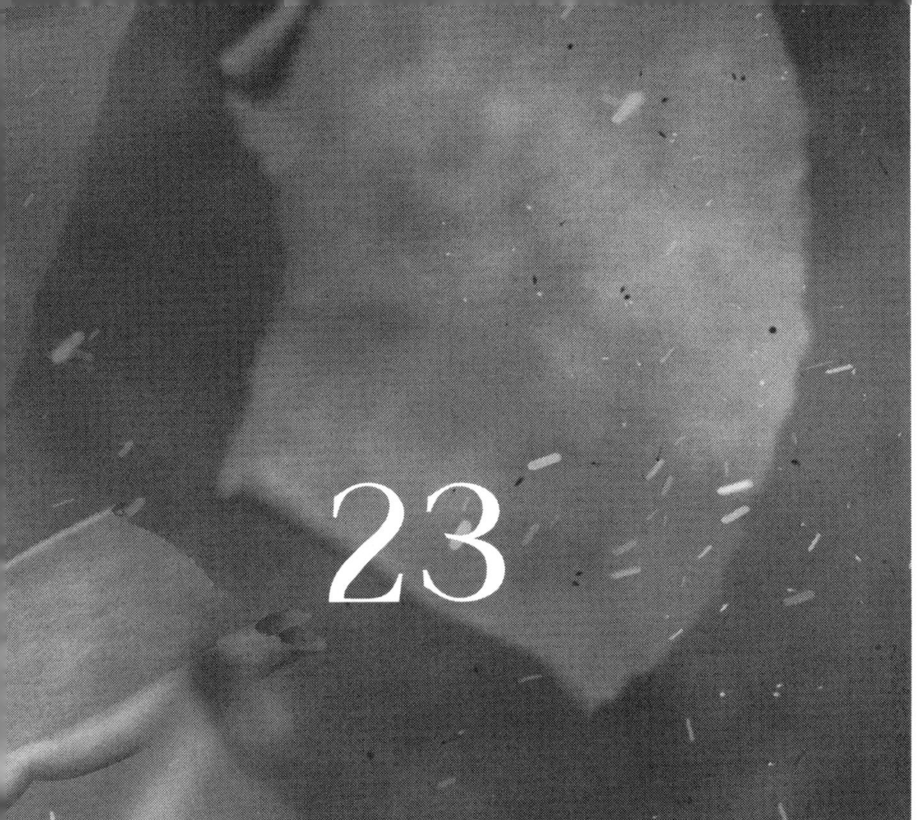

23

Turned out a solid fifteen-foot wall of rock surrounded Goblin Town. I had a suspicion that Skel could jump it, but that wouldn't work with the plan I had going on. Bridgette was right, with her natural ability to blend in and the outfit Gerry had made for me—thankfully the hubbub in Death's Row hadn't slowed her down any—we could do this better and faster on our own.

Not for one second did I believe the goblin king would make a fair trade of my friends for the spell book. And if he wanted that spell book so damn badly, I wasn't about to give it to him. It freaked out everyone who knew anything about the shadow world, which seemed reason enough to keep it safe.

Crash's head lolled onto my shoulder. I tapped him, but he didn't wake up. So much for using him as a backup. "Skel, can you lie down?" I whispered.

The horse went to his knees and then to his belly, and Crash slid off to one side, a low moan the only noise he made. I hopped off and pulled Robert from my boobs and set him on the ground.

A moment later, he was standing next to me, swaying side to side. "Help me move him."

Together the three of us pulled Crash so he lay in the shadow of the wall. A loud bang sounded above us, pinning me to the wall, my butt cheeks squeezing so hard I wasn't sure what might pop out.

A burst of colors in the air eased a little of my anxiety. Fireworks, that was all.

"That's early," Bridgette said. "They shouldn't be celebrating the silver moon already."

The line came back to me then in a rush I didn't like. "The silver moon is the time for the demon skin to be found, and bound, and used to be bidden."

Bridgette whipped around and looked at me. "What did you say?"

I pulled out the book, *Black Spells of Savannah and the Undead*, making sure that Alan stayed in the bag despite his grumbling. "It's from the book the king wants."

She looked up at me. "Our family trees are written on demon skin. They hide some of our darkest spells in them."

My hands started shaking, the book nearly tumbling out of them. I was sure, absolutely certain I'd heard her wrong. I must have. "What did you say?"

"Um. Our family trees are written on demon skin. They hide some of our darkest spells in them." She frowned. "Why, what does that have to do with anything?"

Grimm had said people were after his family tree, but I hadn't believed him. I'd thought it was the coin.

Then I'd thought it was *Black Spells of Savannah and the Undead.*

I swallowed hard. "What kind of spells?"

Bridgette stared hard at me. "Breena, why does it matter?"

I tucked the book under my arm and pulled out the yellow envelope, taking out the freaking *demon skins* scrawled with Goblinese.

She held out a hand, trembling, her eyes scanning it quickly. "This is bad, Breena," she said, looking up at me with large eyes. "The spells in here, they are some of the worst I've ever seen. Bringing back monsters that have been wiped out for generations."

The Silver Lady's words reverberated in my head.

"Is there a way to bring…vampires back in there?"

Please say no, please say no, please say no.

She scanned the pages for too long, long enough to give me hope, and then she shoved them back at me as if she couldn't bear to touch them anymore. "Yes. There's a spell in there to bring a plague of vampires down on us. This is crazy, why would they…" she trailed off, muttering to herself. "I can't even believe this! We've always been taught to stay as far from vampires as possible. To have nothing to do with them."

I looked at the pages in my hands. "Maybe this is why. No matter how you look at it, we can't leave them here, and we can't take them with us."

Bridgette was shaking as badly as me now. "I can't believe anyone would even write that down. Why?"

I shook my head. "No idea. But it's a stupid thing to do."

I put the *Black Spells of Savannah and the Undead* on the ground and dug around in my bag, pausing to point at Alan's stupid face and then snap my fingers to make him stay put.

"What are you doing?" she asked.

"Like I said, we can't take it in with us. Which means we have to destroy it right now." I found the small package of matches I'd stuffed into my bag at a bar Suzy and I had gone to for drinks.

"Won't work," Bridgette said. "Fire will only make the magic come to life. We'll have to find another way."

"Damn it!" I shoved the matches and everything else back in my bag, making Alan grumble. All I could do was hope that my accidental paper swap didn't end up hurting a lot of people. "Skel, you stay here and guard Crash."

I didn't necessarily want to leave him out here by himself, but I wasn't sure we had much of a choice. Whatever whammy Karissa had hit him with, it had hit him hard. Robert, Bridgette, and I jogged away—well, I jogged, he swayed quickly, and she scurried to keep up—down the line of the wall, my hand on the surface of it, feeling for anything we could use to get in.

Because I'd watched *Labyrinth* too many times not to wonder if maybe, just maybe, the writers had been right about goblins liking illusions and mazes and whatnot…

"There's this part in the movie," I said as if they had any idea what I was talking about, "and it was just an illusion, but that illusion made it nearly impossible to see…" My hand dipped into an opening I hadn't seen, and I slid to a stop and stared at the wall. "Hot damn, apparently the movie got it right. You two, stick close."

I stepped into the opening. In front of me was a second rock wall, about two feet away from the first and set up with an illusion that was hard to break. To either side of that second wall were paths that led away from the wall. I stepped around and stared down a long street into what looked like the Strip in Vegas. I'd been there once, years before, and the sounds and lights were spot on, even if the names of the businesses were totally off kilter.

Tits and Bits

All Your Jewels

Gimme Yo Money

To name a few. More notable than the radical honesty of their marketing was the lack of people—or goblins. I stood at the far end of what looked to be a long stretch ending in what could only be a massive set of front doors. A ridiculously tall platform stood in front of them. I dug around in my bag and pulled out the binoculars Sarge had given me earlier.

Alan spilled out because I wasn't quick enough to stop him this time.

"Bree—"

I snapped my fingers at him to shut his face.

Putting the binoculars to my eyes, I scanned the platform.

A big throne had been set up, its back to me, and several goblins stood next to it, one wrapped in thick ropes.

"That's got to be Grimm," I muttered, feeling very 007 as I swept my gaze across to the other side of the throne.

When I saw the tall and very human figure that stood there, I wanted to clamp my hands around his neck and squeeze until his eyeballs popped out. But it was the Silver Lady next to him who really had my attention. She'd been with him this whole time, dragging the stuffing out of him, which was awesome.

It also meant she might know where my friends were being kept here in Goblin Town.

I put my hand up to her, hoping she'd see me.

Nothing.

I lowered the binoculars, trying to think my way through our problem. My gran had always said no problem was impossible to solve—you just had to consider the tools at hand. Robert was invisible to most people, but could goblins see him? I realized I hadn't outright asked Bridgette.

Which reminded me of another potential problem: she wasn't even supposed to be here. "Will they hurt you if they see you?" I asked her.

"They might kick me back out, but they won't hurt me," she said.

And then I looked at Alan.

He glared at me. "What?"

He could talk to the Silver Lady, and he could probably get there without anyone seeing him. "I need your help."

He burst out laughing. "Tough shit. I'm not doing anything for you."

I shrugged, grabbed him by the ear and started to stuff him back into the bag. He pawed at my hands, fighting me, but I had him all the way in except for his head in a matter of seconds.

"Wait. Stop. What if I make a deal with you?" Alan whined. "Don't put me in the bag anymore, and I'll do what I can to help you."

I grimaced and shook my head. "Yeah, you'll have to do better than that. Robert is my backup plan, and he is far more trustworthy. And you're a pain in my ass even as a dead man."

"Friend," Robert whispered.

Alan wormed a hand out of the bag, holding it out to me. "Okay, okay. What if I help you with this…whatever this is, and you…you help find out what happened to me."

I pursed my lips. "But if you get in the way or start yapping, I'll stuff you back into the bag."

"Okay, okay, deal." He held his hand out and I took it, yanking him from my bag. Confusion stole over his face as he glanced around. "What do you need to do in Vegas?"

I pointed to the front gates, not bothering to point out that this wasn't exactly Vegas as he knew it. "There's a woman next to Davin the dick. She's a ghost like you. I need you to get her and bring her to me."

"I hate him."

"Yeah, that makes two of us," I said, and Alan gave me a quick nod.

And just like that, my ex-husband was in on a job with me. The four of us made our way to the back of the podium, ducking and dodging between doors and alleys, staying hidden as best we could. Sure, I could have sent Alan up by himself, but I didn't exactly trust him to do the job. I wanted to be on the scene to make sure nothing went wrong. Or, more realistically, to help turn things around when they inevitably did go wrong.

The clothing that Gerry had made for me made me all but disappear. There was definitely a 007 feel to the moment.

It was only once we got closer that I could see the herd of goblins gathered between the podium and the massive doors. All of them had their backs to us. I ducked under the raised platform and motioned for Alan to go up.

He climbed the wooden structure and disappeared from view.

"Yes, hello," he said. "My name is Alan, and my miserable ex-wife says you need to come see her." A pause. "Ah, no, don't do that. I said don't! Woman, get off me. Ouch, damn it!"

I tipped my head to one side and looked at Robert. He shrugged and lifted both skeletal hands. Bridgette motioned to me. "I'm going to get around the front, see if I can see what's happening."

I moved to stop her, to tell her to stay with us, but she was gone before I could grab her. Damn it, splitting up was not a good idea.

"Stop it, stop touching me, you damn woman and your grabby hands!" Alan screeched, and then he was tumbling off the back of the platform. The Silver Lady followed him, albeit far more gracefully.

Her eyes locked on mine, and I motioned for her to come closer. I knew goblins could hear well, but I was hoping their senses weren't as sharp as Sarge's.

"Can you help me find my friends?" I barely whispered the words, but a scuffle immediately started on stage. I looked up to see a face shoved against the floor, an eye peering at me.

Well, shit.

I stared back, but the eye didn't move.

"Get his face off the floor!" roared someone from above. "Keep him facing forward. I want her to see his slimy face!"

Grimm.

He was pulled off the boards, and the Silver Lady motioned again for Alan to hold out his hand.

"I don't want to touch her," he grumbled. I pointed a finger at him and then to her, using my best angry eyes.

Reluctantly, he held out his hand. "You'd better hold up to your part of the deal."

His eyes widened as he touched the Silver Lady's hand, and then he gasped and pulled back. "She showed me where they are. Under the *Tits and Bits*."

Of course he'd noticed that place. I motioned for him to come with me, gave a slight bow at the waist to the Silver Lady, and then took off. Not exactly running, but hurrying as quickly as I could. *Tits and Bits* was about halfway down the Strip with a big neon sign featuring a naked goblin lady. The typos were the worst; I could only imagine the fun Jinx would have with her red pen in this town. The image above the sign seemed as anatomically incorrect as their typos were grammatically incorrect. Her bits didn't look anything like mine—there was too much here, and not enough there, and pieces that I'm sure were toothlike. I'll say that much and leave the rest to the imagination. But if everyone's undercarriage looked like that, I could understand why some men might think they bite.

As we reached the building, the creak of wood and metal groaned through the air. I twisted around, twinging my back hard, which only made me gasp for the wrong reason. The right reason would have been the fact that the massive doors were opening, which meant we were closing in on midnight. Sarge and Jinx would be out front, hopefully, but they'd only be able to distract the goblin crowd for so long, and I didn't want them getting hurt either if the king lost patience. Our time was running out.

"Hurry." I pushed Alan ahead of me, and he went straight through the door. I tried the handle, but it was locked. I knocked, hoping for a guard we could bonk over the head, preferably one with a massive key ring, but no one came to answer the door. Apparently the goblin king thought the prisoners didn't need a guard.

I stepped back and took a deep breath. "I can do this. I can kick the door down." I swung forward with my foot as hard as I could—and the door bit back.

In other words, it didn't move so much as an inch. My foot hit the door and all that force was pushed back into me. I bounced backward hard, landing on the ground with an expulsion of air from both ends.

Alan stuck his head through the door to laugh at me. "You're an idiot."

I rolled to the side, my butt and ego bruised. "Shut your trap."

I pulled one knife free and used it to cut through the deadbolt. That's how sharp they were, these knives Crash had made for me. Cut through steel, cut through magic, cut through bad guys.

I kept the knife in hand and pushed the door open into what was clearly a goblin strip joint. The room I stepped into was dim; only a few candle-filled chandeliers hung from the ceiling, and most of the candles had guttered out.

A series of stripper poles circled the room, each one in front of a large table covered with black cloth, with a main stage that had three poles set up.

Alan stood in the middle of the room. "Where is everyone?"

What he really wanted to know was where the strippers had gone. I didn't even give him the time it would take to roll my eyes. I hurried through the room, avoiding touching anything. I had friends who danced for a living, and they were honestly some of the coolest people I knew. But given what I'd seen and smelled in Grimm's hotel room, I didn't want to rely on the cleanliness of goblin strippers and, worse, their clients.

"You need to lead the way," I reminded him.

"They're in the back, past the main stage, in the last room on the left," he said as he slipped ahead of us, almost strutting.

I kept moving, Robert a half step behind me.

The door behind the long bar was locked so I headed up to the main stage, passing by the poles, saying nothing as I approached the back to check the door. Alan and Robert could probably get away with speaking since so few people could see them, but I didn't want to draw attention to myself.

"What, you don't want to give it a go?" Alan laughed as he stepped out to the side of me, grabbing a pole and pretending to swing around it. "Remember when you did pole fitness? God, what a joke. Such an embarrassment. You really shouldn't have been shocked that I didn't want to see you quote, dance, unquote, for me."

My chest constricted with that old pain, from a time when I still cared what he thought about me. When I still cared what his friends thought about me. When I wanted him to love me and had yet to realize that no one who loved you would treat you like that. How could that hurt now, in the middle of everything that was happening? I turned away from him, unwilling to let him see the pain on my face. Because I wasn't good at pretending. I just wasn't, and he knew it.

I picked up my pace. I just had to get my friends out of here, that was what I needed to focus on.

Robert bumped my shoulder with his. "Friend."

And just like that, the hurt slid away a little—enough that I could pull my head up. I snapped my fingers at Alan and his jaw snapped shut. Good enough for now. I would deal with him later.

As in exorcise him right out of my life.

The door behind the long black and silver sparkling curtains was unlocked, and I turned the handle, stepping through into the inky darkness. I dug around in the bag at my hip and found a flashlight. Only I wasn't quick enough.

A sharp point pressed against my belly and hands gripped me from both sides.

"We got her now."

24

A light blinked on above my head and my eyes slammed shut. Probably not the best response when I had a sharp, pointy object digging into my belly and several hands restraining me.

Robert gave a low growl.

"Hang tight," I said. The hands tried to drag me forward, but there was very little weight behind them. I forced my watering eyes open and found myself looking at female versions of Grimm with big bat ears, bigger eyes, and lipstick that was about ten shades too neon for their incredibly pale skin.

"Oh, the king will be so giving us so many pleases! This is the one he wants, he showses us her pictures!"

said the one in front of me, the one holding a damn nail file at my belly.

They tugged on me and I dug my heels in. One of the goblin women moved behind me, so I just sat right on top of her.

"Hey, get your big butt off me!" she screeched as she started shoving. The nail file got pushed a little harder and I jerked a hand around, smacking it out of the lead goblin lady's clammy hands.

"Knock that off," I snapped and pushed upward onto my feet, deliberately putting extra oomph into the push on the goblin under my butt. The women—four of them, to be exact—stepped a little away from me.

"You can have the prisoners. He be wanting you the most." The lead bitch lifted her chin and looked down her nose at me. Impressive considering how short she was. The thing was, I couldn't have them running off and getting help, but I also didn't really want to kill them. I mean…even I wasn't that cold.

So I went for a little reverse psychology.

I smiled at the lead bitch. "I'll make you a deal. You run to tell the king I'm here—I'm sure he'll appreciate that you were too afraid to fight me and will reward you for not even trying—and I'll run to get my friends out before you get back."

Before they could so much as shake my hand, I took off as fast as I could, doing my best to ignore the throbbing in my knees, following the natural curves of the back halls. "Eric, Feish, Suzy, Kink!"

The screech of the goblin girls behind me told me that they weren't running to the king, so I'd bought us a little time.

Robert hurried along but kept trying to turn around. "No, don't hurt them. They aren't really that dangerous," I said.

"Oh, she did *not* say we weren't dangerous, did she?" one of the goblin strippers caterwauled, and then something hit me in the back of the neck.

The nail file. And it stuck. "Son of a bitch!" I yelped and pulled it out of my neck, a little trickle of blood running down my shirt. "That was not nice. You are not ladies!"

"Get her!" one of the others screamed.

Robert grumbled, but he kept pace with me, and then I heard a shout of a familiar voice ahead of us. "That sounded like Suzy."

I picked up speed—okay, hobbled a little faster—and rounded the next corner. There was one door, and someone was drumming on it from the inside.

"Back up! Robert, keep the goblins busy but don't hurt them," I yelled as I took out my knife and cut through the deadbolt—better than trying to kick it down from my side. If Eric and Suzy hadn't been able to do it, then there was no way I'd manage. A tiny explosion of purple and green sparkles poofed into the air around the blade of the knife, and a sudden boom of thunder shattered the insides of the building. I wanted to clap my hands over my ears, but figured the damage was already done.

I'd tripped the alarm, and now it was a race against time to get everyone out of Goblin Town.

I opened the door, and Feish fell out and into my arms. "You found me again!"

I hugged her quickly, made eye contact with Suzy, who gave me a nod, and Eric, who followed suit.

"Where is Kinkly?" I asked.

Suzy held out her hands. Kink lay in her palm. "I'm here, but the shitheads broke my wings." I reached for her, but she shook her head. "No fussing our britches now. We have to go, that boom will bring them down on us."

I turned as a body of a tiny goblin stripper went flying over our heads, clothing flapping open and her tits and bits bared to the world as she screeched, reaching for us one last time.

Robert laughed. "Not friends."

The other three lady stripper goblins cowered away from him. "Let's go."

We ran through the building, past the poles, and into the street, where one quick glance proved that Kinkly was all too correct.

The goblins were coming in a wave of bodies, all but trampling over top of one another, the king somewhere behind them. There was no way we'd all make it out without some sort of distraction.

"Robert, show them the way out." I shoved my friends, but their feet stuttered, and I knew they weren't going to just leave me unless I gave them a good reason. "Go," I said. "Tell Crash to come get me, he's waiting outside the wall."

That got them moving. Of course, I didn't tell them that Crash was currently passed out from some spell Karissa had laid on him.

Tomato, tomaaato. The thing was, running from anything was no fun. I'd done it before. I didn't plan on doing it again. I stood in the middle of the street with my arms crossed as I waited for the goblins to reach me. As if I didn't give one teeny tiny poop that they looked like a veritable tsunami of limbs and bodies.

A wash of air rolled toward me ahead of them, and I couldn't help my nose from wrinkling.

"Bums and feet," I muttered. To my right, Alan appeared.

"Shouldn't you be running? I don't want you to die, you know," he said.

For just a moment, a small bit of hope for his personality peeked through the clouds of his asshole behavior. But he kept speaking, as was so often the problem with Alan. "I mean. If you die, then we could be really stuck together in death, you know? That would suck."

I glared at him. "It sucks now, you dumbass."

The goblins slowed in front of me and I gave them a jaunty salute. "Where's your king? Hard to tell as he's not on the throne now, and you're all pretty damn short. Like a sea of toddlers with giant ears."

A low muttering rolled through the crowd along with some serious giggles. If they liked insults, I'd be free and clear in no time. But this wasn't a crowd of giants, easily swayed by bad language and salty phrases.

Goblins had at least twice the brain capacity of giants.

A figure pushed his way to the front of the crowd. Over his head, I could easily see Davin headed our way too, and a set of guards smacked a path through the other goblins as they dragged Grimm forward.

"Three days," Grimm yelled at me. "Three days and you couldn't even do that! So much for your reputation!"

The goblin king stopped about six feet in front of me. His deep green skin made his brilliant eyes pop, and his ears were tufted with black fur. Or maybe it was feathers, hard to tell. He wore a hell of a lot of gold around his neck and across his hands. And his clothing was tailored to his extra small body. A little too tight around the crotch.

"You were with Roderick and the council members in the hotel that morning," I said, certain he was the goblin I'd seen. "Also, a word of advice: you need to let that inseam out, or you're going to have trouble with motility," I said, my mouth working before any sort of a filter kicked in.

He was almost close enough for me to kick him if I took a half step. And I really wanted to kick his smug, patronizing face as he looked me up and down. "You don't look like much. Not really the killer they make you out to be. Though you did escape me in the swamp. I'd have killed you then if I could have and taken back what was mine. But you were too slippery. Not that it matters, this works having you here too."

So he was the reptilian creature that had tried to attack me.

It fit.

I shrugged. "Appearances can be deceiving amongst the fae, can't they? Like you and your big ears."

The crowd gasped and took a visible step back as if I'd thrown a bag of dog poop at them.

Davin was close enough now that I really, really wanted to take a swing at him. "Alan, why don't you pester him?" I said softly. But Alan had slid to the side and was bent at the waist as he inspected a goblin.

"Are these real? Are we on a movie set?"

Jaysus, what a help he was going to be.

The king was talking and I forced myself to listen to what he was saying. "You will hand over the spell book. Immediately."

"Eh." I shrugged. "Tell me what you want it for." His ears perked up, and I knew he'd picked up on the fact that I hadn't outright said no. "I mean, maybe you want to make it worth my while."

Grimm struggled against the ropes holding him. "No, you can't! You can't do it!"

Another shrug from me. "Everyone wants it, but no one wants to say why. I mean, what's so important about this spell book?"

Yes, I knew exactly why they wanted it, but they didn't know I knew.

I put my hand on the bag against my hip. The king's eyes rested on my hand. "A way for us to be... more human," he said softly. The crowd sighed, which only intensified the cheesy smell around them. I swallowed hard and fought the gag reflex.

Clearing my throat, I struggled a bit to speak. "You mean you want to have better glamor?"

"No, I mean the spell would allow us to take part in the human world fully. We would be human. And we would be loved." The goblin king held out a long spindly hand and the urge to take it washed over me.

I laid my palm against his, seeing the differences, understanding why people would never accept them as being part of the normal world. The strange pebbled skin that came in a variety of shades, overly large eyes, the bat ears and the sharper than human teeth. The extra joints in their fingers that made them exceptionally long and bendy. I fought to speak again. "Grimm hid what he was without an issue."

"For a time," the goblin king said, his voice like a song reverberating through my head. "For a time, but it takes strength and magic, and all of it is exhausting, draining." He put his other hand on top of mine, and my knees shook and I went to the ground, staring into his eyes.

Crap.

Big, super-duper poopy crap. The back of my mind said I was in big trouble, that this was what Crash had warned me about when he'd said the fae would try to take advantage of me.

But I was only part fae, a very small part. More of me was...well, whatever my father had been.

"Give me the spell book," the goblin king said, his voice pulling my hands up without touching me, his voice directing me to open my hip bag.

But this didn't feel right. It wasn't his to take. My eyes fluttered closed, and I took a deep breath, the magic in his voice still coaxing me to obey.

Obedience was not something I did well, something Alan knew best of anyone, and in one of the rare useful acts of his existence, he took that moment to remind me. "Oh, look at you doing as you're told for once. I like this. I wish I'd been able to put you in your place more when we were married."

My head snapped up, and the anger that surged through me shot me to my feet. I took three steps back from the startled goblin king.

"I'm not giving you that spell book. By all rights it's mine. With your goblin rules, there are only two ways you can get it. If I give it willingly, which I will not, or—"

A voice that gave me a different set of shivers spoke.

"Or you can duel for it." Crash stepped up beside me. "Those are the rules, Derek. You cannot manipulate people forever. That is not the way of a leader; it is the way of a coward. And the rules of the fae are the same for you as they are for everyone else here."

Derek, the goblin king. Not such a kingly name, that. I stared down at Derek, at his big ears and bright yellow eyes. How in the world had I fallen under his spell, even for a moment? What a douchey face he had, so filled with self-importance despite the fact that he was clearly unable to rule as he should. Sure, I was guessing, but I had a feeling I was right on the button.

He glared up at me, all but vibrating with anger. "A duel then. A pair for a pair?" He flicked his wrist, and the world around us shivered, the pavement under our feet turning to hard-packed dirt, the buildings morphing into a stadium—no, a colosseum. A replica to be sure, but it was *the* Colosseum. Right down to the stone and the broken bits at the top. Hell, I didn't know what they were called, and you know what, it didn't really matter. I was in trouble, but at least I wasn't in trouble alone. The goblins watching were now spread out in the stands, rows upon rows of them cheering and hooting and hollering.

I glanced at Crash. "So I'm guessing he didn't mean pear, like we're having a cooking contest for the best pear compote?"

Crash glanced at me, and while his features were drawn with fatigue, there was also that small spark in his eyes that told me he was trying not to laugh. "Two against two. You hold your own against one of them. I'll kill the one I'm up against, then help you."

I snorted and pulled my two knives. "Or maybe I'll be helping you."

He gave me a bow from the waist. "Most assuredly, it be possible." His accent rolled around me, and I sighed. Yeah, I had it bad.

Alan fluttered up on my other side. "Are you fighting, for real? You can't fight! You'll end up dead, and I really don't want to be stuck with you!"

"Alan, just fuck off, would you?" I growled. "Over there, out of the way." I snapped my fingers a couple times for good measure.

Derek the goblin king strode out to the middle of the arena. "You know, this is a bonus. I was going to have to face you anyway, but now I get to skip a couple of steps. Get the book and kill you both, all in one go." But he wasn't talking to me.

I spun to look at Crash, whose face was about as grim as I'd ever seen it. I opened my mouth, but the goblin king spoke over me.

"You see, Karissa told us you had a spark for this mutt. After our failed attempt with the siren I knew if we pulled her in, you'd follow. Karissa even brought you partway here, using her tits and bits to tempt you one last time."

A flutter of wings could be heard, and there was Karissa, watching us from a perch atop a bank of fog, her long blond hair floating in the breeze, her pet man sitting in front of her on his knees, his face in her…oh my. She lifted a hand and blew a kiss, not at Crash, but at me.

"Checkmate," I muttered. "She didn't try to stop me from taking you because this was where they wanted you."

"And they knew I'd come to help," Crash said.

I thought of the card I'd pulled at Annie's. The devil card, the one of ego and temptation, of the death of friends and relationships. Of danger and choices.

The choice to take on the job Grimm offered. The choice not to tell Crash, who would have known better than to take it on. The choice to come here without Corb. To find Crash first, then free my friends.

I stood a little taller, owning those choices, because right or wrong, I had made them. I stared at Grimm, feeling a connection to the ground below me and the dead who were there. The sensation reminded me of what I felt at the graveyard, the cooling power of the dead calming me and strengthening me. "What are the rules for this fight?"

Derek grinned, showing off slightly yellow, sharp, crooked teeth. "No rules. Use the weapons you have. To the death."

Now here's the thing. A young woman might have thought she'd be all flashy and show off moves, impress the guy who lit her panties on fire with his touch. I just wanted to get this done as quickly and efficiently as possible. I had a list about ten miles long and not enough hours in the day to get it done.

I adjusted the bag on my hip. A finger tapped on my back, hard and bony.

I turned and slid the bag off and put it over Robert's head, a move which produced a series of gasps. Of course, for most of them, it would look like the bag had just disappeared. "Robert, you keep this safe until the fight is over."

"Friend," he muttered and tapped his finger against my chest, over my heart. "Use."

Use my heart? I gave him a nod. "I'll do my best."

Robert tucked his hand into the hip bag and pulled out something, lifted my hand and pressed that something into my palm. I curled my fingers over the cool metal coin. "Use," he said softly.

I tucked it into my back pocket. What the hell was a coin going to do, and why was it in my bag in the first place? He must have grabbed it before he pushed me out of the window of the Sorrel-Weed house.

I did a slow turn to look over the sea of goblins in the stands, but it was Davin who drew my eyes. The Silver Lady was still floating in and around him, drawing energy off his stupid ass if the dark circles under his eyes were any indication.

The hotel…the Silver Lady had said there was a vampire in the Marshall House. The family tree had a spell to bring a vampire plague back, but what did the coin have to do with it?

Crash moved a little off from me, giving us both distance and breaking my line of thoughts as I worked furiously to put the puzzle pieces together. "When this over, we'll need to talk," he said in a low voice.

Oh, I did not like the sound of that. "Yeah? You kicking me out of the house? Breaking things off with me?"

I said it all flippant like because…well, it was the worst thing I could think of on top of how this day was already going. Only the look on his face said maybe I wasn't far off. Damn it.

Son of a bitch. Maybe I really was going from two hotties to nothing in one day. Hell, in a few short hours.

I faced Derek, the goblin king. He grinned at me. "I will face you, little mutt."

"No," Crash growled, and then Davin stepped up across from him.

There was no sound of a gong to start things. One second the four of us stood across from each other, the next Davin and Crash were locked up with all sorts of magic flowing around them.

I wrenched my eyes away from the show they were putting on, from the slurs Davin threw at Crash.

The goblin king tipped his head to one side. "I'm going to crush you."

"Says the guy who's the size of a bug." I flipped my knives around so the blades pressed flat against my forearms. The adrenaline roaring through me smothered some of my fear, reminding me that, whatever Alan thought, I was trained to fight. To keep Savannah and my friends safe.

I sunk into that feeling and let out a slow breath as Derek and I began to circle each other. His teeth glittered at me. "I have killed many of your kind. I helped wipe them out."

"Women? You killed many women? I mean, I've heard that being turned down a lot can make a man vicious." I kept my stance balanced as we moved.

He shot forward, his claws outstretched and his teeth bared like a wild animal. I sidestepped, stuck a foot out and sent him tumbling end over end. He hit the ground hard, rolling through the dirt.

The crowd laughed.

I didn't join them. From the other side of me, I heard a grunt from Crash. I wanted to make sure he was okay, and hell, I needed to see if Davin was sneaking up on me. A quick glance showed me that they'd moved farther from me and Derek, and there was no obvious strong man in the competition between them.

"You bitch," Derek growled. "You tried to humiliate me on purpose in front of my people."

I shook my head. "Actually, you ran at me. I protected myself, and you took a dive in the dirt. That's really on you."

He snarled and his face twisted, skin bubbling and pulsing. The crowd oohed, but Bridgette's voice that cut through the rest. "He shifting into a dark goblin! Run!"

"RUN? Where?" I lifted my hands and indicated the very closed-off arena we were in.

Bridgette had pushed her way to the front tier of the crowd. "You have to kill him, kill him now!"

"HOW?" I yelled back.

"Cut off his balls!" she screeched.

I turned to see the goblin king had sprung up like a weed after a rainstorm. He'd gone from being four feet tall to having a massive twelve-foot frame bulging with muscle. He was naked as the day was long, and his…well, his bits were hanging low.

"ARE YOU SERIOUS?"

"Yes, it's the only soft spot on his hide now," she yelled, and the crowd around her yanked her off the front line. The only soft spot? Of course it was.

Jaysus lawd in heaven, this was going to be gross. The now monstrous goblin king took a step toward me and the reverberation rolled through the ground and into the soles of my feet. Fear kissed the back of my neck, reminding me that despite all the things I'd been through, all the shit I'd had to deal with, I wanted to live.

Which meant I had to be smart about this. I had to outsmart this big ducking goblin.

25

Outsmarting a goblin? All I had to do was piss him off enough that he would make a mistake and give me an opening. That being said, I was still standing with him in a fighting ring, and hoping I could take him down before I got killed or maimed.

No problem, irritating men was a gift of mine.

"I talked to your girlfriend," I said, loud enough that the crowd could hear me. "She said you couldn't get it up again last night." I made a motion to his man bits, and he roared as the crowd howled with laughter.

So much for any sort of solidarity amongst thieves. Or goblins, as was the case. Big dumb Derek let out a roar that rattled my ears and literally sent me shuffling back a few steps.

Crash yelled something at me, but I couldn't hear him through the ringing in my ears.

"Did you tell your wife yet that you have a girlfriend?" I asked.

A screech from the stands said not so much.

I grimaced, still moving, keeping my distance from the giant lug, waiting for my moment. Robert had said to use my heart, but I wasn't exactly sure what he meant by that. Maybe my magic? But I still didn't fully understand what I was capable of—or how it could be of use in this particular situation.

The goblin king held out his hand, and a pool of deep red shadows curled up from his palm, wove through his fingers, and began a slow crawl toward me.

"HURRY! He's using his magic!" Bridgette screeched.

Her yell pushed me forward and I ran toward the goblin king. As I got within his reach, he swung the hand covered in red shadows toward my head. I bobbed downward, came up on the other side as his hand passed over my head.

I snapped up a knife, thinking—or maybe just hoping—I could cut off his hand.

The knife that had just decimated two deadbolts dug into his flesh and bone…and stuck. He wrenched away from me, taking one knife with him.

"Oh dear," I whispered. Looked like Bridgette had been right.

He whipped around and grabbed me with both hands around the waist, circling me with his giant mitts. Lifting me, he snarled, "I'm going to squeeze the shit out of you."

The constriction around my middle ramped up as he leaned into his hold on me, and yeah, I could tell he meant what he'd said. And it was obvious he could follow through too. I couldn't breathe, couldn't so much as gasp around the pressure on my middle.

It would be a matter of a minute, maybe less, before I blacked out. I twisted in his hands, one knife still tucked against my forearm. One knife, one shot at his twig and berries. I pulled my arms above my head as if I were squirming to get out.

A boom rippled the air behind us, almost like thunder had been unleashed in the small space, and the crowd oohed at whatever they were seeing.

Even the goblin king's stupid yellow eyes slid away from me. I snapped my hand forward, throwing the only weapon I had left, praying that it hit its mark. Or marks. I closed my eyes, knowing that I had no time left.

Crash wasn't going to save me. My friends didn't know I was in trouble, and I had nothing left to defend myself with or fight.

The sudden release of the hands on me sent me tumbling to the ground. I hit the dusty packed dirt with a puff of air and had to roll quickly to avoid the flailing feet of the giant goblin. His legs shook and his whole body seized as blood sprayed from between his legs.

I ran to his arm, where my other knife was still embedded, planted a foot on his skin, and yanked my blade free. The goblin king stared up at me. "Damn...un-terrr." The last word slurred as the light went out of his eyes.

Just like that, gone, his body shrinking as the life left him.

There was no time to find my other blade. I turned as Davin strode toward me.

Crash was on the ground behind him, stunned by the looks of it, holding his head in his hands. "Give me the spell book," Davin said, "and you can go free."

"I'm not giving you anything," I wheezed around what I was pretty sure was a cracked rib or two. Maybe even some breaks.

"Well, then, how about give it to me, or I will kill him?" Davin held up his hand and a spell shot out of him, wrapping around Crash and holding him tightly. "My master will not like that he is dead, but we can live with it. We can survive without his help."

I held onto my one knife, keeping it tucked against my forearm. The Silver Lady was still behind him, and I felt the same connection to her that I'd felt before—a link to the power that welled inside of her, just under the surface.

I made myself nod, and the crowd gasped. "Here." I kept my knife hidden and put my other hand to my shirt as if I would pull something out from under it, lunged forward, and slashed my knife through the magic that Davin had wrapped around Crash.

The magic blasted apart, sending us flying in every direction. I hit the far wall, slid down it, and landed with my limbs all askew. Struggling for air again.

Crash was nowhere to be seen.

Davin was running toward me before I could so much as blink, the Silver Lady dragging him back and slowing him down.

The connection bloomed between us, and I lifted my hand. A burst of teal sparkles shot through with black—dust?—curled up around my fingers, and intuition had me flicking it at the ground.

Ghosts shot upward, not that anyone else could see them, and a hundred or more of them spilled toward Davin, clinging to him, pulling him down until he could no longer move. Goblins and humans, tiny fae, and others I couldn't identify. They'd all died here, in this arena. And they were all pissed.

I forced myself to my feet and limped toward him. The pain in my ribs was now matched by a pain in my lower back and left hip. If there was ever a night for double Advil…

He glared up at me even as his face paled, not from fear, but from the energy they were sucking off him. I could see them taking him down in great gulps, their faces and forms solidifying further and further.

"They're killing you," I said. "You have any last words?"

"My master will finish what I started." He smiled, though his lips were cracked and bloody.

I crouched beside him, and the second I did it—I knew I'd made an error. I was too close.

He lunged at me, tackling me and rolling us across the arena away from the ghosts.

Everything happened quickly and slowly. He sat up straddling me, my own knife in his hand. Even though I could see it hurt him to hold onto the handle, he swung it down toward me.

A body shot between us, long black hair and grimy clothes.

"Robert!" I yelled as he took the blow meant for me. I rolled over and pulled out the only thing I had left. The coin from my back pocket.

The Silver Lady touched the center of it, and it thinned and stretched into the weapon she'd held in the vision she gave me at the Marshall House. Robert lay unmoving off to the side of me. Crash was nowhere to be seen.

Before Davin could do anything more, I jammed the thin silver rod up and into his heart.

He bucked on top of me, his body stiffening as I held the tool meant for killing a vampire, but no doubt a silver rod through the heart would kill most people. The ghosts around us scattered, their eyes wide and their bodies shaking as the silver tool pulsed in time with Davin's heartbeat.

"You..." Davin shook his head. "Not possible."

And like all assholes *should*, he died rather unceremoniously after that attempt at a final pithy phrase. He slumped to the side, eyes glazed and chest still.

I crawled to Robert and pulled my knife out of his ribs. "Tell me you're okay," I whispered.

I shifted so I could hold him a little better, harder than it sounds with a skeleton. "Robert?"

I didn't know if magic could help him.

"Whiskey," he mumbled, and I laughed.

"So soon after the last binge? Hell, why not." I struggled to my feet and then reached down to pull him up. He was as wobbly as me.

Every part of my body shook, every muscle was on the verge of seizing, dancing as though I had electricity running through me. But I was alive. Robert was alive, well sort of. Bridgette was alive. I hoped Crash was alive.

Karissa was gone without so much as a see-you-later. No shock there.

The crowd though, they shot to their feet and began to chant a name I didn't know.

"Gov-Nu. Gov-Nu. Gov-Nu."

I turned to see Crash standing across from me at the far side of the arena. His head lowered until his chin touched his chest.

We'd done it.

The crowd of goblins burst over the edge of the arena seating and flowed around us. Some reached out and touched my hands first and then touched their foreheads. Some dared to touch the flat of the blade that I held in one hand.

Bridgette found us after the first wave. "You really killed him," she said, beaming at me. "You have no idea…he's been a monster to our people. You're a hero!"

"Okay." That was all I could manage. I didn't doubt what she'd said, and it wasn't that I didn't care so much as I just desperately wanted to go home and sleep for a week.

Only I found myself thinking of what Crash had said earlier, before the fight. Maybe I wasn't going to get to go home. Maybe…maybe Crash was going to kick me out. Maybe he was done putting up with the crazy danger that came with me.

That gave me pause. "Grimm?" I made myself shout his name, and someone must have set him free from his restraints, because he heard me through the sea of goblins and found his way to my side.

"You really did it. You kept the pages from them." He shook his head. "They are hidden still?"

I nodded. "Yes." Which they were, inasmuch as my bag could be considered a hiding place. "I'll keep them until the silver moon passes tomorrow night. As per our agreement, three days was the time frame. You won't get them back until then."

He smiled and dipped his head to me. "You mean I won't get them back until you get paid."

I pointed a finger at him and clicked my mouth. "You got it."

Grimm went still and crouched, motioning for me to do the same. "The pages…they aren't just a spell, they have the ability to allow the darkest powers of the shadow world to come forward. If there was a way to destroy them, I would do it. Nothing good can come from them. Do you understand?"

I stared hard at him. "Now you want me to try and burn them or something?"

His eyes were all seriousness. "What you are is unique in our world, and it means you are one of the few who could destroy them. When the chance comes, take it."

Grimm looked over my shoulder and his face fell, and if green skin could pale, it did.

"What now?" I asked.

"The SCE is here. Roderick is with them. He wants the pages too. In the wrong hands, those pages could wreak absolute destruction on this town. Maybe even the world."

"Yeah, I got that much. I have them hidden. You want me to destroy them if I can. What about the coin?" Again, I intentionally withheld where they were being hidden.

He tapped my hip bag, damn it, so I wasn't so good at keeping my secrets as I thought. "Keep it, it's a weapon and one you should probably have if you're going to survive this world and what I think is coming."

"Why are you helping me now?" I stared him down, feeling the weight of others coming closer and ignoring it. There were times to hold out on hurrying, and this was one of them.

He pulled me lower to the ground, which was mighty uncomfortable for my hamstrings. "Listen to me. This was one of the first moves in a game of chess where all the pieces cannot be seen, and the players are many and hidden well. We can meet later, I will do what I can to explain more."

A throat cleared behind us.

I made myself stand, noting that the goblins had cleared the area around us.

"Let me guess," I said, dusting myself off, "Roderick?"

"What a well-placed guess," Roderick said. "Again, you are here. Ms. O'Rylee, you are a true meddler."

That spun me around. "Well, that's rather rich coming from you. Who also just happens to show up at all the places I'm at. What are you doing, following me around?"

The thought hit me like a ton of bricks. He'd been at every place of trouble I'd found. Had he been tracking me? Could it be through that damn coin-that-wasn't-a-coin that I couldn't seem to rid myself of?

"My job brings me here," he said.

"As does mine," I fired back. "But don't worry, I've already cleaned up this mess."

His one eyebrow arched and he changed the subject. "What were they fighting over?" Roderick motioned at the goblin king dead on the ground and Crash who was surrounded by jumping, jubilant goblins cheering a name I didn't think he'd ever meant for me to find out. Guv-Na. At least that was how it sounded. Probably wasn't spelled that way. I looked at him, and didn't see him hating the goblins the way Bridgette had said. So was she wrong? Or was he just that good at showing people what they wanted to see?

Yeah, that last possibility was one that stuck in my craw.

I looked to Grimm for help. He nodded ever so slightly to me. "Same old. The crown that Derek wanted and Crash does not."

Roderick sighed. "Lovely. Breena, you were pulled into this mess how?"

Think quickly, Bree. "Because I happened to be with Crash. And they thought he would be upset if something happened to me."

Roderick's eyebrows both slowly rose. "And would that be the truth? Would he be upset if something happened to you?"

We need to talk after this.

Are you kicking me out of the house?

The back and forth from earlier reverberated through my head, through my thoughts. Was I hot and bothered for him? Beyond a shadow of a doubt. But could I really trust him? The moments from our shower together came back to me, his hands and… other things against my skin. Was that even real, or had there been an ulterior motive? I wanted to trust him fully. I wanted to believe he wanted me for me.

But he wouldn't even look at me now. Like suddenly he couldn't be seen with me. He hadn't even come to see if I was okay—which I was not. I was bruised and battered in body and, worse, in the part of my heart I'd slowly been giving him.

"Bree, would he be upset?" Roderick repeated the question, softer, gentler.

"I'm thinking. I…don't know," I finished lamely. "I don't know, okay? Probably not as much as he might claim to be."

He nodded. "Anything in particular you think they were fighting over then, if not you?"

I lifted both hands and lied through my teeth. "Not a clue."

Roderick stared hard at me. "You aren't a good liar. You know that, right?"

"Girl's gotta try when she's been sworn to secrecy," I said.

Roderick looked from me to Grimm and back again. "Fine. For now. The council may want to speak with you again about this."

That gave me pause, a thought rumbling through me, cutting through the aches and pains and the desire to lie down for a week. "Roderick, when I walked through the desks at the council, and all the spells were taken off me, was there a small one, something like a deterrent spell?"

My gran's and parents' files had—according to Tom—a spell on them that was making me not want to open them. But when I'd walked through the desks and all the spells had been lifted off me, Roderick had said I'd only had a slight glamor on me, an old spell.

He shook his head. "No, just the glamor. Why?"

Why indeed? Corb had been suspicious there was a spell, but not sure. Tom had been sure, and then he'd pulled some sort of magic slug out of me. Louis couldn't talk to ghosts. They'd thought Suzy had no power but had brought her on anyway. I frowned. "Just how big of hacks are the Hollows? Like can they make it look like they have mad skills but really have bubkes?"

The sounds around us slowed a little and Roderick gave a sad smile. "The biggest of all the hacks. You were their best shot of moving up in the ranks, and you left. It's why they allow Corb and Sarge to play both sides of the field. Those with any skill in their ranks tend to leave."

The implications flipped all the switches in my head. Taking a nonexistent spell off me was a ruse then? Was that possible that Tom hadn't pulled anything from me at all? I had sneezed, something flew through the air but…he'd said I'd owe him and the Hollows one immediately after he'd "helped" me. Was that how they got by? By tricking people?

Ouch. And I fell for it. I blew out a slow breath. "Great. Thanks."

I pointed a finger at Grimm and mouthed, *You owe me*. He nodded and bowed over clasped hands. Best I was going to do at holding him to his word considering the shape I was in. Not like I was going to be able to grab him and give him a shake to make a point that I meant business and I expected him to pay up.

I pushed my way through the thinning crowd to the body of the dead goblin king—which now was back to his original size with super tiny balls—and found my second knife, scooped it up and cleaned it off on my pants.

A knife that Crash had made for me.

Emotions I did not like swirled up and through me as I made my way out of the slowly dissolving arena. Bridgette did not come with me.

The fake Vegas Strip reappeared, and I walked down it, limping, struggling to get enough breath. I was not going to be heartbroken over a man who'd offered me nothing, a man who had not promised me a single thing. Any heartbreak was on me. We'd had nothing more than a friendship with some benefits. The rest had been in my imagination.

I half thought Crash would follow and tell me it was okay, that we'd talk later. But he didn't show, and the walk of shame was…well, it was shameful. It hurt in more ways than the obvious limping hurt and the crush of my ribs.

Robert swayed alongside me. "I wish you were really here, Robert. I could use a shoulder to cry on."

"Friend," he whispered to me, and slid his hand into mine. I held onto his bones for all I was worth.

"Yeah, you're a good friend."

We made it back to Skel without an issue, and Eric, Suzy, Feish, and Kinkly were all there waiting.

My lower lip trembled. I tried so hard to not cry when I saw them alive and well, but it wasn't going to happen. Their arms circled around me.

"We got you, Bree," Suzy whispered. "You don't always have to be the strong one. Give us a turn."

And for the first time since I'd come back to Savannah, I let them do just that.

26

We arrived at the house that had belonged to my gran, and for the first time, I saw it for what it really was.

Crash's house. Not Gran's, not mine. He'd taken my name off the deed, just in case. And now I had zero standing.

I started to shake, took a deep breath and held it until I was lightheaded, and finally let the air back out with a hiss of pain. Stapled to the door was a piece of paper folded in half with my name on it written in Crash's own handwriting. I opened it.

It was the deed to the house, and my name was most certainly not on it. "We're out."

Suzy put a hand on my shoulder. "What are you talking about?"

I shook my head and tucked the paper into my back pocket. "We aren't welcome here anymore," I said. "Crash wants us out."

Feish gasped. "He kicked you out?"

I gave a sharp nod, ignoring the hurt. Maybe not the most emotionally mature thing to do, but I was exhausted and not in a great shape to deal with this whole scene. "We'll clean up, stay the night, and then go."

In we went, Suzy and Eric talking quietly to each other as they went up to their rooms. I set Kinkly on the kitchen table. "What can we do for you?" I asked, trying to distract myself by keeping my mind on the tasks at hand. "Is there an easy way to heal your wings?"

She pursed her lips. "Celia could have healed them. Karissa could do it, but I doubt the queen will help me now. I can't believe he is kicking you out! Maybe the queen is forcing him to?"

If my gran could have helped Kinkly, then maybe Missy could. I chose to ignore the rest of her questions. "And if we do nothing, will they heal?"

She bobbed her head. "Yes. I'll be more of a target in the meantime, but they will mend on their own in about a week."

I closed my eyes and rubbed a hand over my face, or was going to. My hand was caked with dark brown stains—Davin's and Derek's blood had dried in a thick layer on my skin. I lowered my hand. "You could try Missy, but I don't know who else would be able to help you."

She shrugged and winced. "I'll get my two sisters to come and stay with me in the oak tree. I'll spy on Crash for you. See who's going in and out for the next week. It'll be okay, Bree. It will."

I smiled and managed to give her a wink. She gave me two thumbs-up. As if everything really was going to be okay.

Up to my bedroom I went. I still hadn't acquired much stuff, and I easily packed it into two bags. I flipped open my hip bag, and Alan slid out. I barely remembered stuffing him in there. "Damn it, I hate you, Bree."

I didn't even bother to look at him. Like I needed a Jiminy Cricket twittering on about my failings and insecurities—my own mind was perfectly good at throwing those at me. I had to find a way to remove him from me.

"Gran," I called out, "I need to talk to you."

Gawd, I was going to have to say goodbye to her. I mean, I'd only just gotten her back, and if I left, would she disappear completely? And just where the hell was I going to go? I couldn't go back to Corb's for obvious reasons, and I was fast running out of money thanks to my spree on the camouflage uniforms earlier.

Gran didn't come in, and I was just too tired to find her. I forced myself into the shower despite the memories that assailed me of my time with Crash. I might have cried a bit, but you can prove nothing and I'm admitting nothing. When I finished, I crawled into my bed and flicked off the light.

My dreams were as dark as they'd ever been, the Sorrel-Weed house front and center in them, the blood-born demon taunting the crap out of me.

Then someone was begging for me to help them. Then screaming for help. At the edge of my consciousness, I could almost recognize the voice.

"No, don't hurt her!" I called out in my sleep, partially waking myself.

A hand touched my face and I sat up, batting it away. Corb was crouched by the bed. "Bree, what happened?"

"Did you know that there was no spell on me from the envelope?" The question blurted out of me and I put a hand on his arm. He didn't tense, and he didn't look away.

"I was afraid there was. Tom said there was." He frowned. "Damn it, he used helping you as a chance to tie you to the Hollows again."

I nodded and slumped back on the pillow, not taking my hand from him. I didn't think he was lying. Not this time. I was too tired and feeling too alone to be smarter than that.

"Stay with me," I said.

He didn't hesitate, just crawled into bed, fully clothed, and carefully put his arms around me. The wash of his magic pushed the darkness back and my body relaxed, floating as if I were indeed in the water, the coolness soothing some of the hurt in both my body and my heart.

No dreams haunted me after that, and when I woke in the morning, Corb was not there. Maybe he'd never been there and I'd only imagined it. I sat up slowly, my body aching but my ribs not nearly as bad as they'd felt the day before.

"I can't believe you slept with him," Alan snapped from his corner of the room.

I twisted around. "So he *was* here?"

"He held you all damn night." He shook his head, his nose wrinkled and lips pursed. As if it were disgusting that Corb had showed he was worried about me and had given me far more care than Alan would have done if the roles had been reversed.

I rubbed my face and slowly pulled on my jeans, a clean bra and shirt, and my work boots. I put my knife sheaths over the jeans—I wasn't going out without them anytime soon. Scooping up my bags, I took them out onto the second-floor landing.

"Gran, I have bad news," I said softly.

She flickered to life in the doorway to her bedroom. "I also have bad news."

I narrowed my eyes at her. "You sound weird, are you okay?"

She spread her hands wide. "I am not your grandmother. My name is Matilda."

I wasn't quite sure how to react to that, so I just stared at her a moment before I could speak. "Shouldn't you have been kept out by the spells and garden?"

"The other witch removed the protections as she left, the one you call Missy," she said. I noticed that her terrible wounds were healed. She touched her neck. "Yes, the energy here is healing for the undead. Which is what has finally allowed me to speak. The blood-born demon has your grandmother. She's been trying to help me these last few days, but that was what he wanted all along. He wanted her. I was here, and she was busy hiding me from you. We didn't realize what was happening until it was too late. We didn't realize he wanted her knowledge."

"Why would she help you?" I snapped, not sure I wanted to believe her words. "You were like two small dogs barking at each other across the fence."

She spread her hands in front of her. "Because the demon made a grab for you. We all saw that. She thought to weaken him by bringing me here."

And that made perfect sense to why Gran would do what she did. To protect me.

I was up and running before she could say anything. I grabbed my hip bag and threw it over my shoulder.

The blood-born demon had my gran.

I was going to kick his balls so hard that they lodged in his throat if he so much as hurt a hair on her undead head.

I yanked the front door open and was outside with a single jump. "Robert, he has Gran!"

Robert was at my side in a flash, and I was sprinting across the lawn, hopping the fence and pounding up the front steps of the Sorrel-Weed house as if I didn't have cracked ribs and a wounded heart. As if I'd never been remotely scared of it.

The door swung open for me, but the eeriness of that didn't bother me. I was burning with rage that he'd dared touch my gran. Never mind steal her away.

In the main room I stood, breathing hard, Robert next to me. I reached out and touched him, my magic flaring as I brought him from skeleton to a fully formed man.

"Bree," he growled. "The magic here is darker now. Just in that short time since we were here last, it's been growing."

"The basement," I said, pulling my knives from their sheaths. "That's where the tour guide said not to go, so that's where we go."

Robert nodded and took the lead. He opened the door and reached for the light. Nothing.

"In my bag," I said. "There's a flashlight."

He opened the bag, pulled it out and flicked it on. "This is going to be rough."

"I'll probably pee my pants at some point," I said. "Don't tell anyone."

He grunted and took the first few steps down. "I'll probably pee my pants too. Your secret is safe with me."

I kept close to him and wasn't surprised in the least that the door slammed behind us. Not surprised, but I did still jump and wobble on the stair edge.

"This feels funny," I said as we made our way down the steps. "Like the air is wrong."

"A demon's home is never funny," Robert said. "Smelly, horrid, but not funny."

At another time I would have laughed.

Okay, I did smirk. Give it to Robert to pull even that much out of me. We reached the bottom of the steps, and he swept the flashlight over the room. Beside him was a light switch on the wall, and I reached over and flicked it on, figuring there'd be electricity due to the tourist visits.

Robert didn't flick off the flashlight. We crept forward. The basement had some ground-level windows, and there were pieces of furniture all over the place, scattered haphazardly.

"Gran," I whispered her name.

I knew you'd come.

The blood-born demon's voice curled around my ear and I spun, slashing with one knife, cutting through absolutely nothing. Laughter rippled around us and the lights dimmed but didn't go out.

"Where is my gran?" I yelled.

I'm going to enjoy killing you.

A whoosh of air behind us, a sudden shriek, and I hit the ground, rolled onto my belly and found myself looking straight at Robert. He'd pulled the same move. "We have to kill it."

"I know," he said. "But you ran in here without any thought about how you were going to do that."

"I killed the other demons."

"They were amateurs." Robert grunted and pushed up to his feet, those icy blue eyes sweeping the room. He grabbed my hand and tugged me in close, his mouth against my ear. "You can't hurt him until he takes solid form. Let him grab me. He can't hurt me."

He let me go and took a few steps away from me. The air behind him moved, shimmering with a form I could almost see.

"Robert, look out!"

But I wasn't fast enough, and neither was he. The blood-born demon wrapped itself around Robert, holding him tightly as the critter bit into his shoulder, tearing into him.

The demon was solid, and that meant I could kill it.

The creature swung Robert around to face me.

You have to kill him to kill me.

Which meant the life I'd given Robert had—temporarily, at least—confused the demon. It didn't seem to get that he was already very much dead. It wouldn't kill him to have the knife stuck through him. Again. The thing was, I didn't want to hurt Robert. And the chance that my knife could indeed finish him off was there.

I wouldn't risk it.

I lifted one of my knives then lowered it. "Take me instead."

Robert shook his head. "No, Bree, don't!"

The demon threw Robert behind him and rushed me. All the darkness in the world seemed to exist within him, within that critter that had been born evil.

Once more, the thoughts that had harried me most of my life chewed through me.

Not good enough.

A joke.

Embarrassing.

No one wants you.

Plain.

Old.

Slow.

Useless.

I made myself open my eyes and look into the darkness, and it surely looked back at me.

It knew my faults, my worst fears. It blasted me with them.

"You're wrong," I whispered those two words.

The demon wavered in front of me, even though it held me tightly. I stared hard into it, feeling every bit of the fear it had stirred in me. Hell, I was pretty sure I really had peed myself. My knives had dropped from my numb fingers, my body chilling as the demon drew my energy down.

I was dying. I could feel it in my bones. I'd died just the week before and I could tell death was coming for me again.

I forced my hand into the pocket that held the silver coin, barely managing to hang onto it as I pulled it out. The silver metal warmed in my hand and swiftly turned into the same two-foot tool that I'd used on Davin. A tool to use against evil.

The Silver Lady had used it on a vampire all those years ago.

Someone was screaming my name, someone who loved me for me, and it was all I needed to hang on long enough.

"Where is my gran?"

The demon cocked his head to the side and the spindles of darkness drove themselves deeper into me. *You are dying, and you still want to know?*

"Yes."

She was taken by my master to his home in…

I didn't ask where again, maybe I should have, but I was out of time. Fully and completely out of time. With the last of my strength, I plunged the silver rod into the demon. For a split second, I thought it hadn't worked. That the silver wouldn't kill him. That I would be the one to kick the bucket instead.

The tendrils digging into me loosened.

No. NO!

The demon fell away from me, his body fully solid as he slammed against a set of chairs, toppling them. Then he tumbled to the floor and shriveled where he lay until there was nothing left but a hunk of pale skin the same color as the "paper" Grimm's family tree was written on.

I went to my knees, the lights flickered on, and Robert stood across the room from me, still fully fleshed out for the moment. Still the man he'd been.

"Well done, Bree." He smiled and winked at me. "You are amazing."

And then in a blink, he stood there with raggedy long black hair, his bony body swaying side to side.

"Thanks, Robert," I said, scooping up my knives and the silver coin. I'd killed the demon. I'd killed him and I'd survived.

But Gran wasn't here. She'd been taken somewhere else.

And Robert…Robert had been the one who'd called my name and kept me from succumbing to the darkness of the demon.

I struggled to breathe a moment. The knowledge that, while I survived, I'd lost the person who meant the world to me.

"Where the hell are you, Gran?" My words echoed and a chill worked down my spine as if my words were a portent of things to come. Something I didn't like one ducking bit.

27

Alan's apartment had three bedrooms and was as swanky as all get-out. Fully furnished and rented for the next two weeks, already paid. How did I know all of this?

"I can't believe you think you're going to stay in my apartment," Alan shouted. "And the ugly ones are coming too?"

Corb had given us the keys and the address, and said he'd meet us at the apartment later. Thank all that was holy, Alan's body was not in the apartment. Which begged the question, just where was his body?

I twisted around to look at my three friends. Eric, Suzy, and Feish were behind me. I wasn't exactly sure how it was going to work with Feish, seeing as she was technically Crash's slave. But that she was striking out with us could not have made me happier. My smile faded.

Gran had been taken by someone that a blood-born demon would call master. How the hell was I going to bring her home?

"Alan, shut your trap." I snapped my fingers at him. "We won't be here long. Just enough to sort out a few things."

"That's still too long. You know how I hate people in my space. Touching my things. Getting my floors dirty," he grumbled, pacing the room.

His apartment—well, really it was a flat—was the best option for all of us at the moment. Other than Corb, no one knew where we were staying. Not that I was worried about the goblins anymore—they all loved me for helping kill off their tyrannical king. No, I was more worried about whatever baddies had sat behind the wheel of this one—Davin's and the demon's bosses. Were they one and the same? Whoever we were truly dealing with, they weren't done causing trouble.

I knew it with every instinct I'd honed over my forty-one years.

And I also knew this next bit was part of the larger whole. I sat at the kitchen table and pulled out the yellow and slightly battered envelope I'd retrieved from the Sorrel-Weed house, pulling the contents out one at a time, flipping the sheets over to face me.

The reports were the easy part. They were full of a lot of jargon that I'd heard from all the cop shows Alan watched.

DOA.

No suspicion of foul play.

Died of natural causes.

That was about Gran. For my parents, it should have been just a traffic accident. It was not.

There were only two pictures, no other paperwork. A note was stuck to them, pinning them together and also hiding part of the image.

All the information was shredded. This goes deeper than any case I've ever seen. Be careful.

Suzy was on one side of me, Feish on the other, as I pulled the note off the first picture.

The image didn't make sense at first, then I realized that it was two bodies. Not in a car or any other vehicle for that matter but on a lawn of grass. Maybe a meadow in the woods, that was harder to say. "These are my parents," I said. I made myself pull the picture closer. The shot showed them curled around each other, spooning as if they were just sleeping.

I swallowed hard.

"They have the same wounds as Alan," Eric said from right behind me. "You see there, around the neck and shoulders? They look like they were attacked by a shifter, ragged wounds claws and teeth would make."

I put that picture down and picked up the other. Gran was in a chair, her head lolled forward as if she were simply sleeping.

Eric took the picture from my shaking hands. "Let me see. Yes, these are the same kind of wounds. Though on Celia, they are harder to see because of the way she is bent forward. Your gran, parents, and Alan were all killed by the same creature. The cops who wrote these reports must have been spelled. Or scared enough to lie. But two of the real pictures got preserved."

Alan paced in front of me. "Before you ask, I don't remember anything. I just remember waking up and then walking to your gran's house."

"Ghosts rarely remember their actual death," I said. "They get frightened, they get angry, but they don't remember details," I said, the words from Gran's book echoing through me.

I picked up the case information and read it over, looking for something…and when I found it, I couldn't believe I'd not seen it before.

"Place of death…" I rubbed my finger over the city on all three death certificates. Not Savannah like I would have thought. "They were all killed in New Orleans. No one told me that's where they died. Why would the paperwork be here?"

Of course, there were a lot of unanswered whys.

A knock on the door turned us all around as Corb let himself in. I didn't know what to say to him. I was angry. I was hurt, and he'd held me all night so I wouldn't be alone. The bags under his eyes said it all.

It had not been a restful night for him either.

"Grimm sent me with something for you," he said, holding up a bag that looked like a watermelon was in it, and it clinked. It freaking clinked. "And he asked me to remind you to hold on to his family tree until you can destroy it." He cleared his throat. "For safekeeping."

I touched the bag on my hip and nodded. "Yeah, that's probably for the best given what's written on it."

All eyes turned to me and I sighed. "A spell to bring about a plague of vampires. You know, nothing major."

What could only be described as shocked silence descended on the room. "Why?" Suzy was the first to splutter the question I was sure we all wanted answered.

I shrugged. "Who knows? But it's on that paper, and Davin wanted it. Derek wanted it. Maybe Derek thought the vampires would help him? Or that they'd be forced to help if he brought them back to life? I don't know."

I gathered up the papers from Eric and stuffed them into the manila envelope. "Everyone pick a room. We've got this place until the end of the month when his rental is up."

Alan stomped around the table toward me. "I will not let you live here!"

Corb cleared his throat. "I've been doing some digging, Bree. I do have some good news for you."

I slumped into a chair and he pulled up one beside me. "Fire away."

He grinned and glanced at Alan. "It really is good news."

I didn't trust it, but his smile was contagious. "You know, you have the slightest dimple on that side." I poked at his cheek, and he caught my hand.

"You know that Alan moved all his debt onto you, and really seemed to cross all of his T's and dot his I's," Corb said. I nodded, wondering how this could lead to good news.

"Yes, I do seem to recall that he did that," I said.

"Did you know that he forgot to cross one very important T?" Corb was full-on grinning as he pulled a single piece of paper from his back pocket and smoothed it on the table. "Alan, you recognize this?"

Alan pushed between us, making my skin crawl with a cold breeze. "No, oh shit, no!"

Anything that would make Alan curse had to be good. I leaned forward and stared at the paper.

"It's a life insurance policy?" I scanned the page quickly, shock settling in, and then scanned it again. "Alan's life insurance policy. Is it really correct? Is that what I think it is?" I jabbed my finger at the beneficiary named on the policy. Which happened to be me.

Alan all but threw himself around the room, cursing and yelling that it wasn't fair. That his secretary was supposed to have made those changes. That he hadn't meant to forget.

"He probably thought he had years, that it would be the last thing he needed to change," Corb said. "The policy is enough to cover all the debt and leave you with a good nest egg."

I squeezed Corb's hand. "This…this is good. Thank you."

His smile faded. "But?"

"Gran is missing. I have to go after her, Corb. I know that some people would say she is just a ghost, but she isn't. Her *soul* is missing," I said, the words choking me. "I have to bring her home."

Corb stood and pulled me to my feet, green eyes steady on mine. "Then we go get her."

"We?"

He grinned. "I'm officially out of work. I broke ties with the SCE. Actually, I was hoping you'd give me a job. I think Sarge will be asking soon too. The Hollows won't take him back. And after the stunt Tom pulled, I'm not sure…"

"Tom, what does he have to do with this?" I asked.

Corb grimaced. "There was no spell on you from your gran's paperwork. I overheard him and Eammon talking this morning. They put a simple spell on the paperwork to make you need their help, nothing heinous, just…a pain in the ass." He rubbed a hand over his hair, messing it all up. "They always intended to take it off so they could have a favor to call in. Only you didn't have a spell on you when Tom found you." He reached over and touched the talisman I wore around my neck. "Your gran's talisman protected you from it, probably felt strange when the two collided, I'd bet?"

The feeling of ants crawling all over my skin when I first opened the envelope came back to me. "Yeah, it did."

"I didn't know," Corb said.

I looked him in the eyes, wanting to believe him. "For now, I'll take that."

Corb leaned in to kiss me and Alan shot between us, so I'm not sure if I would have let him put his lips on mine or not.

"Don't you dare," Alan snapped. "I hate you both."

I cleared my throat. "So. New Orleans then? You think Sarge will come?"

Corb nodded. "Yeah, he saw Jinx back to Factors Row. Apparently she's taken a liking to him and she tried to entice him, turned into a wolf and everything. He turned her down, so he's going to need a few weeks out of town."

I grimaced, wondering what kind of trouble a lovestruck trickster could cause and decided I really didn't want to know.

He took my hand. "What do you say?"

There was really no other answer than…"Okay, let's go. But you realize that until I find a way to remove my ghostly attachment, Alan will be with us?"

Corb grimaced. "Yeah. No fun, but let's go anyway."

Suzy stepped into the doorway and I smiled. "You coming too?"

She shook her head. "I can't go, I'm not…my powers are still not under any sort of control. And I need Eric to stay with me. He's becoming my touchstone, a place of calm when the emotions and power begin to swirl out of control."

Corb nodded. "That's good. He'll ground you."

Feish bobbled forward. "I am coming. No more do I have a boss, and he can't be ordering me about. Also know New Orleans good." She gave us a wide grin showing off her gills.

Her words made me realize—or maybe realize wasn't the right word, maybe forced me to remember was more accurate—that I hadn't had any sort of wrap-up with Crash.

There had been no goodbye. Not even a thanks for saving my ass, Bree, appreciate that. Twice. I'd saved his ass twice. Not even a note. No kind of explanation for his abrupt turnabout. Even Grimm had sent me payment for everything I'd done.

"Then we go. We'll save Gran, and when we get back here, we can go house hunting." I forced another smile, because inside my heart was breaking more than a little. Because I knew that something had happened, something I didn't understand, and whatever was between Crash and me was not as it seemed. Gran's soul was missing, and the home that I loved was never going to be mine.

I drew in a big breath, pulled on my proverbial bigger girl panties, and tipped my chin up.

"Look out, New Orleans, we're coming for you."

A knock on the door turned us all around, and a booming voice echoed through with the use of a megaphone.

"Bree O'Rylee?"

"Who's asking?" Corb shouted back.

"We have a warrant for her arrest for the murder of Alan Walker."

Well, shit.

15
DEVIL
15

I hope you enjoyed this installment of the Forty Proof Series. Be sure to keep an eye out for the next book, **Midlife Ghost Hunter**, which will be available December 2020.

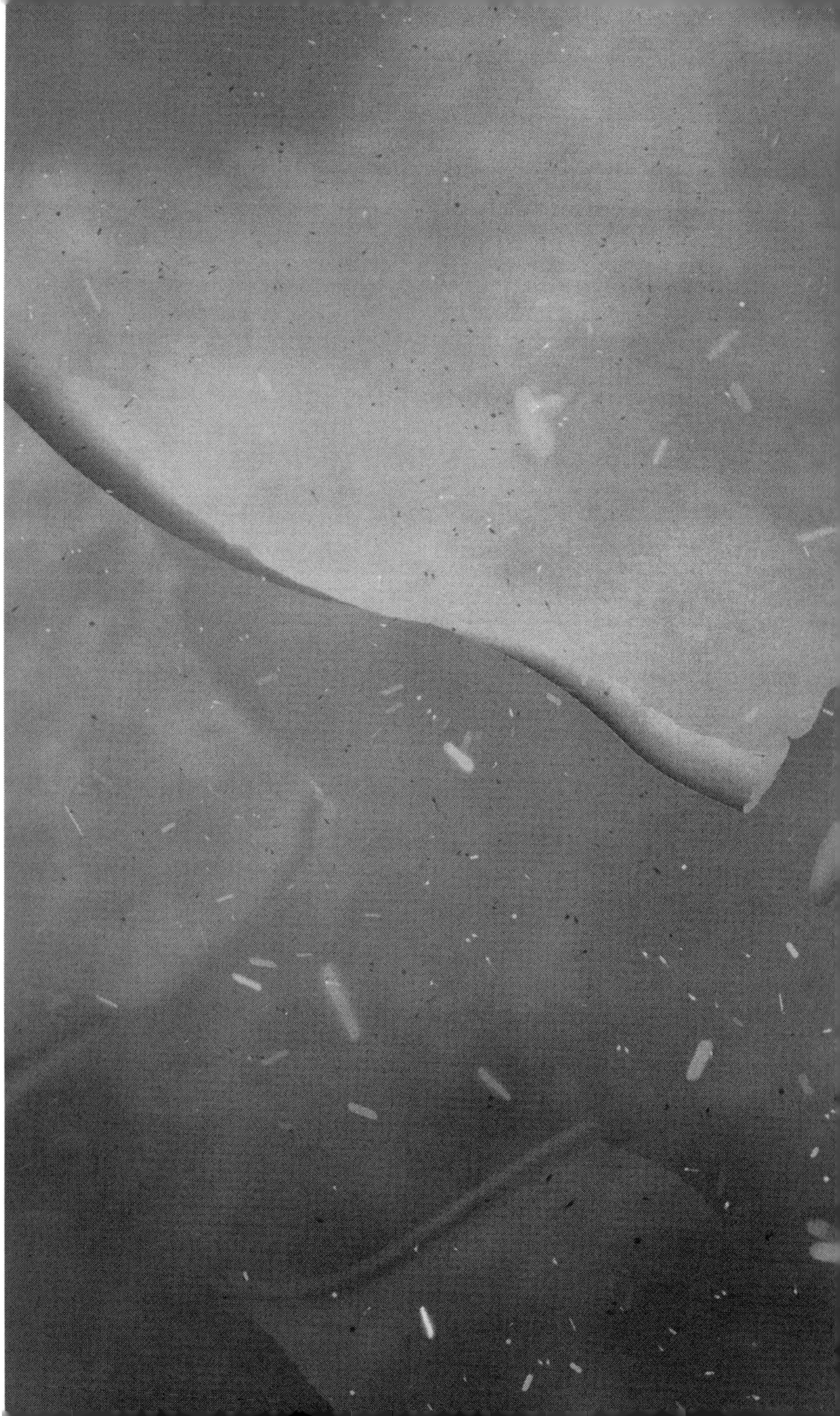

Need more than that to tide you over? You can check out more of the amazing authors in paranormal women's fiction genre at:

www.paranormalwomensfiction.net

OR you can check out my big list of books at:

www.shannonmayer.com

Printed in Great Britain
by Amazon

63478953R00201